YOU AND I

www.transworldbooks.co.uk

www.transworldireland.ie

YOU AND I

Emily Gillmor Murphy

TRANSWORLD IRELAND

TRANSWORLD IRELAND
an imprint of The Random House Group Limited
20 Vauxhall Bridge Road, London SW1V 2SA
www.transworldbooks.co.uk

First published in 2012 by Transworld Ireland,
a division of Transworld Publishers

A CIP catalogue record for this book
is available from the British Library.

ISBN 9781848271425

Addresses for Random House Group Ltd companies outside the UK
can be found at: www.randomhouse.co.uk
The Random House Group Ltd Reg. No. 954009

The Random House Group Limited supports the Forest Stewardship Council (FSC®), the
leading international forest-certification organization. Our books carrying the FSC label are
printed on FSC®-certified paper. FSC is the only forest-certification scheme endorsed by
the leading environmental organizations, including Greenpeace. Our paper procurement
policy can be found at www.randomhouse.co.uk/environment

Typeset in 12/15pt Bembo by
Falcon Oast Graphic Art Ltd.
Printed and bound in Great Britain by
CPI Group (UK) Ltd, Croydon, CR0 4YY

2 4 6 8 10 9 7 5 3 1

To my family for their constant support,
and to my friends for their endless inspiration.

1

Olive

THE ICE-COLD WIND GOT CAUGHT IN MY THROAT. I OPENED and closed my mouth helplessly as I struggled to get the words out. The wind seemed to be coming from every direction. Any piece of skin that wasn't protected felt numb.

'The . . . Newman Buildings . . . please?'

I double-checked the many pieces of paper that the college had sent me, praying that I hadn't said it wrong. Luckily, the foreign man knew exactly what I was talking about and he instantly pointed me in the right direction. I quickly mumbled, 'Thanks,' wrapping my scarf tighter around my neck and racing off in the direction he had indicated. I couldn't help but notice the irony, the foreigner directing the Irish person around a Dublin college. But I felt like a foreigner too, lost and confused in a big city that I didn't fully understand. I grew up only two hours away, in a small country town in Wexford. But Wexford and Dublin might as well be on opposite sides of the planet. Where I grew up you could not look around yourself without seeing green. Green fields, green trees. It was easy and comfortable, you knew exactly what to expect. But here, here you saw something new every time you blinked.

People hurried by me, covered from head to toe in scarves, gloves and jackets. Even the weather seemed different here. Of course it was cold in Wexford also, but this seemed like a different type of cold – harsher and more bitter. It was daunting, but at the same time I couldn't help but be excited.

I knew I had reached the right building when I saw a large *Welcome to UCD Freshers* sign hanging from the roof. From the outside this building looked like a grey, concrete block, unwelcoming and emotionless. The gloomy and cold atmosphere changed, however, the moment I walked through the doors. On the inside I was completely taken aback by all the colours and music that engulfed my senses.

There were at least twenty to thirty stands on either side of this enormous hallway, each with its own title and bright decorations. To my left was a stand that seemed to represent the Dutch Society, but as I looked closer I could see that all the posters depicted people drinking Dutch Gold, a very cheap and foul-tasting beer. On my right was an equally odd stand. The letters LGBS were staring back at me in many different fluorescent hues. On closer examination I could see that this was the Lesbian, Gay and Bi-sexual Society. There was also a very small sign, almost hidden in the corner, that said *Straight people are welcome too*.

I slowly progressed further into the room, which was packed with people who looked just as confused and lost as I was. I jumped as I suddenly felt someone tap my shoulder, and turned around to see a very tall, slim girl with bright purple hair and matching eye-shadow.

'Hello,' she said. 'Are you a first year?'

'Um, yes,' I said hesitantly. The girl was wearing a black T-shirt with white writing on it that read *Drama Society*. 'What's all this?'

'This is Freshers Week. Did you not read about it in your student guidebook?'

I shook my head, feeling a little embarrassed. UCD had sent me a guidebook once I had been accepted. It was an extremely tedious book and I had given up on it after the first few pages.

'Not to worry. Well, Freshers Week is the first week of term. It's where all the societies put up stands and try to encourage first years to join and take part.'

'Oh, OK,' I replied, still confused.

'Do you have any interest in joining the Drama Society? We do about eight different plays each year.' She had a great saleswoman voice.

'I can't act—' I began, but she interrupted me before I could finish my sentence.

'That doesn't matter at all. We have lots of different activities that don't involve acting. For example, writing, set design, make-up design, director, stage manager . . . Also, it's a really good way to meet people.'

I knew there was little point in arguing – this girl was never going to let me go until I agreed to join.

'OK.'

'Brilliant. It is just two euro.'

I searched through my over-full bag until I finally found my wallet. After handing her my money, she handed me back a small bag full of sweets, coupons and a membership card. I didn't want to take part in the Drama Society but I knew she wasn't going to leave me alone until she'd got that two euro.

'Do you know what time it is?' I asked, while trying to force my new goodies into my bag.

'Yes, it's twelve-fifteen.'

'Twelve-fifteen? Shit, I am late.'

'Don't worry, everyone is late on their first day.'

But I had already stopped listening to her, saying hurriedly, 'I have to go . . . Thanks.'

'No problem!' she shouted after me, but I was already jogging in the opposite direction. It took all my self-control not to start sprinting. I was so angry at myself for being late. I had wanted to go to this college for years – last summer it was all I could talk about – and now I was late. I was never late, I was always together and organized. Thankfully, it didn't take me long to find the lecture hall. It was the biggest one in the building and there were numerous signs for it. Taking a deep breath, I calmed myself before going in. There was a small circular window on the door that allowed me to see that the theatre was mostly full, but there were a few empty seats about halfway down the steps. I took another deep breath. I was calm and collected. I was OK.

That was until I finally stumbled into my lecture. When I say stumbled, I mean literally fell down what felt like the steepest steps in history. This was, of course, followed by the entire contents of my bag – books, pens, purse and lunch scattering down the steps and under people's seats. Luckily my dramatic display didn't break the lecturer's rhythm, but I could feel every other eye in the theatre staring at me. It was impossible to ignore the sound of suppressed laughter.

I gathered up what hadn't disappeared from my sight, and jumped into the nearest free seat. I knew my face must have matched the colour of a tomato; this only made my panicking worse. I tried to take long, deep breaths to calm myself down, but as I did this the boy beside me gave me an odd look, and I realized I was hyperventilating quite loudly.

It's OK, I told myself. Just concentrate on what the lecturer is saying. The lecturer had a large projection behind her – *ENG10100 Literature in Context* – and she was discussing what we were going to study for the rest of the year. I opened my A4 pad and went searching for a pen, only to realize I had lost all my pens when I had tripped down the stairs. Over six pens that I had bought only an hour ago and now they were all gone. I looked around me to see everyone with their heads down writing furiously; the boy next to me was already on his second page even though the lecturer could not have been talking for more than ten minutes.

I didn't know what to do; it must have been obvious to the lecturer that out of 500 people I was the only one not writing. I didn't want to ask the boy next to me for a pen, I was afraid the lecturer might think I was just talking; also I was scared that he would yell at me if I disrupted his frantic note-taking. I decided there was nothing I could do but listen, try to remember everything I heard and write it down later. It soon became evident that this was going to be an impossible task. The lecturer talked so quickly and seemed to jump from one subject to another without taking a breath. One minute we would be talking about Shakespeare's *Hamlet* and the next we were on to *Harry Potter and the Philosopher's Stone*.

By the end of the lecture I felt more flustered and confused than ever. I wanted nothing more than a few moments to sit and try to take everything in, but this, of course, did not happen. Sitting at the end of the aisle was a huge mistake; before I even had time to repack my bag, the boy beside me plus another dozen people behind him were all standing, waiting for me to move so they could leave. My humiliation had hit its limit at this point so I just stood aside, mumbling apologies as an endless number of people pushed by.

By the time I was able to finish packing my things the theatre was empty except for a few remaining stragglers. I jerked and nearly dropped my bag again as I felt someone come up behind me. Everyone seemed to be making me jump today. The lecturer was standing there with two of my pens in her hand; she was a petite woman with blonde hair.

'These fell down into the front.' She handed me my pens.

'Thanks,' I replied, feeling the heat rising to my face again. 'I'm really sorry I was late. I just got lost and distracted – I swear it won't happen again.' I was beginning to ramble.

'Don't worry,' she said kindly. 'The first lecture is pretty irrelevant anyway.' The boy next to me wouldn't be happy to hear that, I thought. She smiled at me and then started walking towards the door.

The rest of my lectures that day were not as disastrous as that first one. I still had no clue what was going on in any of them, but at least I was able to find the theatres and take some notes, except for my Irish Literature class, where the lecturer had such a strong Northern Irish accent that I wasn't even sure if he was talking English.

When my day was finally over I felt exhausted. I wanted nothing more than to just go home, but that wasn't an option. I was sixteen years old when I decided that I wanted to go to UCD. At first I had thought that I would just go to the local college, like all my friends at home. It would have been comfortable, easier. I would have kept the same friends that I've always had, dated the same boy and then nothing would have changed. I think that's what scared me the most. That sudden realization that I could spend my whole life in one place, and never experience the anxiety and excitement that come with doing something that is completely out of your comfort zone. That is what my parents did. They met in school, went to the same college and then got married and started having children straight away. I don't look down on my parents, they love each other and the life they have. But it was not what I wanted. I wanted more. I decided then that I would rather be afraid of the unknown than live a life that I knew was not enough for me.

Once again, I had to ask passers-by for help. I tried to

approach the friendliest people that I could find and ask them where the Merville Buildings were; these were the dorms where I was going to live. The first two people I asked sent me in completely the wrong direction. Finally the third person I asked, a man who reminded me greatly of a character you would see in one of Tim Burton's films, set me on my way. The Merville Buildings were at the far end of the campus. I had been told that nearly all first years lived here and that it was Party Central. The building reminded me of the Newman Buildings that I had been in earlier. It was shaped like a giant block, lacking any sort of homely quality. I only prayed that, like the Newman Buildings, the interior would be a pleasant surprise. I double-checked my letter from UCD before opening the door to my new home, Block F Room 4.

I was met by a smell that I didn't recognize and a girl practically shouting while talking on the phone.

'Oh my God, yeah, that sounds amazing. I am like so there! I have to go; my roommate has like just arrived. I'll get her to come too. Bye, bitch.' She hung up the phone and before I could even get in the door she was standing in front of me.

'Hi, my name is Rosanna, but everyone calls me Roz. Are you living here too? I'm afraid that we have all grabbed rooms already, but like don't worry – they're like all exactly the same. How was your first day? Oh my God, I like completely missed all my lectures. I just met up with my girlfriends who all go here too and we all just got like so distracted. I'm going to be like the worst student ever.'

I stood there stunned and amazed at how many times she had used 'like' in one sentence. Rosanna was very tall and very pretty. She had straight blonde hair and wore a lot of make-up, but it seemed to suit her face. Her eyes were slightly unfocused; I had a feeling that this was somehow connected with the odd smell that got stronger as I walked further into the apartment.

'Hi, I'm Olive,' I said. 'Am I the last person to arrive?' I looked over her shoulder, trying to see where I was going to live for the next year. It was small.

'Yeah, you are. The other girl's name is Beth – she's so nice, a Medicine student, so I'd say she's like a super-nerd. She was here at lunchtime to unpack and then she had to go back to her labs. She has labs till nine – like nine! Can you believe it? I'd like die. Oh my God, I'm completely blocking your way! Come in! Come in!' She started ushering me into the dorm.

My new home consisted of three very small, identical bedrooms, one bathroom, and a kitchen that was connected to a tiny living area that had a couch. It was decorated in dull browns and there were already dirty dishes sitting in the sink. How were three people supposed to live in such a small place? I looked up at the ceiling to see multiple stains and a T-shirt wrapped around the fire alarm. Rosanna must have noticed me looking at the T-shirt.

'Oh my God, I'm so sorry about that. I was just having a smoke and normally I swear I always go outside, but today it's just fucking Baltic. So I wrapped the T-shirt around the fire alarm so I wouldn't set it off and get like everyone in trouble. I can open all the windows, if the smell bothers you?'

It took me a minute to register everything that she was saying to me. She just stood there smiling like a china doll, waiting for my reply.

'No, no, it's fine,' I said, a little dumbfounded, still unsure what to think of her. 'So what are you studying?' I asked as she started to roll up another cigarette.

'Politics.' She lit her cigarette. 'It's such a load of bullshit. But my dad insisted that I do it. He's like a twat.'

I couldn't help but think how funny it was that I could be sitting with one of our future TDs who was definitely high.

'What about you?' she asked.

'Arts,' I replied, still absorbing my surroundings.

'Oh my God, I am so rude. Do you want a smoke?' She offered me her lit cigarette.

'Um, no, thanks,' I said. I had never smoked before. 'Is that weed?' My curiosity had gotten the better of me.

'No, no. Weed makes me way too fucking sleepy. This is some chemical shite that I got in the head shop. No idea what's in it, but it gives you like a fucking amazing buzz.' It was only then that I noticed her hands were shaking. 'Are you sure?' she said, taking the cigarette out of her mouth and offering it to me again. I just shook my head politely. 'Well, hun, if you want some later, just tell me, OK?'

'Thanks,' I replied. Rosanna was really a very likeable girl, if not a bit annoying.

'This girl I met earlier on today, her name was Alison. She just lives two blocks away. She's having a big party and then we're all going into town later. You have to come!'

'But it's a Monday?' I asked, a little confused.

'So?' Rosanna looked at me as if this was the most insignificant fact. I guess I needed to get used to being a step behind everyone.

'I have no proper clothes with me,' I explained. 'My dad is bringing all my cases up tomorrow. I just have the basics with me today.'

Roz waved her hands as if this was not even an issue. 'Oh, don't worry, doll. You can borrow mine,' she said without hesitation.

I was about to say that it was fine but she started talking again before I had a chance.

'I can't believe your dad is like bringing you all your stuff. That's so sweet.'

'I guess it is,' I said, not really sure if she was being genuine. It was hard to tell with her. 'I didn't want to be dragging around a suitcase all day so he offered.'

Roz jumped up from her chair suddenly and walked around the room in circles. She didn't seem to be able to sit still.

'Oh my God, your dad sounds like such a sweetheart. My parents are like so annoying, my dad is like "money this and money that" . . . Like who gives a shit really? And then my mum cares more about her reputation than me. She is fucking thrilled I am out of the house.' Roz speaks so quickly that I can barely keep up.

'Where are you from?' I asked awkwardly, once more uncertain if she was joking or being serious, this time about her own parents.

'Dublin.' She took another long drag.

'Oh. Then why are you living on campus?' I asked, baffled.

'Because I couldn't take another year with those nut jobs that are my parents.'

I could feel the heat rising to my face. 'I'm sorry – I didn't mean to be nosy,' I said. 'You don't have to talk about it.' I started picking my nails nervously, trying to think of a way to recover.

'Don't worry, hun, it's not like I give a shit. Basically I am the outcast in the family. I have one brother, a complete entrepreneur, started his own delivery business – I actually don't have a clue what he delivers. I would love if it was drugs. Would make him a bit more interesting.' Roz laughed out loud at her own joke. I laughed too, not really understanding what was so funny.

'I doubt anyone knows what he actually does, but my dad doesn't care because he is making a lot of money. That is the only important thing to my family – money – so he is the Golden Child. But my brother is as boring as shite, just like my parents. I, on the other hand, am *not* boring.'

I just stood there nodding, too afraid to say anything. I thought it was probably best to just let her ramble on in her hyperactive state.

'I am the Wild Child.' Rosanna winked at me when she said

this. 'I once came home plastered and got sick on my mother's new Valentino dress. The look on her face was priceless! So once college came around they were only too happy to get me out. Out of sight, out of mind, you know what I mean?'

'Yeah, I guess,' I mumbled, shocked that this girl I had just met was telling me her life story.

Roz sat back down, completely unfazed about everything she had just said. She was sitting still now but her hands were still shaking as she went to take another drag. I couldn't understand her. How could she be so distant from her family? My family were everything to me. Was it the drugs talking? Did people just ramble on about nonsense when they were high? I only knew one other girl who took drugs. She had been a year ahead of me in my old school in Wexford, and the only side-effect she ever got was an uncontrollable hunger and yet she was caught smoking weed nearly every week by the teachers. Needless to say she became increasingly overweight.

I was lost in my own thoughts when Rosanna spoke again.

'So, are you going to come out tonight?'

'Oh, I don't know,' I answered, having forgotten how the conversation had even started.

'Come on. It will be such a laugh.'

I was about to say that I would rather just get a good night's sleep, but Rosanna was the first person to be really nice to me all day, even if it was in her high state, and as immature as it sounds I desperately wanted her to like me.

'OK,' I replied eventually. 'Thanks.'

'No bother, hun. Tonight is going to be like unreal.' She then took a very long drag from her cigarette.

2
Tom

I TWISTED AND FIDDLED WITH THE KEY IN THE LOCK. THE LOCK was old and would sometimes get stuck. I eventually heard the click and was able to push the heavy door open. I was met by the sound of crashing dishes and swearwords coming from the kitchen.

'It's only me, Mum!' I shouted down the hall.

We lived in a dodgy area of town, near a council estate that was full of unemployed bums and drug dealers. We had been broken into a couple of times; it made my mum constantly nervous. I walked into the kitchen to find she had smashed the two plates she had been holding and was now trying to pick up the shattered pieces.

'Sorry. That old lock – so loud. Gave me a fright.'

I bent over to try and help. I suddenly noticed a large cut on her right hand that was bleeding a lot.

'Oh, God, Mum, you're bleeding!'

She looked at her hand in complete surprise. 'How clumsy of me,' she said, while running towards the sink and turning on the tap.

My mum was a frail woman, a lot younger than she looked; her dark hair was always pulled back, which made the worry lines on her forehead look more pronounced. I threw away the broken pieces as she began to wrap her hand with bandages from a first-aid kit we kept in the kitchen.

I stood there awkwardly, never quite sure what to say around my mother.

'Are you happy to be back in college, Tom?' She was pulling out another two plates from the cupboard; I noticed that we only had four unbroken plates left. I guess it didn't matter much since it was only the two of us.

'College was fine,' I answered, still hovering. I was studying Science in Trinity, specializing in Physics. It was something many people seemed to be shocked to find out about me. My parents had sent me to the local school when I was younger. It was close and it had been all they could afford. Half of my class had been travellers. The other half consisted of people like me, kids who didn't really fit in but had no other choice because their families had no money. When I started secondary school at the age of twelve, there were over a hundred students in my year. But by the time I was sixteen, more than half of them had dropped out. Most of the girls had gotten pregnant and a lot of the boys were arrested for dealing drugs or getting into fights. When we reached our final exams, there were only two of us who went off to college. My mum told me that the school still used me as an example of what you could achieve. I didn't feel like I had achieved anything really.

The truth was, I found college easy. Theorems and formulae were simple to remember, and I always managed to get the bare minimum to keep my grade point average respectable. College was my escape. I often avoided going back to Mum's for days, if I could. I would crash at friends' houses, sleep on couches, floors. Anything to avoid coming back here. That's probably why she had got such a fright when I came in the door. Our building was completely run down. We were on the ground floor and were able to hear our neighbours upstairs walk around their part of the building. Our walls were damp, leaks seeped through the roof and the wallpaper had started to peel off. None of our furniture matched – most of it was bought in second-hand shops. The couches and seats were covered in old stains that my mum couldn't get out, no matter how hard she tried. We didn't have many photos either. There were some from when I was little, holding my mum's hand, but she destroyed any of herself and my dad when they were together. Nothing about this place seemed like a home, but it was the only home we had.

'I'm making curry, do you want some?' she asked in her quiet voice.

'Yeah, thanks.' I sat at the table while she handed me a plate.

'Are you staying in tonight?' There was a note of hope in her voice.

'No.' I was abrupt. 'I'm going to see Paddy.'

'Oh, OK,' she barely whispered as she sank a little more into her seat.

Paddy was my dad and I had absolutely no intention whatsoever of seeing him that night or anytime soon.

'I'll probably sleep over as well,' I added, just to make sure I was covered. She only nodded this time. I was actually planning on heading to a house party in UCD; I had no clue where I would end up sleeping – at some girl's house if I was lucky. My parents had been divorced for over ten years now; it made lying and sneaking around very easy. It wasn't that I needed to sneak around – I was twenty, for heaven's sake – but it was easier to lie to her than tell her the truth and have her question and judge. She was emotional when it came to me and it was always safer to keep her in the dark.

My dad was a musician and my mum was a cleaner, therefore

neither of them could have afforded a legal battle over me. It eventually came to a point when the lawyers asked me who I wanted to live with, who I wanted to have control over me and what I did.

I had experienced more than four years of shouting and fighting, feeling absolutely powerless. Then this decision was forced upon me. My mum had cried and begged – she told me I had to pick her, that she wasn't able to live without me. So I did, I picked my mum. I feared what she would have done if I hadn't. However, when I made that decision, I had had no idea what lay ahead of me. My mum gained complete control over me, including when and where I was allowed to see my dad. A man I had seen every day for ten years, I was now only able to see once a month.

I would go to his small apartment in Dublin, while my mum waited in the car, refusing to see him. We would exchange awkward small talk. He would ask, 'How's school?' And I would ask, 'How's work?'

It was uncomfortable, and before the ice could be broken, my mum would start to beep the horn, insisting it was time to leave. When I turned eighteen, I realized I could visit my father whenever I wanted; my mother no longer had legal control. At first I did actually visit him when I said I was going to. I wanted to connect with my father again, but he had a new life – a new wife and a new child. I had no relationship with my father now, and I blamed my mother for that. I would tell her I was with my dad, not because I needed an excuse but because I knew it hurt her. I could feel myself getting tense: I needed to leave. The longer I stayed, the angrier I got. I knew it wasn't fair on her, but I couldn't help it. I blamed her, I blamed both of them.

Finishing my curry quickly, I left the table without a word. I went into my room, which was a mess – dirty clothes and magazines scattered across the floor. My small single bed was unmade and my guitar was leaning up against the wall, carefully protected by its hard case. It was the only thing in my room that I kept safe. My dad had taught me to play when I was eight; I often played at parties and open-mike nights when I was in school. These days, I didn't play as much as I used to. It only reminded me of a life that I no longer had and would never have again. I decided against bringing it with me tonight.

I knew Alison, and tonight was going to be messy. I pulled out an old shoebox that I kept under my bed; it was filled with small plastic bags of weed and skins. I grabbed one of the plastic bags and placed it in my back pocket; I then pushed the shoebox back under my bed. Luckily my mum never searched my room. I wasn't sure if she would care if she found anything. It would be hypocritical of her. The first time I had smoked weed was when I was fourteen. My friends and I had found it in my mum's room. When my mum had caught us, she freaked out. She had claimed that it belonged to my dad and she'd had no idea it had been there. But she had been lying, I knew it was hers. I had never been punished for it, but she began to change her hiding places constantly after that. I had always managed to find it though. My mum stopped once the recession hit.

I looked in my wallet – twenty euro and a couple of coins; it wasn't much. I would have to take some drink off Damien; I knew he had a bottle of vodka at Peter's apartment. I changed my shirt and put a beanie on my head before heading back out. My mum was still sitting at the kitchen table; she had barely eaten a thing. She just sat there, pushing her food around, looking aimlessly into space.

'I'm off, Mum.'

She jumped at the sound of my voice. She hadn't noticed me walking back into the kitchen.

'Oh, OK. What time will you be home tomorrow?' she asked, looking up at me with water in her eyes.

For God's sake not again, I thought. 'I don't know,' I said curtly, before walking out the door.

The cold air hit me like a slap in the face. I threw on my hoodie that had been tied around my waist and started walking towards the bus stop. It was extremely cold for September and most people were wearing jackets and scarves. Dublin was quiet, people were already home from work. There was only the odd straggler waiting for a bus or Luas. Peter's home was just off Grafton Street, the centre of Dublin city, and it didn't take me long to get there. He lived in an apartment that his dad paid for – on the one condition that he finished his course in Trinity. His apartment was one of those modern places in which everything is white and simple. No pictures, posters or colours. The only thing that lets you know that someone lives there is that it is always dirty. Plates, cutlery and empty beer bottles are dumped everywhere.

I knocked and was answered by Peter shouting, 'For fuck's sake, Tom, it's open!'

I pushed the door open to find Peter and Damien sitting at the table, both well on their way. Peter was a big guy; he often resembled a bear with his hairy beard. Damien was small and skinny and had typical Irish red hair that you could not miss. I had met the two of them on my first day in Trinity. Damien had managed to get himself in trouble with two much older and much tougher guys. I was never quite sure what he had done – said something stupid or hit on one of their girlfriends, probably. Either way I hated seeing two rugby idiots pick on someone who clearly was not up for the fight. They had cornered him and it looked like punches were about to be thrown when I came along.

'Hey!' I had shouted, not really sure of what I was going to do. 'What do you think you're doing?'

The taller one looked me up and down and then shrugged. 'Fuck off,' he told me.

Damien looked terrified; there was no way I could have walked away. I shoved the tall one as hard as I could.

'I said what do—' I never got to finish my sentence because the guy turned around faster than I had expected. And before I knew it, he hit me so hard that I fell straight to the ground. His fist had felt like iron. Before I had time to recover, I felt a hand wrap around my arm.

'Come on, mate. Time to move.' Damien had me up quickly, and a moment later the two of us were sprinting out the door.

'Fuck!' I exclaimed when we were finally out of eyesight. 'That hurt.'

'Yeah, it sure looked like it did.' Damien was grinning at me. 'You always take punches for strangers?'

'Only for the ones who look like *they* can't take it.'

The two of us started laughing.

Later on that day, Damien introduced me to Peter. The two had been friends from school. When I told them that I didn't know anyone in Trinity, they essentially adopted me.

'Tom, Tom, get the fuck over here,' Peter slurred. 'Damien actually managed to get laid the other week, and he was just telling me what happened.'

I walked across the room, sat down next to the others and poured myself a large drink.

'Go on, Damien, tell us about your sex antics,' I said as he went bright red.

'To be honest, guys, it was a bit weird. The girl was like . . . really rough.'

Peter burst out laughing and I asked sceptically, 'What do you mean, rough? Like, was she a knacker?'

'No,' he answered, going redder by the minute. 'She hit me and bit me a lot – I have the bruises to prove it. I eventually just lost my hard-on and she told me to fuck off.'

For a moment, Peter and I stared at Damien in complete

silence, then the two of us practically fell off the chairs, we were laughing so hard.

'Damien, you didn't get laid. You got raped!' Peter shouted, still laughing uncontrollably.

Damien seemed unsure of what to do so he just poured himself another drink and tried to change the subject.

'You plan on scoring Alison again tonight?' Damien asked, looking at me.

'Don't think so,' I replied. 'She was boasting about some rugby boyfriend last time I saw her.' Having a boyfriend didn't normally stop Alison from doing anything; in fact, last time it was only after we had hooked up that she felt the need to mention him. But I had heard from around Dublin that he had already beaten up some lads for scoring his girl and Alison was definitely not worth a broken nose.

'Well, I hope there are some decent birds there tonight. Alison's friends can be so fucking stuck-up!' Peter exclaimed while knocking back his drink.

Peter was right. These were the type of girls who wanted to know how much money you had, what part of Dublin you lived in and most importantly your social standing before they would even consider looking your way. But I found that was only in the public eye. Get these girls alone and it was like shooting fish in a barrel. The words 'I am a musician' seemed to be the secret password to get them naked, and I had no problem taking full advantage of it.

'Peter, can I crash here tonight?' I asked.

'Fuck's sake, Tom. Do you ever go home?'

I felt the anger boiling up inside me. *It's none of his business.* 'Hey, I was just asking. Forget about it then.' I said this a bit more aggressively than I had meant to, but there was no taking it back now.

'Chill out, Tom, of course you can crash. Just saying it's a bit weird.'

'Well, it's not – OK?' I could see Peter and Damien give each other funny looks but I pretended not to notice.

We sat there drinking in silence for a couple of minutes; you could have cut the tension with a knife.

'But if I was willing, technically it's not rape then?' Damien suddenly blurted out, and with this the three of us were in hysterics again. Finally, after what felt like hours of drinking and laughing, I managed to get myself under control and suggested that we get a move on. We grabbed the nine o'clock bus and started making our way over to UCD. Trinity certainly had a great social life, but UCD was also known for its partying and drinking. Trinity halls were scattered across the city, but UCD residents all lived in the one place. This meant that house parties were common and always a lot of fun.

Alison's party was exactly what I had expected it to be. I knew everyone there and they all knew me. The girls wore tight dresses and the boys had on jeans and polo-shirts. The first time I went to a party like this, I had been so intimidated. The girls acted like they could crush you with their stiletto heels and the boys were never afraid to pull a punch – but I soon learned that it was all about the image. So I started to pretend I thought I was better than anyone else there. I pretended that I was a sexy musician, even though I had never played for them. And suddenly the girls wanted me and the boys envied me. It was exactly where I liked to be.

Peter disappeared pretty quickly; he had spotted a blonde that we all knew to be easy. Damien and I stuck together. Girls like these could attack you at any second, and back-up was often needed.

'For fuck's sake, Damien. Why do we bother with these things?' We had found ourselves a comfortable corner that allowed us to view and inspect everyone at the party.

'Come on, Tom, sometimes they are a bit of fun. If nothing else you have Alison. I heard the boyfriend is shagging some Trinity bird. She will be looking for someone to use as revenge.'

'Great,' I grumbled. I would have liked to believe I could say no to Alison, but she was so hot that I never turned down an opportunity with her.

'Tom – Tom! Weren't you with that girl last year?' Damien was elbowing me and gesturing towards two people who had just walked in the door. His lack of subtlety was jarring. The girl on the right was blonde with poker-straight hair. I vaguely remembered her from a drunken night in Oxegen, a music festival that I had gone to in July with Peter and Damien. She had been pretty wild. I had never seen the girl next to her. She was petite, with dark hair, and looked a little out of place.

'Yeah, I think her name was Rosanna.' I wished Damien would stop staring at them.

'She's hot – who's the other girl? I wouldn't say no to her either.'

'She's not bad,' I said, shrugging. Not bad was a huge understatement. She was stunning. Her slim legs were emphasized by black leggings. She had sexy, curly brown hair. I watched her as she pulled it back out of her face, and then I was able to see her properly. Her huge green eyes were almost impossible to look away from, but I forced myself to stop staring. I didn't want Damien to know that I was interested. He would only say or do something stupid.

Rosanna and her friend had started talking to a large group of girls. I knew I needed to get her alone at some point tonight.

3

Olive

ROSANNA'S CLOTHES WERE NOT EXACTLY THE TYPE OF THINGS that I was used to wearing. Everything seemed tight, short and extremely revealing. Her suitcase was full of underwear, tops, skirts and leggings, all in luminous colours. Luckily, she owned one black jacket that she was willing to lend to me.

'Don't worry, hun. I don't feel the cold.' Rosanna was very kind even if she was a little eccentric; she tried to encourage me to wear a short black skirt and a low V-necked top that would make me run in horror. She eventually gave up when I kept insisting that I was not willing to show my legs.

'I swear my legs are not suitable to be seen by the public eye. They are covered in bruises.' I was extremely pale and my legs bruised easily. This meant that they were not an attractive sight.

Rosanna just laughed and shrugged, saying, 'Suit yourself – take whatever you like. So where are you from, Olive?' she asked, handing me a pair of black leggings.

'Wexford,' I answered, while attempting to use Rosanna's make-up. Her skin was a lot darker than mine and I was finding it hard not to look caked. 'I have been to Dublin loads, just never lived away from home before.' I tried to sound relaxed, but the thought of living on my own still scared me. I couldn't forget about everything I had left behind me and what it might cost me.

'I am so excited to be living away. My mum's ultimate dream is to become a MILF. She was thrilled to have me out of the house – less competition.' Roz laughed as she was saying all this but I couldn't help but feel a bit sorry for her. Her home was this small dorm and she had nowhere else to go.

'Shit, I have like nothing to wear,' she said, pulling off her top and bra, leaving herself practically naked. I didn't know whether I should just look away, or if I did look away would she think I was being a prude.

'Um, that looks nice,' I said, pointing to a random piece of clothing that was sitting in her case. She picked up a bright pink string top and a pair of white shorts, then put on a pair of leopard-print heels that made her nearly a foot taller than me. She stood up and looked at herself in the mirror, hands on hips, chest out, mouth pouting.

'Does this look good?' she said without breaking the pout. She looked stunning. Her legs were perfectly bronzed and her boobs looked huge.

'Yeah, you look really well,' I said, staring at her in awe.

'Are you sure? I feel like a fat lard.' She was pulling at non-existent fat on her stomach.

'No, really, you look great,' I said, consciously holding in my own stomach.

'I guess,' she said, turning away from the mirror still pouting. I wondered was she planning to do that all night.

'I seriously like need to straighten my hair; it's just so disgracefully curly.'

She ran out of the room to grab her GHD, which I had seen earlier in the bathroom, while I began to wonder should I do the same. I never used to do anything with my hair other than brush it, but I now felt that I wasn't making nearly enough of an effort. It was hard not to feel bland, standing next to a girl like Roz.

'Do you have a boyfriend?'

I was startled by the sound of Rosanna's voice; I hadn't even heard her come back into the bedroom.

'Not really,' I said.

'Not really? Oh my God. There so *is* a guy, isn't there? Come on, tell me everything! My love-life is like so pathetic, I have to live through my friends'.'

I could feel myself blushing. 'I had a boyfriend in Wexford,' I said, 'but we're not really together any more.' I had hoped that would satisfy her curiosity but I was wrong.

'Oh no – why?'

I thought carefully before I replied. I didn't really have an answer to that question.

'It's just because he went to Maynooth for college and I went here. Geographical differences.'

The truth was, John and I had never officially broken up. We just both left for college. He had been the textbook perfect boyfriend – good-looking, kind and smart. My friends had loved him and he had always been very considerate with my family. But John was safe and I was no longer willing to settle for safe.

'Oh my God, that's so sad!' Roz said. 'Did you love him?'

I was a little stunned at her bluntness. 'I think so,' I replied. 'He was my first, so I guess so.'

'Oh, hun, trust me – you don't have to love a guy to sleep with him. My first was on my fifteenth birthday, I was completely wasted. The guy was like the biggest disappointment ever. His penis was like two inches long! Was your guy any good? Was he big?'

I sat there, glad Rosanna's make-up was so thick because I knew I must have been bright red under it

'I d-don't know,' I stammered. 'I think he was average.'

She gave me a sympathetic look. I felt like the slow child in the class, the kid who just didn't get it.

'Oh my God, Olive, you are actually so cute and innocent. I wish I was more like you. I would talk about sex with a complete stranger,' this I found easy to believe, 'but seriously, hun. A little bigger is always better, unless he's like fucking massive. Then you start to have friction problems.'

As we got ready I slowly grew used to Roz's pure bluntness. I was jealous of her ability to be completely unashamed of anything she did or said. In the space of an hour she told me about five different guys she had slept with – some very disappointing and some apparently earth-shattering. I tried to add to the conversation with the little sexual experience that I had. I always thought that college was the time that you had sex and took drugs, but Rosanna seemed to have seen and done it all before, and she talked about it as if it was common-day life.

It was 9.15 before our third roommate came home. Beth was a smallish girl with straight mousey-brown hair tied back in a ponytail. She practically fell in the door under the weight of all her books.

'Beth!' Rosanna screamed. 'This is Olive, our roommate. She's like so nice; we've just spent the whole afternoon getting ready for this party two houses away. You have to come.'

Beth gave me a tired smile and said, 'I'm really sorry, girls. I've had a very long day and I'm up at seven tomorrow. Honestly, all I want is sleep.' She was very softly spoken, and you could hear the exhaustion in her voice.

I knew Rosanna was about to try and persuade her but I interrupted quickly with, 'Don't worry, I'm sure there will be loads of other nights out,' and she smiled at me with gratitude before making her way into the kitchen.

Rosanna talked non-stop on the way to the party. I began to wonder was it a side-effect of whatever she had been smoking. Beth had seemed nice, and now I wished I had stayed and talked to her longer. I was beginning to feel that this party was a huge mistake.

'Alison is such a doll. You'll love her, and her boyfriend should be there too. Oh my God, he is like such a babe – you will like die of jealousy when you see him. I know I did.'

I was learning pretty quickly that Rosanna didn't really need much encouragement from me. A couple of ooh's and ahh's seemed to keep her happy. As she rambled on about this really hot guy that she had seen earlier and how he had been completely flirting with her, I let my mind wander to my first day at college. I had thought that from day one I would be learning about all these amazing novels. I would have been told to read the work of Shakespeare, Wilde, Yeats, Shelley. I would have been on time. Taking pages' worth of notes; understanding everything. I would have met hundreds of people as passionate about literature as I was. Instead, I had been humiliated in front of hundreds of strangers, and would for ever be known as the girl who fell. So as we reached the door to Alison's dorm I thought, It can't get any worse.

The small dorm was packed with people. We could barely get in the door.

'Alison!' Rosanna screamed as she ran across the room to a blonde girl who was standing next to a tall guy who looked like he was concentrating very hard on frowning.

'Hey, Roz, how are you? You know my super-amazing boyfriend Cian? He is on the Leinster Under Twenty-ones rugby team.' Alison gushed over Cian like he was a celebrity.

'Hi, Cian,' Rosanna said with a huge smile across her face. Cian merely grunted in return; maybe he was afraid speaking would ruin his *look*.

'Alison, this is Olive. She's my roommate – she is like so cool.'

Alison flicked her hair while turning towards me, and said, 'Hi, Olive. Oh my God, I like *love* your clothes.'

I smiled back. 'Thanks. They are Roz's. She was kind enough to let me borrow them. My dad is bringing up my stuff tomorrow, so I had absolutely nothing to wear this evening.'

Alison's facial expression never changed as I spoke. 'Oh really? That's nice,' she replied.

Our conversation had clearly ended as she turned back to her group of friends and they began talking. Rosanna joined in but I couldn't tell what any of them were saying, they were all talking so quickly. These girls had strong Dublin accents that were hard to understand when they spoke so fast. Eventually one of Alison's friends must have felt sorry for me, as she moved around so that she was standing next to me.

'This is such a fun party, right?' She was quite a short girl – I had to lean down when she was speaking to me.

'Um, yeah, it's great.'

'You guys have any problems finding the block?' Thankfully she spoke slowly so that I was able to understand her.

'No, Rosanna seemed to know where she was going. Also, we passed a couple kissing on the stairs. So we guessed that we must be close to some party,' I said, attempting to make a joke but this girl didn't seem to get it.

'Yeah, that's Peter and Alex. Oh my God, Alex has been like my best friend for ever but she is like the biggest slut. You know what I mean?'

'Oh . . . OK,' I replied, feeling at a loss. She just seemed to stare at me; she was obviously waiting for me to say something, to react somehow. 'I'm just going to go to the bathroom,' I said hurriedly, then turned and walked away before she offered to come with me. I knew that she was just trying to be nice, but I did not understand the girls here. Was it sarcasm? Or did they all really not like each other? I eventually forced myself to go back. I wanted to make more of an effort.

As the hours began to pass slowly, I did my best to socialize. I stuck to Roz mostly but I began to worry that I was becoming an annoyance, especially when she started talking to some guy that I didn't know. I decided to try and find somewhere to sit.

People were beginning to couple off. I guessed this was because there was plenty of alcohol flowing and there seemed to be nothing else to do. By now, I was feeling tired and wondered if I could slip away without anyone noticing. I found an empty chair in the corner of the hall. There didn't seem to be as many people out here so I decided to at least sit down for a few minutes before leaving. Rosanna's shoes were killing me. I sat down and took off the heels and started rubbing my feet. The shoes were a full size too small but Rosanna had insisted that I borrowed them.

'Bored?' I looked up to see a tall, thin guy with blue eyes and scruffy hair.

'No, no, just tired – first day of college and everything,' I said, slipping my heels back on. The pain was even worse now. He shrugged. He had a beanie on his head, which seemed odd because it was boiling in the hall. His hair and skin were quite dark and his face seemed thinner than it naturally should have been.

'Are you a first year?' he asked.

I nodded. 'English major.'

He smiled. His face seemed warmer, kinder, when he smiled. 'Ah. So you have come to UCD to experience the great and romantic Yeats, the scandalous Oscar Wilde and the very, very, *very* boring Joyce . . .'

I started to laugh. 'Well, yes, I have. And let me guess . . . You are a Philosophy major, spending your days smoking and drinking and contemplating the big questions in life – like where have we all come from?'

He patted my shoulder as if he was trying to be sympathetic.

'Not even close, my dear,' he told me. 'I am a Science student, specializing in Physics. I don't even go here – I go to Trinity, a real college. But I *do* spend my days smoking and drinking.'

I stared at my feet because I knew I was blushing, and mumbled, 'I can't imagine that smoking and drinking helps you understand Physics?'

'It doesn't – but it certainly makes it less painful.'

I laughed. I knew he was flirting with me and I let myself enjoy it.

'What do you think of your first UCD party so far then?' He took a sip from his beer. He seemed to exude an air of extreme confidence.

'Good. Everyone has been really nice.'

The boy in the beanie started to laugh. 'Nice is not the word I would use for the people here.'

'What do you mean?' I asked, unsure what he was trying to imply.

'Well, I think shallow, selfish and annoying are a much more accurate description of the individuals at this party.'

'That's not really fair,' I protested, but he rudely interrupted me.

'Fair? Come on! Nobody here understands what is fair. Most of the people here are just going to college to waste time until Daddy's trust fund kicks in.'

I was really beginning to get annoyed now. 'What makes you think that *you* are so much better?' I demanded, and he seemed taken aback, as if he had expected me to have no opinion on what he was saying – or worse, agree with him. I didn't know these people but I wasn't going to judge them so harshly, like he was. But then he started to smile again.

'I'm sorry, but don't pretend. I could see from a mile away that you are so much smarter than those other girls, especially Rosanna. She is the dizziest of the lot. Most of the people here probably think Freud is a cosmetics line.'

I wanted to slap that cocky smile off his face. 'Look, I don't know who you are,' I said quietly.

'I'm Tom.'

'But you seem like an asshole to me.'

I stood up and went storming out the door. What a little shite, thinking he was so much better than everyone else there. I passed the same couple that I had on the way in, except now the guy had managed to get his hands under her top. I tried to run past them but Rosanna's heels meant that I could go no faster than a brisk walk. I was nearly at the bottom of the stairs when I heard someone following me. I prayed it was Rosanna but I was wrong.

'Hey, wait up!' Tom had jumped in front of me so that I couldn't walk away. 'Look, I wasn't trying to insult you – I was trying to give you a compliment.'

'OK, fine,' I said, making to walk around him, but he stepped in front of me again.

'Wait. You never told me your name.'

'Olive!' I practically spat out. I was grumpy and tired.

'Are you going home already?'

'Yes,' I replied. I had accepted the fact there was no way I was going to get around him in Rosanna's heels.

'Well, can I walk you home then?'

'No, thanks,' and with that I popped off the heels and walked as fast as I could back to the dorm.

4

Tom

I WALKED BACK UP THE STAIRS TO ALISON'S DORM COMPLETELY confused. What was Olive's problem? What had I said that was so wrong and insulting? She could not have gotten away from me fast enough. Peter seemed to be making good progress with the blonde. I kicked him as I walked by; he didn't even look up to see who it was. He just gave me the finger. Damien was in the same place where I had left him; he looked like a drooling dog as he stared at a group of girls standing nearby. My friends were such twats.

'Damien, stop.'

'What?' he asked irritably. I had clearly disturbed his trance.

'You look like you're about to hop on top of one of them. Down, boy.'

'I am not a dog, Tom.'

'Then stop acting like one,' I said, stealing the beer out of his hand and gulping it back in one mouthful.

'Fuck off, Tom, get your own drink.' He grabbed it out of my hand but it was already empty.

'So did the brunette burn you then?' Damien asked smugly, knowing the answer.

'She was a complete weirdo. I tried to give her a compliment and she freaked out. The girl looked bored out of her mind, thought she might have wanted a bit of a laugh.'

'I knew she wouldn't go for you.'

'How?' I asked, getting annoyed.

'She looked like a girl with some standards.'

I was starting to get really annoyed now. 'Fuck off, Damien, I could have had her if I'd wanted her. I'm just not bothered.'

'Of course you're not bothered. You're not bothered with any girl that you have to work at, because you know you won't get anywhere.'

I wanted to punch him; he was smiling because he knew he was getting to me.

'A girl like that wouldn't touch *you*, let alone score you.' I slammed the empty beer bottle down on the counter; it was so loud that a couple of people standing nearby were now staring. 'Watch your mouth, Damien. I'm serious.'

He looked a little afraid of me now. I knew I needed to calm down, that I was overreacting. But I couldn't help it. Everyone always expected me to fail, even my own friends.

'Chill, Tom. I am only taking the piss out of you.'

I smiled and gave him a gentle shove. The anger was still there, but I had to pretend that I was fine.

'She was pretty decent though, wasn't she?' Damien went on, and I nodded, fearing what I might say if I spoke. 'Maybe *I* should have a go with her – ask that Rosanna girl for her number?'

I don't know why, but the thought of Damien hitting on Olive made me feel worse. 'Don't, Damien.' I started to imagine the two of them flirting, kissing – it made me feel ill.

'Why not? You're not going to have another go, are you?'

'I might.' I was trying desperately to stay calm. I shoved my hands in my pockets because they were beginning to shake.

'What if she rejects you again?' Damien was sounding snide.

'She won't,' I said sternly.

'Why not make a little wager on it then?'

I looked at him to see if he was being serious. 'Fuck off. I am not doing that.'

'Why not, if you're so sure? Come on, I will give you a hundred euro if you can get her to sleep with you in two months.'

I knew I shouldn't be considering this. It was stupid, immature and a really easy way to lose money. But the cocky look on Damien's face was really pissing me off. He thought I couldn't do it. No one ever thinks I can do or achieve anything. For once I wanted to prove them all wrong.

'Make it six months?'

'Five.'

'Fine.' As I shook his hand I felt a lump form in my throat.

'And you can't stop me from trying with her if you lose.'

'OK . . . I'm going to the jacks.' I needed to get away from him, from everyone.

The bathroom stank – it was clear that someone had been sick in it earlier. I splashed cold water over my face and leaned against the sink, my hands still shaking. *Who the fuck did Damien think he was?* I couldn't understand why I was so angry. I seemed to be angry all the time these days. The smallest thing would set me off and then I would be full of rage. I hated this situation that I was trapped in: nothing I did ever seemed to make a difference.

Why had I bothered to make the bet? But I had, and I needed to pull it off. I didn't have 100 euro to lose. In fact, I barely had 20 euro, and asking my mum for money was not a good plan. Her reaction was unpredictable; she might scream at me or start crying – or give it to me with a smile. More than likely it would be one of the first two. Damien would definitely not forget about the bet either, especially since I had made such a big deal over it. *Shit, how was I going to convince this girl to sleep with me? She hated me already.* I stared at myself in the mirror.

'What am I doing?' I murmured. I didn't want to be this guy any more, the guy who didn't care about anything or anyone. The guy who did stupid shit with his friends and hurt people along the way. I hated myself and yet I knew I couldn't stop.

Just then, I heard someone knocking on the door.

'Sorry, not done!' I shouted, but the person just kept knocking. I had only been in here for two minutes. 'Wait a second,' I called, but the person kept going. I unlocked the door to find Alison standing in front of me – well, not standing exactly, more leaning up against the doorframe.

'Hi, Tom,' she giggled, looking me up and down. 'What you doing?'

'Nothing. Do you need the bathroom?' I asked, pretending to be innocent.

'No,' she said, still giggling.

I could smell vodka off her breath. 'Then why were you knocking?' I asked.

''Cause I wanted to talk to you – *privately*.' She pushed me back into the bathroom and locked the door behind her. 'My boyfriend cheats on me all the time, Tom.'

'Your boyfriend is a twat.'

'I think so too.' She jumped up on to the sink counter so that she was sitting in front of me. 'You think I'm hot, don't you?'

I knew exactly what was going to happen but it was fun to play along. 'Yeah, of course I do,' I replied, smiling. We had both done this so many times before but I still got a rush from it. I walked over to her and put my hand on her bare leg. She really did have very nice legs. She pulled my face to hers and started kissing me aggressively. I responded by grabbing her by the waist and tugging her hips closer to mine. She started undoing my belt and I pushed up her skirt.

'Tom, don't tell anyone.'

'No problem.' I needed the rush. The rush would make me forget.

I woke up the next morning to the sight of Damien's feet. We were both on the floor with whatever blankets Peter had allowed us to borrow. The one over me was actually a towel. I didn't remember much from the night before. After my encounter with Alison in the bathroom, Damien, Peter and I had managed to drink a litre of vodka between us. Something that I definitely regretted now, as my head was pounding. I managed to drag myself up from the floor and look around Peter's apartment, though I did have to lean against the wall for support. Everything was filthy as always – the bin overflowing, beer cans scattered across the floor and the counter-tops were sticky.

I somehow managed to get myself to the bathroom, turn on the taps and splash my face with water. At this point I noticed a number scribbled on my hand and the name *Sinead* above it.

Confused, I walked back into the main room and gave Damien a kick.

'Fuck off,' he mumbled, turning over. He had slept fully dressed like me, but at least I had managed to take my shoes off; his runners were still on his feet. I kicked him again, harder this time.

'What?' he shouted, not even opening his eyes.

'Who's Sinead?' I asked, trying desperately to remember what had happened after we left Alison's.

'Jumbo,' he sighed, still refusing to open his eyes.

I was completely lost. Who on earth was Jumbo? 'Who?'

Damien opened his eyes this time. He had obviously realized that I wasn't going to leave him alone.

'Some fat bird that was stalking you last night. It was fucking hilarious.'

'Shit, I don't remember anything.' I rubbed my pounding head.

'Not surprised. You were pissed out of your mind – you could barely speak. Don't know how you got into Coppers.'

'We were in Coppers?' The whole night was a complete blank to me.

'Yeah, Jumbo practically raped you there.'

I suddenly felt like I was going to be sick. 'Fuck, did I score her?'

'Nah, not really. She kept trying to but you just kept falling asleep. It was pretty funny to watch.' Damien started to sit up now. 'Shit, my head is spinning,' he said, while rubbing his face. 'That vodka nearly killed me. At least I wasn't as bad as you, Tom. Peter and I had to carry you here.'

I sat down on the ground next to Damien, laughing. I didn't exactly find anything he said funny but I found it easier just to pretend to laugh at my drunken idiocy.

'How wrecked was Jumbo?'

'Pretty awful,' he replied, 'but, sure, you had no clue what was going on. I don't think that will help you win our bet.' Sadly, this was part of the night that I remembered clearly and Damien knew it too.

'Ah, sure, that will be a piece of cake,' I said, trying to sound as if I didn't care.

Damien was laughing now. 'Whatever, mate. All I know is that next semester I will be a hundred euro richer and you rejected.'

I gave him a shove before standing up and walked to Peter's kitchen. I opened his fridge to find it was completely empty.

'Does Peter ever have any fucking food?' I slammed the fridge closed and prayed that Damien wouldn't bring up the bet again. My only hope was that maybe he would eventually forget about it. That was unlikely, though. He didn't have much luck when it came to girls. He was always jealous that I barely had to do anything and I would still get laid. Any chance to humiliate me and he would take it. I had no idea what I was going to do. I never asked girls out, and I didn't know how to convince Olive to sleep with me.

Damien was right about one thing. Olive wasn't like the girls I normally went for: she wasn't easy. She had seemed honest and loyal. Characteristics that were painfully hard to find these days. I would be lying if I said that I wasn't attracted to her. I had been attracted to her from the second I saw her. She had surprised me – something that other girls never seemed able to do. I was going to have to act the nice boy role; girls were supposed to love that. Sure I'd just find out where she lived from Rosanna, if I still had her number. I'd tell Olive that I just wanted to be her friend – she would surely agree to that. Once I got her alone for a while I'd be able to get her to fall for me. Maybe this wouldn't be as difficult as I'd thought. Give her a few compliments, dish out some flowers and chocolates; it was more than what most guys did for sex.

Peter had finally arisen from his room. 'Lads, what time is it?'

I looked at my phone, which was still in my pocket, thankfully. The state I had been in last night meant that I could have easily lost it.

'Eleven,' I answered. I also noticed three missed calls from my mum, but I chose to ignore them.

'Eleven? Fuck, my dad's coming over in half an hour. This place is a state, he's going to kill me. You guys have to go!'

'Why is he coming here?' Damien asked, still not getting up.

'He wants to discuss my future.'

Damien and I both looked at each other and burst out laughing.

'Fuck off, lads. Seriously, if he thinks I'm dossing he will just cut me off – no money, no apartment, nothing.'

'That would be pretty shit,' I said, still laughing. But Peter was not impressed; he started to clean manically and shoved the two of us out the door.

'Hate to be him. I'm going to head home and get a shower. See you later, Tom.' Damien turned around and started walking down the stairs.

As I watched him I began to wonder, Where can I go?

5

Alison

'ALISON. ALISON? *ALISON!*' I COULD HEAR MY DAD, HE WAS JUST across the table. He sounded angry. He had a very short temper, especially when it came to me. So I decided it was best to answer him before he caused a complete scene in public.

'What?' I sighed, not even looking at him.

'Katie asked you how your first week back was. Answer her, please.'

'Fine.' I shrugged. Katie was my dad's second wife, a child bride really. When I am forced to go to public places with them like this, people usually assume that we are sisters. That is, until the PDA (Public Display of Affection) starts anyway. Then people either look away in embarrassment or stare with shock. Dad had become so vain ever since he had met Katie. He had hired a personal trainer and went to the gym several times a week. He regularly dyed his hair so that there were no longer any traces of grey to it. It almost seemed like he was getting younger rather than older in the last few years. My friends shamelessly flirted with him when they came to my house, claiming that he was by far the best-looking dad. I pretended not to care when they went on about him, but truthfully it made my skin crawl.

'I used to love UCD. I can't believe it's been six years since I left – I feel so old.' Katie was twisting her blonde curls in her fingers and smiling towards my dad. She looked like a two-year-old who wanted attention – and my dad was always ready to give it to her.

'Come on now, Katie. You don't look a day over twenty-five.'

She started giggling at him. 'Oh, Robert, stop, you're too kind.'

'Well, she is only twenty-eight,' I mumbled, regretting it once I said it.

'Stop with those smart comments, Alison. You're acting like a moody teenager!'

I could see the red reaching my dad's ears, and knew I was pushing my luck. Katie didn't get it, she never did. I didn't know whether this was because she was dim or whether she pretended to be dim; either way, my dad loved it. She continued to curl her hair in her fingers and look at the two of us, the smile never faltering.

We were sitting in the tea room of the Four Seasons Hotel. My dad had been trying to organize this 'get-together' for days now but I just kept putting it off. I hated being in a public place with the two of them. It felt like a bad performance. Katie was the perfect stepmother and I was the polite and understanding stepdaughter. Except I was not polite and I did not understand. I did not understand why I had to pretend we were one big happy family when it was all so fucked up. I despised my father: he had destroyed us.

When my dad had started to date Katie I thought it was some sort of mid-life crisis after his divorce from Mum. My mother had left him for a younger man but not quite as young as Katie. I thought the phase would pass and he would dump the gold-digger. But after only six months of dating they announced their engagement. Then four months later they had the wedding. Katie claimed that she just could not wait to be a wife. I think that she just could not wait to be rich. My dad loved to spend money on her – new house, new car, multiple trips away, half of which he didn't even go on. Katie liked to call these 'girl weekends' but I knew better than that.

Dad ran his hand through his balding hair; he did this when he was going to say something that he knew I wouldn't like. Since Katie had arrived this was nearly all the time.

'Alison, Katie and I have some news for you . . . Good news, actually.'

I had been waiting for this. He would not have taken me somewhere so civilized and public unless he was worried I was going to throw a tantrum.

'OK.' I was half-hoping they would announce that they were moving so I didn't have to deal with them any more. Mum had moved to Barcelona with her toy boy. This made her a lot easier to deal with.

'Katie and I are having a baby.' Katie was smiling even more broadly now. Dad was smiling too but it looked rather forced. I didn't think a baby was something that would satisfy his desperate need to feel younger.

The two sat there staring at me, waiting for a reply, Katie with her picture-perfect smile and Dad's smile turning into a frown.

'Oh, good,' I said, mustering up as much fake enthusiasm as I could.

'It's going to be amazing,' cooed my stepmother. 'You will have a little baby sister or brother. Though I really hope it's a girl. I have always wanted a little girl. Wouldn't that just be amazing, Robert?'

It was now my dad's turn to be stuck on the spot. He looked trapped – I guess he was.

'Yeah, it would be great,' he said heavily, looking down at his shoes.

Katie squealed. 'Oh, it's all just so exciting!'

I felt my phone buzzing in my pocket; the text simply said *I'm outside.* I picked up my Juicy Couture handbag and stood up, announcing, 'I have to go.'

'Where?' my dad asked with aggression in his voice. He didn't like people walking away from him.

'My friend is outside,' I said, thinking, Let him get angry. He never did anything about it except yell.

'Ooh, is it a boy?' Katie asked in her annoying squeaky voice. 'Is he hot?' she added curiously. She really enjoyed flirting with my guy friends; she would wear low-cut tops and giggle at their pathetic jokes. I walked away without even answering her. What was the point.

A baby? A baby! My dad was an idiot. He was forty-five; he would be in his sixties when the kid went to college, if he even made it that long. His anger issues might kill him before then. Katie wouldn't be that sad, since she would inherit everything. She wouldn't have to pretend to like me then. Maybe Dad isn't the father; it could be the result of one of Katie's 'girl trips' to Vegas or something. That would be great; Dad would definitely get rid of her then.

Cian was leaning up against his car – a black BMW – in the Four Seasons' car park. He had gotten it for his eighteenth but he wanted a new one for his twenty-first this year and he would probably get it. Cian was the 'ideal' boyfriend – good-looking, affluent, in UCD on a rugby scholarship. All the girls wanted him, and he was mine. Well, technically anyway; he didn't call anyone else his girlfriend. I knew he slept around. I pretended not to know because it was easier. It seemed my whole life was based on fantasies and lies. No one seemed to care that everything was fake, that I was fake.

Not my family, not my friends and especially not Cian.

He was wearing navy cantos and an Ireland rugby jersey. He didn't wave or smile when he saw me, merely nodded his head. I walked over to him.

'Hey,' I said, trying to act cool.

'Hey,' he replied, doing the same thing. Then: 'So what was the story with your party last week? Jordan said you had sex in the bathroom with that druggie Tom guy.'

It was a bit ironic for Cian to call anyone else a druggie. He took tons of steroids every day to keep himself big and muscular. He claimed that they were just supplements but I wasn't as thick as Cian thought I was.

'Jordan is a shit-stirrer. What about you? The girls said that you got head off that slut Rebecca in the disabled toilets in the club.'

'Your friends are jealous bitches.'

We stood there in silence for a while. I knew that Cian had been with Rebecca and he knew I had been with Tom, but as long as no one else knew, it didn't matter.

'Can we go?' I asked, getting into the passenger seat of the BMW. Cian merely grunted and got into the driver's side. He turned on the engine and then revved it aggressively. He skidded out of the car park leaving behind some angry-looking people who clearly worked in the hotel. So this seemed to be my life. Acting like everything was fine when actually it was all fucked up. Pretending to be happy when all I really wanted to do was scream. Destined to be exactly like my parents even though I despised them. Maybe Katie and I had more in common than I had originally thought.

6

Olive

THERE WAS NO POINT IN WORRYING, BUT I COULDN'T HELP IT. At the start of the day I had reassured myself that he might have lost his phone or maybe had forgotten to charge it – he could be forgetful at times. But as the day progressed I found it impossible to think about my lectures and tutorials; I could only think about him. Why hadn't he texted me or called me back? It wasn't like him. I started to consider ringing my mum. I didn't want to worry her, but I couldn't think about anything else all day. By five o'clock my lectures had ended and I was sitting in our apartment alone. Beth had classes till nine and Rosanna was probably outside the arts block smoking. That was usually where she could be found.

The past two weeks seemed to have flown by. College was no longer as intimidating as it first had seemed. I had learned where most things were and my lectures were starting to make sense to me. The evenings were still the strangest. I wasn't used to having to cook for myself and I made silly mistakes, like forgetting to defrost the chicken or leaving food in the oven too long and then it would be burned to a crisp. I had learned very quickly that cooking was not one of my secret talents. Luckily Roz never cooked and I was able to join her and her friends when they went out to dinner. I loved Roz's company. She was always warm and friendly towards me, but I still found it difficult to talk to her friends. I felt like such an outsider when I was around them. I was always the person who just didn't get it.

Being alone in the dorm didn't help my anxiety, although I tried watching TV for a while. My dad had bought me a miniature set and had brought it up with my clothes. I kept it in my bedroom, not because I didn't want to share. In fact, it had been Beth's idea to put it in my room in the first place. We worried that if it was in the common room, where there was a large window, we might get caught by the TV licence inspector. They were always skulking around the UCD campus.

After thirty minutes of failed attempts to distract myself, I called my mum.

'Hey, Olive. Everything OK?' She sounded panicked and flustered. This wasn't a good sign.

'Um . . . yeah. Just wanted to ring and say hi to everyone.'

'That's nice, hun. Is that all?' It was obvious that something was up.

'Mum, is Andy there? I rang him three times last night and twice this morning, and he is not picking up.'

My mum went silent for a second; this confirmed that something was seriously wrong.

'Your brother had a bit of a bad day yesterday but he is fine now, so don't worry.' My mum had always been an awful liar.

'What do you mean, a bad day?' I asked, really getting nervous now.

'He just had one of his mood swings. He didn't really calm down so we brought him to the clinic to spend the night. We're picking him up later.'

While my mum had been talking I had run into my room and started packing my bags.

'I'm coming home,' I told her.

'No, you're not. You can't be missing days upon days of college. Andy is fine. It's just the football season is over and you are gone . . . I think he got a little upset last night. The clinic rang today and said everything was under control.' This really meant that they had used drugs to calm him down.

'Are you sure I shouldn't come home, Mum? I think I should be there when he gets out.'

'No, you stay where you are. I didn't tell you about it because I knew you would want to come home, which is completely silly. Don't worry – I'm sure he will call you once he is back.'

'OK,' I choked. I could feel the tears brimming up. I said goodbye and went to the bathroom to wash my face.

I felt so guilty – I should be there. Andrew was my little brother. He was fifteen, and even when he was only a toddler my dad knew there was something different about him. He would have these awful mood swings. He once cried and screamed for three days straight. He eventually passed out and Mum had to bring him to the hospital, where he was treated for sleep deprivation. My mum always claimed that there was nothing wrong with him. 'Boys are always moody,' she would say. My dad, who was convinced he was ill, had many arguments with her, trying to persuade her to bring him to see someone. Bless my mum, she always refused. His mood swings were completely inexplicable; he would be happy and laughing one moment and depressed and crying the next. It got worse when he started school; he found it hard to make friends and was often the subject of bullying.

Andy was twelve years old the first time he tried to commit suicide. He had hanged himself in his room. Downstairs we heard the crashing of the chair. My dad went up to see where the noise had come from. When he found him he shouted for my mum to call an ambulance, saying that the two of us were to stay downstairs no matter what. I remember that day so well. The paramedics ran into our house and my mum was crying, telling them to go upstairs, that her son had just tried to kill himself. I always wondered how she knew that was what had happened. My dad had said nothing other than to call an ambulance, and yet she knew. It was so scary, hearing the sounds of the paramedics' voices; they were shouting urgent orders at each other. After what felt like hours, they came back down the stairs with my brother on a stretcher and a breathing mask around his face.

'He is alive,' they simply said before putting him into the ambulance. There were silent tears running down Mum's face and my dad was as white as ice. After the sight of Andy's bruised neck, I ran to the bathroom and started to vomit violently. Next time Dad suggested that Andy see someone, my mum didn't argue.

He visited what seemed like an endless number of doctors and specialists. They decided his attempted suicide was a combination of bullying and severe hormonal imbalance. For a while it seemed as if all Andy's problems were over. My parents took him out of school and he was taking medication: it all seemed so simple. Everything was fixed with one pill a day. It didn't last long, though. The mood swings started again, and with them came more and more medication. It was awful when he got angry: he would scream till his face went blue, and start breaking everything around him. I saw him punch through his mirror once. When he finally calmed down we took him to hospital to get stitches. It got harder when he grew older, since he was stronger now. When he was a child my mum would just hold him still until he stopped; now he was nearly as strong as my dad. I knew there would come a day when he would overpower Dad, and I didn't know what would happen then.

Even worse than Andy's anger fits were his stages of depression. Unlike his anger, his depression would sometimes last for weeks. During these times, he didn't speak, he didn't eat. He refused to get out of bed. When he was depressed, he was never left alone. One of us would sleep on the floor of his room, and we would take turns checking on him every fifteen minutes during the day. It was exhausting, but all of us feared what would happen if we didn't do it.

After a year of very little improvement the doctors suggested that Andy move into the clinic where he could be monitored at all times. My parents and I were unified in the decision to keep Andy at home. We were a family and we would face problems together, not alone. Although there had been the odd time that we'd been forced to take him to the clinic, either because we were unable to calm him down or were afraid he was about to do something, he had never spent longer than a few days there.

It was two weeks after his fourteenth birthday that Andy tried to take his life again. His mood had been relatively normal so we hadn't been keeping as close an eye as we usually did. I had come home from school to find Mum in the kitchen starting to get dinner ready. Dad was still at work. I was absolutely ecstatic. I was seventeen and John had just asked me to be his girlfriend, and I wanted everyone to know.

'That's fantastic,' Mum said. She had always been a fan of John; he was the typical nice country boy that mothers loved.

'We're going on our first date tonight – he is taking me out to dinner. I am so excited. Where's Andy?' I asked. I knew he would be thrilled. John always came over to play computer games with him. He never teased him for his oddness; he was probably Andy's closest thing to a real friend.

'I think he is upstairs taking a bath. Tell him it's time to get out. Dinner is nearly ready.'

I ran up the stairs two steps at a time, absolutely jumping for joy, and banged on the bathroom door.

'Andy! Andy, get out. I have some amazing news.' There was no answer. 'Andy!' I shouted louder – still nothing. I opened the door; there were no locks in our house, not after his first attempt. I don't think there is anything in the world that could have prepared me for what lay on the other side of that door.

Andy was lying naked in the bathtub soaked in his own blood. His left wrist was slit open, and in his right hand he had what looked like a butter-knife. I let out a scream of horror and crumpled to the floor. I heard the clatter of my mum dropping something and then her footsteps running upstairs.

'Olive! Olive! What is going on?' She stopped mid-run when she saw Andy. '*No*,' she whispered, the entire colour draining from her face. I lay on the floor in absolute hysterics, not able to stand I was crying so hard. My mum turned to me and hoisted me up from the floor.

'Olive, you have to listen to me. You have to go to the phone and call 999 and tell them what has happened. You have to do that now, Olive, OK?' As I nodded, she shoved me in the direction of the phone and went to help Andy.

I don't remember much of my conversation on the phone, but the operator seemed to know from my hysterics and sobbing that something had gone terribly wrong. Within minutes Andy was being put into an ambulance. The paramedics let my mum and me ride in the back with him. When we got to the hospital, the doctors announced that he would survive. The knife had not been sharp enough to cut the veins properly, but it had been an extremely close call. The nurses took me away and treated me for shock. They wanted to treat Mum too, but she kept on insisting that she was fine and she wanted to wait and see her son.

Mum didn't call Dad until they announced that Andy would

live. He was over within minutes. He came running into the hospital, shouting, 'Andrew Fitzsimmons! Andrew Fitzsimmons! Can someone please tell me where Andrew Fitzsimmons is?'

I remember thinking it was like a dramatic scene in a film but it was real. And my dad wasn't an actor, he was a real person and his terror was real. When they finally let us see Andy, he was fast asleep. They said his body needed time to recover and he would be awake in a few hours. We all stayed in Andy's room that night. I fell asleep holding his hand.

The next day I woke up to see Andy sitting in his bed eating toast. It was surreal to see him like this, acting as if nothing had happened. He saw I was awake and gestured towards his food.

'Good breakfast,' he said between mouthfuls. I said nothing. I merely looked around the room. Mum and Dad were nowhere to be seen. Andy must have noticed me looking for them. 'They went to get some coffee. They said they would be back soon.' He stared at me nervously, waiting for an answer.

'How can you just sit there? How could you do that?' I could feel the tears welling up in my eyes. 'You are so selfish! How could you do that to me? I thought you were dead, Andy. I really did! How could you put me through that hell!' I was screaming now. 'Do you hate me that much, Andy? Do you?'

Andy was staring at me with shock on his face. 'I felt like I had no other choice. No one wants me,' he muttered.

I got up from my chair and slapped him across the face.

'How dare you? How dare you blame us for what you did.' I suddenly felt someone's arms wrap around my chest.

'Let go! Let go!' I screamed.

'Calm down, Olive.' My dad was leading me towards the door but I fought every step of the way. When he eventually got me outside I just collapsed into a heap. I don't know how long it was I cried for, but my dad sat next to me, soothing me the whole time.

I tried to shake away the memories; sitting in my college dorm was not the time to think of such dark moments.

'He is getting better,' I whispered to myself. I had to believe that. I looked in my book bag and found what was definitely the heaviest one: Chaucer's *Canterbury Tales*. We had been told to compare different translations and to come up with negatives and positives to each translation. It was boring and difficult work; it was exactly what I needed.

7
Tom

I HAD AVOIDED THINKING ABOUT OLIVE AND THAT RIDICULOUS bet for nearly three weeks now. I had convinced myself it was because I didn't care, but I knew I was kidding myself. I didn't want to be rejected; I didn't want to fail again. If I didn't try, then I wouldn't fail. But I had to try and it wasn't just because of the bet. It was because I wanted to prove to myself that a guy like me could get a girl like Olive. I wanted to prove everyone wrong.

It was a Saturday and I was actually glad of an excuse to leave the house. Mum was in one of her weeping moods again, ranting on about the house falling apart and the lack of work. I left as soon as she turned on me; it was the easiest thing to do.

At the bus stop I held up the queue as I took my sweet time counting my change.

'One twenty . . . one thirty . . .' Then I would pretend to search in my pocket for a while. 'One thirty-five . . .' I smiled to myself as I heard one guy in a grey suit holding a briefcase say, 'For fuck's sake!' The queue disappeared quickly after I had counted all my change together and sat on the bus. Everyone who came in behind me gave me a filthy look, except for this old granny who had a smile plastered on her face. She probably had no idea that she was even on a bus.

When I reached UCD I was amazed to see how quiet it was. Maybe it would be easier to find Olive than I thought. I made my way over to Merville, which looked like a complete ghost town. I began to pray that she hadn't gone home for the weekend; my plan was getting more flawed by the second.

I had been wandering around for forty minutes and was about to give up when I spotted her. Not exactly who I wanted, but it was better than nothing.

'Hey, Rosanna!' I shouted. She was walking out of Centra chatting with another dark-haired girl. She turned around at the sound of my voice. When she saw me she frowned with a look of confusion on her face.

'Tom? Hi.'

I jogged over to her and gave her a hug; this made her look even more confused. 'How are you?' I asked.

'Good. Horrifically hung-over, but good. This is my roommate Beth.' She gestured to the petite girl standing next to her. There was a bit of an awkward silence and Rosanna looked like she just wanted to walk away. I decided I had better get to the point.

'I saw you chatting to that Olive girl at Alison's party. I was just wondering if you knew her?' I wished I had been a bit more subtle but I couldn't take it back now.

'Yeah, she's our roommate. Why?' Rosanna sounded sceptical and I started to panic about what to say next.

'Oh well . . . Just, I was chatting to her at the party and she seemed cool. Is she around?'

'No, she went home for the weekend. She said she wanted to see her brother.'

'Oh, right.' I began staring at my feet. 'Do you know if she is single?'

'Yeah, I think she is.' Rosanna scrutinized me as if 'desperation' was tattooed across my forehead.

'Oh, cool. Great . . . So could I maybe get her number off you?' Beth was looking at Rosanna and me as if we were speaking a different language. I frantically tried to think of ways to not sound so pathetic. I couldn't think of any.

'I don't know . . . Olive is kind of a private person. I don't think she would want me to give out her number to random people.' Rosanna sounded sympathetic. It was obvious she felt sorry for me. My embarrassment level had reached its limit and now I just wanted to get as far away as physically possible.

'Oh, OK,' I said, giving up all hope.

'Hey, Tom!' Rosanna called as I started to walk away. 'We live in Block F, Room 4. She will be back on Monday, if you want to talk to her yourself?'

'Um, yeah, I might be around.'

She smiled at me before she and Beth started walking in the opposite direction.

There was no doubt in my mind that Rosanna pitied me; she didn't think I had a chance. Her offer for me to come to the dorm was only because she felt bad for me. I didn't know how I was supposed to be doing this. I had come from a school where no one asked anyone on dates. Instead we would all meet up as a group and go underage drinking in a field or down a street corner. I had lost my virginity on one of these nights when I was fifteen. The girl had been two years older than me and a lot more experienced. I had had no idea what I was doing; I just did as she told me. It had been really awkward and a huge let-down. When I tried to say hello to her the next day in school she ignored me completely. I soon learned that the less talking you did with the opposite sex, the better.

When I reached the bus stop, I didn't know what to do. I couldn't stand still. I found myself walking back and forth, back and forth. I didn't know where to go. Peter's? He hated when I turned up out of the blue, especially at weekends. Damien's? He lived in the back arse of nowhere. Anyway his parents didn't like me, thought I was a hippie or something. Dad's? That was never an option. Back to Mum's? She might not be over her mood yet. Back and forth, back and forth. I eventually jumped onto the bus heading into the city centre. Mostly because it was there than for any other reason.

'Oh my God. She is such a bitch! Not only did she score Johnny but she then claimed she didn't know anything was going on between him and me! Like, oh my God! Everyone knows Johnny and I have been scoring for months! We're practically a couple.'

I wished I hadn't sat down here; these two absolute fools could not be any louder. I had 'Paint the Silence' by the South blaring in my ears and yet I could still hear those two crows shouting about this stupid guy Johnny. Surely this was not a conversation that these two girls wanted to be overheard by the whole bus? Not that anyone would have been interested. The two girls looked young enough. If I had to guess, I would say fifteen, maybe even fourteen. It was hard to tell, with the mountain of make-up on both of them. One was blonde and the other had red hair which looked as if she had unsuccessfully tried to dye it blonde. The blonde was actually not that bad-looking, but as soon as I heard the posh Dublin twang, I was instantly repulsed.

'I swear if I see her tonight, I'm going to tell her to back the fuck off,' said the girl with red hair while texting on her pink phone. You could see the build-up of fake tan in between her fingers. I was starting to wish I had taken another bus.

The day was getting bitterly cold. It was a typical Irish autumn day and most people were well wrapped up, but these two girls had nothing more than tank-tops on and a hoodie wrapped around their waists. I flicked my iPod on to 'Rootless Tree' by Damien Rice. At full blast it was just about loud enough to drown out the two crows.

My mind started to wander to the conversation, actually argument, that Mum and I had had before I left that morning. She had many moods. Sometimes she would be depressed and I would spend the day making her cups of tea and telling her how much I was enjoying college. Talking about college always made her feel better. I think it proved to her that I wasn't going to end up like my dad, working in a pub, barely making enough money to survive. Other days she would be full of energy, and she would run around the house, cleaning, singing, talking about all the fun things she did when she was younger, and all the exciting things that were just waiting for me and all the opportunities I had. When she was in these joyful moods she always made these exciting plans for us. Going abroad to see New York or the Eiffel Tower or maybe even Italy? I loved it when she was like this. It was impossible not to be sucked in by her excitement, and I would even begin to fantasize what New York looked like.

But it was always with a hint of sadness that I would go along with her dreams. I knew we would never be able to go anywhere. She was only a cleaner, and any spare money she made went to paying for college. Free education? What bullshit! It was 1,600 euro just for registration fees, and because our economy was shit at the moment it looked like the fees would double next year. But the mood she was in today was definitely when she was most difficult to handle. She would just become so angry at our financial situation and she would then turn on me.

'Maybe if you were ever home to help, I could take more cleaning jobs and we would have more spare money.' I knew she was just saying this. She couldn't get any more cleaning jobs. We were in a recession and people weren't hiring. Having a cleaning lady wasn't a necessity and my mum was getting less work every week. But she liked having someone to blame and I was an easy target.

'I'm going out.' I already had my coat on and the door half-open before she replied.

'Just like your father!' she shouted. 'There's an issue that needs to be discussed and you just leave. You will never—' I had closed the door before she could finish what she was saying. I never said anything to defend myself when she was in these moods. What was the point? She was incredibly stubborn, and I would just say something that would hurt her and she would just get depressed again. No matter what I did, I always seemed to hurt her.

I suddenly noticed that the two girls in front of me had stopped talking and were looking at me. They both looked very angry and annoyed but I didn't know if that was directed at me or whether that was just the way they always looked. I took my earphones out and was sure I must look pretty confused; I would laugh if they were going to give out to me for eavesdropping.

'I'm sorry,' said the blonde, who did not look the least bit sorry, 'but your music is very loud. I can't hear my friend.'

I couldn't help but laugh out loud at this, which made the blonde one look even more angry. No way was I turning my music down so they could continue their pointless conversation. I flicked through my iPod and tried to find the loudest music possible. I put on 'Cassius' by the Foals and made sure the volume was on full.

'Better?' I asked with a massive smile on my face.

The two girls looked disgusted and turned around and started whispering to each other. My music was so loud I only caught the odd phrase such as 'fucking bastard', 'so fucking rude', 'what's his problem?' Swearing really was very unattractive on girls; I smiled to myself in satisfaction. I had fun trying to choose what I felt would be the most offending music to them for the rest of the bus journey and by the time I reached Grafton Street I almost felt cheery. As I stepped off the bus, the cold air filled my lungs. The street was full of people going somewhere, having stuff to do, friends to meet. I loved how busy town was – it always revived me. I started walking to Murder's Foulest Things, a small bookshop just off Dawson Street. The underfoot was wet from the rain the night before and cars flew by, splashing puddles of water on unsuspecting victims.

The door of Murder's Foulest Things clinked when I walked in. The middle-aged woman who had been reading a book at the till looked up and smiled when she saw me. She was a fair woman, who had many worry lines across her forehead. But you could tell she had been very pretty when she was younger.

'I didn't expect you back so soon, Tom. You can't possibly have finished those two books you bought last Tuesday?'

I had first met Moiraine about a year ago, when I had entered Murder's Foulest Things for the first time. I had been so intrigued by the unusual selection of books that you could find here. Moiraine loved murder mysteries and the small shop was packed corner to corner with books about crime. There was a small area devoted to what she considered to be romance novels but which were, in fact, books about sex with maybe the odd vampire romance thrown in every now and again.

'I had a lot of spare time the last few days. Just my lack of social life,' I said, smiling back at her.

From the first day I walked in, Moiraine had chatted to me as if she had known me for years. She would often lecture me on my health and well-being, but she always said it with a hint of a smile, as if to say, 'I know what it is like to be your age.'

'Lack of social life?' She laughed. 'Darling, I can tell you're nursing a massive hangover. You want a cup of tea?' She was already heading into the back room, which had a small kitchen with a sink and kettle.

'Well, I did go out with Peter and Damien last night.' There was just something about Moiraine. I could never lie to her.

'You boys. Do you have to go nuts every night? Your liver is going to be in bits when you're thirty!' Probably earlier, I thought to myself. She came back out from the kitchen and handed me a cup of tea, saying, 'So how's your mum today?'

Moiraine was the only person I ever spoke to about my mum. I think it was because I knew that she and my mum would never cross paths. Maybe it was also because I knew Moiraine would never judge me.

'She's having one of those days. Blaming me for everything that is wrong with the world – well, our world anyway.' I instantly wished I hadn't said anything. I trusted Moiraine, but she didn't need to know every problem me and my mum had.

'I bet you clean up pretty well,' was all she said. I thought I saw sympathy in her eyes but, before I could be sure, she had stood up and started moving books that had been on her desk to the many shelves. 'If you cut your hair, maybe take a shower, I could introduce you to my daughter.'

I smiled at her. Moiraine was so good at telling when someone was upset, and she would change the topic so suddenly that you would forget what you had been talking about before.

'Your daughter is five years older than me and married.'

'Yeah, but I never much liked her husband,' she said, laughing back. 'Come on, Tom. There's no special girl?'

I thought of Olive; she was the type of girl that Moiraine would actually approve of – pretty, but not over the top, loyal but not a sheep, and she was definitely not afraid to put me in my place. I didn't know why I thought I knew Olive. I had only met her once and she had spent most of the time yelling at me. Still, she had definitely left a lasting impression on me.

'No, there's no girl.'

'Playing the field, are you?'

'I guess you can say that,' I replied, sipping my tea. I grinned, thinking of Alison. I was proud of our little rendezvous in the bathroom. She was incredibly annoying and spoiled rotten, but she was hot and no straight man with a penis would say no to a situation like that.

'So,' I said to Moiraine, clearing my throat. 'Any new books to show me?'

I bought three new books, all of which Moiraine let me have at half-price. I refused at first, but she insisted that she did it with all her loyal customers. I never saw many other customers in Murder's Foulest Things. I always worried that I would walk up to it one day and the doors would be boarded up and the shop empty. But if Moiraine did have money problems she never let on.

Ever since Moiraine had asked me about my love-life, I couldn't stop thinking about Olive. My encounter with Rosanna and Beth was pathetic to say the least; it had definitely been a bad idea. I needed to be someone that Olive would be interested in. But what type of guy did she like? Definitely not one who made fun of her friends. I had learned that pretty quickly. I needed to be more determined. She was probably used to guys who would hit on her once and then give up. I needed to be stubborn, and annoying. I wanted to be able to do this.

I spent the rest of the day wandering around town, looking in various music and book shops. I wasn't looking for anything in particular but more avoiding going home. I considered for a moment ringing my dad, asking him could I stay the night, but

I quickly decided against that idea. The evening would be filled with awkward conversation. Robin would make a huge production of the whole thing. Big fancy dinner followed by stereotypical fun family activities such as Monopoly or Scrabble. She would be so tense and stressed for the whole evening. I would never get the chance to relax – to talk and catch up with my dad, or even just spend time with Pamela. Pamela was my stepsister. She was eight years old and she always looked at me as if I was her best friend, even though months would go by when I wouldn't see her. Thinking of Pamela made me feel guilty; she was one of the few people in my life who seemed to genuinely enjoy my company. I shoved it to the back of my mind; there was no point in thinking about things that I couldn't change.

It was a weird feeling, wandering around town. I felt sick from the drinking the night before, and the lack of sleep was starting to catch up with me. I just wanted to crawl into my bed and switch off, but I felt as if I had no home to go to. Just various places where people were obliged to let me sleep.

By the time I reached the bus station I knew I had no other option. I had to go back to my mum's house. She was the only one who was expecting me, who wanted me to come back – well, at least I *think* she wanted me there. Sometimes it seemed that she would be better off without me, like everyone else in my life. I was just an inconvenience, a bother to everyone. I just had to hope that her mood had passed but then I began to worry that I would come home to her depressed. I had to deal with whatever faced me when I got back – I had no other choice.

Across the bus I saw a couple sitting together. The girl was resting against the guy's shoulder. Both had their eyes closed; they could have been sleeping. If I had been with Peter and Damien we would have made cheering sounds, making fun of the guy for being so whipped. But sitting here on my own, I felt envious of that guy; he looked so comfortable and secure. It seemed like he had everything and I had nothing. I was alone. I had never wanted a girlfriend before. I preferred having the freedom to do what I wanted. But looking at that couple I didn't feel free, just sad and lonely. I gave myself a shake and made myself look away from them. It's just been a long day, I thought to myself. I'm not the boyfriend type and, anyway, who would I want to date? All the girls I knew were more concerned with your bank balance than your personality, and I didn't want to be someone's rebellion against Daddy.

When I got home I opened the door to the apartment slowly and cautiously put my head around it, as I didn't know what to expect. Screaming, crying? With my mum it could have been anything. But the smell of chicken was what greeted me. I walked in and closed the door behind me. My mum rarely cooked anything other than curry and chips.

'Tom?' I heard her shouting from the kitchen. She didn't sound angry. I guessed that was a good sign.

'Yeah, it's me,' I shouted back. I walked into the kitchen to find her working away at the hob.

'Hi, hun,' she said, looking back at me. 'I was hoping you would come home soon. I made dinner.' She was smiling. There was no sign of her being upset, but her eyes looked a little red and I knew she must have been crying earlier.

'Wow, thanks, Mum.' I was surprised. She only made dinner on special occasions.

'I felt bad about earlier.' She wasn't looking at me now. I could tell this was difficult for her. 'I don't mean to take everything out on you. I know – I know you're not your dad. You're better than him, smarter, kinder.'

'Dad isn't a bad guy, Mum.'

She looked a little taken aback at this. 'I know that,' she said, a bit quieter now, 'but I'm just saying you're a different person and I shouldn't have gotten so angry with you before. Work is hard to get because of the recession and I'm just worried about you.'

'I know. I'm sorry if I'm making it worse.' I knew that when she said she was worried about me, she meant she was worried I would never make a life for myself.

'You don't make it worse.' She was speaking barely above a whisper now. 'You really don't. You make a lot of things better, actually. I would just like you to come home a bit more often – after nights out and everything.'

I knew that what she really wanted to say was, could I not go to Dad's – but I appreciated her apology and knew it would upset her if I didn't agree.

'I promise I'll come home more.'

She smiled at me and placed her hand gently on my arm. I smiled back, embarrassed, but I appreciated her attempt at affection.

8

Olive

MY WEEKEND WAS SURPRISINGLY PLEASANT. BY THE TIME I HAD arrived home Andy had seemed to be doing better, and he was over the moon to see me. His schizophrenia made his mood swings impossible to predict. Sometimes they were mild and would only last for a few hours, other times they could go on for days or weeks. I had spent Friday and Saturday night with Andy. We watched films that he liked, and football matches that Dad had recorded for him. We stayed up for hours just talking about life. He didn't mention his trip to the clinic – he never did mention his trips. It was always the case. I never brought it up either; I wouldn't do anything to risk his good mood. I wanted to spend Sunday morning with him as well, before I had to get the bus back to Dublin, but Mum convinced me to call up some of my old friends from school. A lot of them had gone to the local college so they still lived at home. It wasn't until I saw them all that I realized how much I had missed them. I missed how easy it was with them. Rosanna was kind and fun, but I always felt she was too cool for me, and she knew it. Beth was a complete enigma. Some days she was so chatty and warm, other days she barely said two words. I missed the simplicity of my Wexford friends.

By week four I felt like I was beginning to get the hang of college, and I finally started to figure out how the UCD website worked. My lectures were hard-going, but at least I was in the right place at the right time and I was taking notes. Rosanna spent most of her days either in bed recovering from the night before or hanging out with her friends in college. I had yet to see her open a book. I was getting to know Beth better. She didn't like to go out much and she rarely drank. Sometimes when I didn't feel like making awkward small talk with Roz's friends, I would convince Beth to come out with me to the student bar. We would play pool and buy pitchers of cheap beer. I have never felt more like a student than I did on those evenings. No worries, just happy and enjoying life.

With Beth, I was able to be myself. The two of us would say silly things and make stupid jokes. We were very comfortable around each other. Beth had seemed awkward and stiff at first, but it wasn't long before she was able to relax with me and I soon learned that she was incredibly sweet. Beth's only negative was that she sometimes got withdrawn. She would become quiet and distracted and would often disappear to her room without a word. Roz went out nearly every night, so the two of us would usually end up having dinner together in our dorm.

'Why did you decide to do Medicine?' I asked Beth. She was in one of her good moods, which always made dinner more enjoyable.

'I don't know,' she said, in between mouthfuls of spaghetti. In the past few weeks I had learned that pasta was the easiest thing to make for dinner. It was hard to get it wrong. 'I just always wanted to be a doctor, you know? There was never really anything else I wanted to do.'

I nodded along as I munched through my pasta. I hadn't eaten lunch today to try and save money, so I was absolutely ravenous. I was trying to teach myself how to budget. My parents gave me a monthly allowance but living on my own was much more expensive than I had expected. I knew that they would have given me more money if I'd asked for it, but I didn't want to add to their many worries.

'Why choose English?' she asked me in turn.

I shrugged. 'I always liked English in school, so I thought why not?'

'You miss living at home?' she asked casually.

'I miss my brother mostly. But at least I can go home on the weekends.' I hadn't told Rosanna or Beth about my brother's problems. It was just easier not to. 'Where is home for you?' I knew from her accent she couldn't be from Dublin.

'Limerick,' she replied. 'I don't really miss home, but I miss my boyfriend.'

I was a little taken aback; Beth had never mentioned a boyfriend before.

'Is he from Limerick as well?' I said.

She nodded. 'But he's going to the local college there, so I never really get to see him.'

I could hear the sadness in her voice, and suddenly I felt guilty for not knowing more about her.

I let her talk about her boyfriend for the next hour. It was odd listening to her, she could not have been more in love. They had been together for five years, practically a marriage.

'I am guessing that you don't have a boyfriend?' Beth said, while washing the plates.

'Yeah,' I answered, a little surprised. Was it so obvious? I was pretty enough and I had had boyfriends before. It's not like guys were repulsed by me. Beth seemed to notice that I found her comment odd.

'I don't mean it in a bad way.' She turned towards me. 'It's just because there was some guy looking for your number off Rosanna. So I guessed you must be single?'

'Who?' I asked, racking my brain, thinking of every guy I had spoken to in the last week. There weren't many.

'Some guy called Tom. Kind of scruffy-looking, but hot.'

'Tom?' I tried to think who he could be. There had been a guy who had talked to me in one of my lectures. He had been very good-looking and charming, but I wouldn't have called him scruffy. I started to hope it was him, even though the possibilities were very slim. We had only talked for two minutes and we hadn't even exchanged names.

I began to create an elaborate fantasy about this 'Tom'. He was in love from the first second he saw me, and from our short conversation he knew he had to have me. He had wandered around UCD, asking anyone if they knew me, desperate to track me down. I was in the middle of thinking what he would say to me when he found me – something romantic, sweet and funny – when I heard a knock on the door. Beth was still cleaning and Rosanna was out as usual, so I got up to see who it was.

I looked through the peep-hole. We had already had plenty of drunk or stoned visitors, usually looking for Rosanna. I saw a guy with baggy jeans and a blue T-shirt; he had dark, messy hair that looked like he had tried unsuccessfully to flatten it down. He was fidgeting a lot and kept looking down at his feet. He appeared oddly familiar. Probably one of Rosanna's many boys, I thought to myself. I pulled open the door and he jumped when he saw me. He recovered quickly though and smiled as he said, 'Hi.'

I definitely knew him from somewhere, but I just couldn't place it. 'Hi,' I said back. 'You looking for Rosanna?'

He seemed a little disconcerted and mumbled, 'No.'

'Beth?'

'No.'

'Then I think you have the wrong place. Sorry.' I was about to close the door when he started laughing.

'You don't remember me, do you?' He didn't look embarrassed any more, just amused.

'No, I don't,' I said, starting to feel the heat rise to my face.

'Brilliant. I am Tom,' he said, offering me his hand with a cheeky grin growing on his face.

Suddenly it clicked; I remembered who he was. 'You were that guy at Alison's party?' I asked.

'Damn,' he said. 'I was hoping that we could start over again. I don't think you thought much of me last time.'

I stood there unsure of what to say or do, and then I remembered what Beth had told me.

'Have you been trying to get my number?'

'Yep,' he replied with no hesitation. 'Rosanna wouldn't give it to me, so I decided just to pop in.'

'OK,' I said, at a loss.

'Can I come in?' he asked.

'All right.' I stood aside to let him in. I was completely dumbstruck – why was he here?

He sat down on the couch and put his legs up on the table.

'Nice,' he said, moving his bottom about, trying to make himself comfortable. 'Most of my friends' dorms are filthy and you usually end up getting stuck to the couch. But your place is really nice.'

Beth was now sitting at the table with her laptop. She looked at Tom with familiarity.

'Hi, Tom. How are you?' she asked, while smiling at me. It must have been obvious from my face that I had no idea what was going on.

'I'm good. Just chilling, you know?'

Beth laughed and returned to the work on her laptop, while

I stood in the middle of the room, wondering what to do.

'Do you want some tea?' I asked, for no other reason than to just break the silence.

'Um, yeah, sure.' He was looking a bit ill at ease himself now. I filled the kettle and then waited for it to boil. My mum and dad had donated their old kettle to us. It took ages to heat up and made a lot of noise. I handed Tom his cup of tea, hovering over him, still completely unsure of what to do next.

'I would ask you to sit but it's your house,' he joked.

I sat down quickly and felt the heat rising to my face again.

'So, Olive. How's college life going for you?'

'So why are you here?'

We had both spoken at the same time and I could hear Beth giggle in the background.

'I don't know,' Tom said, while shrugging. 'You seemed like a cool girl and I just thought I'd come by and see if you wanted to hang out.'

'Hang out?'

'Yeah. Hang out – like just you and me?'

It took all my self-control not to let my jaw drop. Was he actually asking me out? We had met once, it hadn't exactly gone well. I had been a grumpy bitch and he had been a cocky shite.

'Well, it's nice of you to ask, Tom, but . . . I don't really know you.'

'Exactly,' he said. 'You don't know me, but I am giving you the opportunity to get to know me.'

His stupid grin was starting to really annoy me. 'Look, I am flattered,' I said, 'but you are not my type.'

'You just said you didn't know me. So how do you know I am not your type? Come on, let me take you out tonight.'

'I am busy,' I told him, trying desperately to think of a way out of this.

'No problem. What about tomorrow?'

'Yeah . . . I'm busy then too.'

'Really? Doing what?' He called my bluff.

'Oh . . . college work. Yeah, I have a ton of work to do.'

'It's less than a month into the first semester.'

'Yeah, well, you know. I want to get a head start on everything.'

He sat there looking a little put out.

'I get it,' he said, standing up and giving me a wink. 'You want to be chased. I can play that game.'

'No, no, I don't want you to.'

'Don't worry, Olive. I am a stubborn fucker. You will be seeing me again soon.'

'No, you don't understand—'

'I will see you soon, beautiful.' And with that he was out the door and down the stairs.

I turned to Beth, who had been sitting at the table the entire time.

'What just happened there?'

She looked at me and burst out laughing. 'I don't know, but the look on your face right now is priceless.'

'He just would not take no for an answer.'

'No. Like he said, he is pretty stubborn. But it was kind of sweet as well.'

'Sweet? He thinks he is God's gift to women.'

'Yeah, he does a little. But he likes you.'

'Well, I am definitely not interested in him.' I picked up his untouched cup of tea, and got a whiff of what can only be described as smoke mixed with some sort of cologne. It was actually quite pleasant. His smell was probably one of his only redeeming qualities.

By the time Roz came home my curiosity had got the better of me. She was in her room getting ready to go out again. I tried to sound casual as I asked her what she knew about Tom.

'He is a bit of a womanizer but amazing in bed,' she said while lathering on the make-up as always.

'You have slept with him before?' I asked, surprised at the disappointment in my voice.

'Oh yeah, half the girls in Dublin have. He is a bit of a legend really. Why are you asking about him anyway?'

I told her what had happened earlier, but without much enthusiasm. A small part of me had been excited by the fact that someone fancied me. Now I felt like just another target in a long line of girls.

'He came here and asked you out?'

'He asked me to hang out, yeah.'

'Well, I have never heard of Tom doing that before.'

'But you just told me he has dated hundreds of girls.'

Roz shook her finger at me as if I was a student who was not listening in class.

'I said he had slept with a lot of girls. I have never heard of him having a girlfriend or even taking a girl out on a date.'

'Then how does he get so many girls if he is not dating them?'

Roz gave me a *you're so innocent* look; she often gave me those looks.

9

Beth

MY BOOKS PRACTICALLY TOPPLED ME OVER AS I FELL INTO MY bedroom. I dropped them all hopelessly on the floor before letting out a sigh and deciding to just leave them there. I rubbed my shoulders as I sat on my bed. The strain of carrying heavy books every day was starting to give me back pain. I lay down on the duvet and closed my eyes. It was six in the evening. I had an hour off before I had to go back to my labs. The dorm was empty. Olive was in the library getting started on one of her essays and I had no idea where Roz was.

I was starting to regret the fact that I had promised Olive that we would go out for dinner this evening. In a way I had been looking forward to it, since we had planned to go to the TGI's restaurant in Dundrum, where the portions were huge – and I hadn't eaten properly all day. But then again I was already exhausted, and I still had two and a half hours of lab work to do. A part of me wished I could just cancel on Olive and go straight to sleep when I got back later, but I knew I couldn't do that. Olive was my friend, genuinely and truly. It was something that I took very seriously. Roz had texted us both earlier, trying to convince us to go out with her to some club this evening. We had both declined like we normally did, but I liked the fact that she still asked.

I found Roz hard to understand. With Olive it was simple. She was a country girl who was trying to break out of the mould that life had created for her. She liked to have fun but she always had her guard up. Sometimes I thought she was hiding something, but I never asked. I definitely understood the feeling of wanting to keep things to yourself. With Roz, it was different. I seemed to envy her and pity her at the same time. She was so spontaneous and lively, she lit up any room that she entered. Boys followed after her like puppies, and anyone who met her instantly liked her. But she was also flighty. She lacked any sort of drive. She didn't seem to think about what she wanted in life; instead she just went with the flow, taking things as they came. I couldn't understand how she was able to do that. I had always wanted to be a doctor. It was why I had worked so hard in school; it was why I had wanted to come here. It was the reason I got up at ridiculous hours in the morning and why I worked until I was nearly crying with exhaustion. It had always been my goal and I thought it always would be. I couldn't understand Roz because I couldn't understand her lack of direction. I always needed to know where I was going and how I was planning to get there.

I tried to let myself relax, but it was hopeless. My mind was still going a million miles a minute and I couldn't stop thinking about all that we had discussed in our lectures this morning. I opened my eyes and rolled over onto my side. I kept a picture of Michael and me on my counter. He was wearing a white shirt and I had on a light-blue dress. I was only sixteen in that photo. It had been when the two of us were still in the same school. Before Michael had met my parents, before I had moved to that horrible school. My biggest regret was ever telling my parents about Michael and my relationship. My parents and I have never been that close. They are both doctors and when we talked it was normally about their work or my plans for the future. It wasn't only my dream to become a doctor; it was theirs too – the only bond we shared. I didn't speak about my personal life and they never bothered to ask.

I had kept my relationship with Michael a secret for over two years. Everyone at school knew, my teachers, my friends, but my parents were left in the dark. I had met Michael's family on numerous occasions. His mother I had found hard to deal with. She knew I came from a wealthy family and she had asked me for money a couple of times when she got me alone. Michael was furious and humiliated when I told him; he had a huge row with his mother over it. Ever since then his mother was polite but didn't say much when I came over. I loved his grandfather. He was kind and charming, reminding me a lot of Michael.

It was only after we had decided we wanted to live together that I knew I had to introduce Michael to my parents. It was weird telling them that I had a boyfriend. I had never mentioned anything to them about my friends or boys. It wasn't because I was trying to hide anything, it was just because I didn't think they would be interested. When I went out at the weekends they wouldn't even ask where I was going or with whom. They just wanted to know that I wouldn't be home late. Telling them was strange; I didn't build up to it or anything. I just walked into the room and spat it out without any sort of warning. At first my dad just frowned at me, as if I had said something that didn't make much sense, but my mum spoke up quickly.

'We should like to meet this boyfriend of yours. Invite him over for dinner tomorrow night. Does that suit you?' She turned to my dad, whose expression still hadn't changed.

'Yes. Tomorrow – that is fine,' he replied.

They didn't say anything else about it. I didn't know whether their reaction was good or bad. This was all new to me.

Michael was terrified when he came the next evening. I opened the door to find him shaking like a leaf.

'Are you OK?' I asked, surprised to see him looking so nervous.

'Yes. Just a bit anxious.'

I tried to reassure him. 'They are going to love you.'

Michael raised his eyebrows and gave me a sceptical look, saying, 'Come on, Beth. We haven't avoided this meeting for so long for no reason. I am dirt poor and come from a broken family. As long as they don't completely despise me I think we will be doing well.'

I kissed his cheek. 'You impressed me. I am sure you will impress them.'

Michael smiled back at me but I don't think he believed me.

The first twenty minutes of the meal went OK. We struggled through the awkward introductions and Michael's manners seemed to meet my parents' extraordinarily high standards. We stuck to safe topics such as school and college aims. Michael was incredibly gifted. The cleverest person in our school, there was no doubt that he would do well in the all-important Leaving Cert. I even think my parents were beginning to warm to him when he told them he was passionate about chemistry. Disaster struck when my mother asked Michael where he lived.

'I live in an apartment just next to St Mary's Park in Limerick City.'

My mother stopped eating and stared directly at him.

'St Mary's Park? Well, that is certainly an interesting part of the city.'

Michael physically tensed. My mother had never been near St Mary's Park but she had certainly heard of it. It was known to be one of the poorest and roughest parts of Limerick. Even

I was nervous going there. Michael would walk me to and from the bus station, claiming that it wasn't safe to walk around on one's own. Even in the middle of the day.

'Do you live with your parents there?'

'Just my mum and my grandfather. My father is not around.'

I could tell that my mother was getting nosy. Up until now she had assumed that Michael was just like us. Middle-class. I had never told her anything otherwise.

'I'm sorry to hear that. Divorce is such a sad thing.'

'Actually, they were never married.' Michael looked as if he wished he had never corrected her, but it was too late now. My mum just nodded. I knew she would be judging him, coming up with her own assumptions. But there was nothing I could do to stop her. I knew my mother and she would think whatever she wanted to think.

'What does your mother do?'

'She's not actually working at the moment. But my grandfather is a mechanic.'

'How do you afford school?' My father had been silent for most of the evening. I hadn't thought much of it. He didn't talk much in most situations; he was more of a silent observer. But I was shocked when he asked such a personal question.

'Dad!' I exclaimed.

'I am sorry, Beth, but it is not such a ridiculous question. If Michael lives near St Mary's Park in an apartment and his grandfather is the only one bringing in any sort of income, then it is safe to say that there is not much spare money in their household. St Peter's is a private school and it is one of the highest fee-paying schools in the country. I would just like to know how he and his family manage.'

I was about to protest again but Michael placed his hand on my arm.

'It's OK. I am on a full scholarship, sir. They give one out every year. I applied for it when I was thirteen. I had to do an entry exam and an IQ test. I got the highest result out of everyone who applied, so I was awarded the scholarship.'

'That is very impressive. And what about college? Are you hoping to receive another scholarship to pay for that?'

I couldn't believe that my dad was interrogating Michael so heavily, but I also knew that there was no way I was going to stop him.

'I shall apply for scholarships, but I also work at the weekends in Tesco. I have been saving my money for the last few years, so I will be able to pay for college myself.'

My dad said nothing; he just nodded.

After that the conversation returned to safer topics. My mum was polite and my dad just remained silent. My parents left us alone to say goodnight.

'Well, that could have gone better.' Michael sounded defeated.

'It went fine,' I tried to reassure him. 'I know my dad is a little intimidating, but that is just his way.'

He nodded, but I knew he was unconvinced.

'I will see you tomorrow in school.' He kissed me gently on the lips but it wasn't with much enthusiasm.

When I walked back into the dining room, my parents were still sitting in the same positions. They had grave looks on their faces. I knew then what was coming.

'Would you mind sitting down, Beth?' My mum gestured towards the seat across from her but I didn't move.

'Why?' I asked accusingly.

'Now, there is no need to be melodramatic. We just want to talk to you.'

'What is going on?'

'Sit down!' My father's voice was stern and forceful. I did as he said. When I was sitting he gave my mum a look and she started to talk again.

'We don't think you should see Michael any more.'

'What? Why?' I hadn't expected this. I didn't know what I had expected from them, but it wasn't this.

'He is a lovely boy and obviously very clever. But he is not right for you.'

I could feel the tears brimming in my eyes but I held them back. I didn't want them to see me cry.

'But you don't know him! He is so ambitious and smart. You are just judging him because he doesn't have as much money as we do.'

'That is not what I am saying at all.'

'You are both just so judgemental and materialistic. There is more to people than money . . .'

'Beth! Stop it!' I jumped at the sound of my dad shouting. He had never shouted at me before. It scared me. He seemed to collect himself together before speaking again. 'Michael is clearly very clever and ambitious and I would wish the very best for him. But I do not want you to be involved with him any more. I have seen boys like him before. No money, born in a broken family. Unfortunately, people like him find it very hard to move out of their bad situations, no matter how determined they are. You have so many opportunities in front of you, Beth. We are just afraid that you will settle for less in life if you are with a boy like that.'

'Dad, please,' I begged. My voice was barely above a whisper.

'You shouldn't be dating anyone at the moment anyway. What you need to do is concentrate on your studies. That is what you want and it is what we want for you.'

I was so angry that I was not able to speak. I knew I was about to cry so I just left the room. I cried all night. My parents didn't come in to me again. That was the way they were. They discussed a matter once, gave their choice, whether I liked it or not, and then it was not brought up again.

I avoided Michael in school the next few days. He was obviously aware there was something wrong, but I couldn't tell him what it was. I knew he would be devastated. A week passed and I had barely said a word to him. Eventually he cornered me in an empty classroom. It was nearly eight o'clock; school had finished hours ago, but I had stayed in late to do my homework. I always found it easier to do it in school. I had also been avoiding my parents the last week. I looked up as I heard the classroom door open. I didn't think there was anyone left in the school. Michael stood there, looking pale and nervous.

'I was hoping you would be here. I ran into Miss Murphy as she was leaving. She said she left her classroom door unlocked so you could do your work.'

'Yeah. I asked her could I stay in for a while. I didn't want to go home.'

'Why?' Michael asked bluntly.

I wanted to tell him. I was so used to telling him everything. I felt so alone without him. 'I got into a fight with my parents . . .'

'Over me?'

I just nodded. The tears were starting to pour down my face.

'Look, Beth, if you don't want to see me any more, I understand. I don't want to get between you and your parents.'

I stared at him, shocked. 'I don't want to break up.'

'You don't?' he asked, sounding surprised.

'Of course not. Do you?'

Michael instantly shook his head. 'No. I want to be with you. I am completely in love with you.' He walked over and put his hands on either side of my face.

'I love you too.' I was no longer crying.

Michael leaned in and kissed me. It was different from any

way he had kissed me before. I could feel him craving me. It was faster, more intense. I felt myself begin to shiver and get excited. He lifted me up onto the desk without our lips parting. His hands began to venture down to under my shirt and I pulled him in closer.

I was completely lost in the moment when I heard the door click behind us. We jumped apart instantly but it was too late. Standing at the door was our headmaster. His mouth was slightly open and his hand was still on the door.

'Michael, Beth. What on earth do you think you two are doing?' He was furious. It was obvious that he had seen us. We both remained there frozen to the spot, unsure of what to do next.

'Miss – Miss Murphy said I could finish my homework here,' I stammered.

'It doesn't look as if you two are doing homework to me. Both of you go to my office now. I will call your parents and they must come and get you immediately.'

We were both suspended for a day. I got sent straight home but Michael was made to stay in. He told me that the headmaster sent him to the school guidance counsellor where he was given an extremely uncomfortable sex talk. We were both virgins then and I don't think it would have ventured any further in that classroom, but that was irrelevant. It had looked really bad, and that was what mattered. My parents were furious. My dad wouldn't even speak to me. He wasn't there when I got home. I wasn't sure what the school had told them, but it sounded like they made it out to be a lot worse than it actually was.

'After we had specifically told you to stop seeing him! What on earth were you thinking?'

I sat there silently. There was no point in defending myself.

'Do you want to throw your life away? God forbid if you get pregnant.'

'You can't get pregnant from kissing . . .'

'Don't you dare be cheeky, Beth.'

I went back to staring at the floor. I knew there was nothing I could say to make this better.

'Your father and I have decided that it is best for you to do your final year of school somewhere else. There is a very good boarding school in Cork that will take you.'

'No, Mum.'

'Beth, this is not up for discussion.'

'No, Mum. Please, please don't send me out of Limerick. All my friends are here.' I didn't dare say Michael's name.

'I am sorry, Beth, but there is no way we are sending you back to that school where you can be so easily swayed by that boy.'

'Then send me to the public school. Please just don't send me out of Limerick.' I couldn't imagine being locked up in a boarding school for the next year. No life, no freedom, no way of being able to see Michael.

'I am not sending you to that public school.'

'Please, Mum. It is just one year. It's not going to make the slightest difference to my results, I swear. I will still get Medicine in UCD, I know I will.'

My mum appeared to quietly consider it for a moment. I hoped desperately that she would agree.

'Fine. But if you don't get the results we expect, then you are to re-sit your exams at whatever school that your father and I choose.'

I let out a sigh of relief.

My final year in that public school was hell. It was obvious I didn't fit in and no one was going to let me forget it. But it was worth it because I was still able to see Michael. I managed to keep my relationship secret from my parents for that final year, but by the time I had gotten my UCD place they had realized we had been together all along. They weren't happy but they knew now that I was moving out, they couldn't stop me. It wasn't as if I had ever been close to my parents, but after that incident with Michael there was this invisible wall between us. We no longer looked at life the same way. I no longer sought or cared for their approval. All I wanted was to be with Michael.

I looked at my watch and realized that the last hour had flown by. I crawled sleepily out of my bed and tidied the books that I had dumped on the floor. I took out my phone and texted Olive that I would meet her later. I had cut my parents out of my life – it had been my choice. But I wasn't going to lose my friends. I needed them.

10

Tom

TRYING TO CONVINCE OLIVE TO GO ON A DATE WITH ME WAS A lot harder than originally planned. I stopped by her dorm three times that week, and every time she would come up with multiple excuses for why she was busy. But at least she spoke to me for those short times I came to visit, and as the week ended and rolled on to the next and then the next, I realized that the visits were getting longer and that she had actually started to laugh rather than cringe at my failed attempts at courting. We even began to have fun together. Her humour was unusual but hilarious, and she would talk for hours on end about her schooldays. She was a serious country girl. I began to wonder was I slowly wearing her down?

As we began to head into the end of October, I knew I had to do something more to convince her to go out with me. When we talked it was always in a friendly way, not flirty. Any time that I tried to flirt with her, she would either get offended or ignore me. I was running out of ideas, and that 100 euro was slowly drifting away. I needed help.

I heard Roz before I saw her; she was flirting with some guy behind the counter. He looked about sixteen, and seemed absolutely thrilled with himself as Roz twirled her hair and giggled. I had a feeling that this performance was more for my benefit than the waiter's. I had found Roz's number in my phone earlier this week. She had obviously given it to me sometime when we had been hooking up. Our hook-ups had been the result of seriously messy nights and few other options. She had always been the life and soul of the party but liked having boys fight over her, which I would have been unwilling to do. It was probably the reason why she had lost interest in me so quickly. I texted her, asking would she meet me in town. Her reply said, *Only if it's in Starbucks*.

She was wearing a lot of make-up as usual. Her blonde hair was perfectly straightened and her eyes outlined in black pencil. She wore leather leggings that looked like a second skin they were so tight, and a baggy white T on top that revealed one bare shoulder. She flicked her hair over her shoulder before sitting down opposite me.

'Hi, Tom. Oh my God, I like couldn't believe it when you texted me. So how are you?' She looked at me with her usual big smile plastered on her face.

'I'm pretty good, how about you?' I asked, trying my best not to be sarcastic or rude. I desperately needed her help.

'Oh my God, it has been like mad the past few days. I have been out like every night and I haven't been to like any of my classes. It's like such a disgrace. I am like so going to fail my course.'

'Ah, I am sure you will be grand.' I had forgotten how much Roz liked to talk; getting a word in was difficult with her.

'So like why did you want to meet up, Tom? It better not be to get some action because I need some serious alcohol in my system before I would even consider that.'

I wasn't sure if she was joking but I laughed anyway.

'No, actually, I was hoping . . . um . . .' I hadn't thought about how I was going to phrase this. I didn't want to directly ask for help, as that would seem desperate.

'This is about Olive, isn't it?'

I looked at her, a little surprised. 'Yeah, how did you know?'

'Well, Beth said you were like stalking the girl . . .'

'I am not stalking her. I just want to hang out with her a little.' My hopes of not sounding desperate had gone out the window.

'Do you fancy her?'

'We're not twelve years old, Roz.'

'Oh my God, you so do.'

'I just think she is a cool girl.'

Roz was laughing at me now, and I started to think I should maybe just run for the door and forget the whole thing.

'Well, I hate to tell you, Tom, but she is really not your type.'

I was starting to get sick of everyone saying that. What does 'type' have to do with it anyway? People are all the same; pretend to be perfect on the outside but on the inside we are all completely fucked up.

'What is her type then?' I asked, deciding I might as well throw caution to the wind.

Roz took a sip from her coffee before answering me. She had an expression of concentration on her face.

'I think Olive is a bit old-fashioned, you know? She would be looking for the fairytale type of guy. Well-groomed, kind, charming and romantic. I'd say she likes being treated like a princess.'

'What do you mean? Like flowers and poetry and all that shite?'

'Yeah, that's exactly what I mean. Girls like Olive want to be courted, not hit on.'

I sat there in silent thought for a moment. Most girls I had been with would have been thrilled if you had even bought them a drink. I didn't know how to court someone. I started to become overshadowed with doubt. What was I doing? This stupid bet had gone too far, I was going to hurt someone. I always ended up hurting people and for some reason I found it impossible to stop.

Roz's voice surprised me; I had nearly forgotten that she was sitting with me.

'Look, Tom, I have to like go. But I just want to say I like Olive. She is a bit vanilla but very sweet, and if you are like messing with her head for some sick joke, I will have to castrate you.' Roz was already standing by the time she had finished talking. She was staring at me, waiting for a reply.

'It's not a joke. I just . . . like her, that's all.'

Roz looked unsure whether to believe me or not. 'Well, if that is the case,' she told me, 'then get ready to work your ass off.'

The sixteen-year-old waiter stared as Roz walked out, obviously hoping that she might stop to flirt again, but Roz didn't even look in his direction.

I looked at my watch, and found that it was only two-thirty. I was surprised that Roz had left so quickly. Not that I really wanted her to stay but her company would have kept me occupied. I hadn't been home in the last three days, and I dreaded the thought of going there. Mum had called a few times. I didn't answer, just texted saying that I was staying with Dad. That had stopped the calls. The truth was, I had been staying with Peter. He as usual didn't mind me crashing on his couch, and because he lived alone, there were never any questions from parents as to why I wasn't going home. But I could tell this morning that I was getting on Peter's nerves, so I made sure to leave before I pushed my luck too far.

Living at home was getting worse every day. The lack of work was making my mum emotional and I just didn't know how to handle her. One day I would be her pride and joy. The next I was the thing that destroyed her life. When she looked at me I knew she saw me as the result of a failed marriage, a failed attempt at happiness. I found it easier just not to deal with it; nothing I did made it better anyway. I knew I would eventually have to go home today but I wanted to delay it for as long as possible. Maybe I should go to the cinema. I looked in my wallet to see how much money I had. Four euro: definitely not enough for a cinema ticket. I did, however, notice a small plastic bag of weed and a couple of skins. Why not? I thought. I had nothing else to do. I left Starbucks, giving the sixteen-year-old waiter a wave as I left. He waved back in confusion and I laughed to myself at my own private joke.

I never used to smoke as much as I do now. I started when I was in school. Everyone else was doing it and I didn't want to be the odd one out. This seems like such a pathetic reason, but it was why I started. I soon learned that weed wasn't the only thing that people were taking in school. Coke, E, speed, crystal meth – you could get your hands on anything you wanted. I would be lying if I said that weed was the only thing that I ever took. I had tried coke a few times when I was eighteen; I quickly stopped though. It made me aggressive and I usually ended up in fights when I was on it. I still took pills the odd time, but I kept it quiet. Peter and Damien didn't really do drugs. They might smoke weed if it was being passed around, but they would never go out and buy stuff like I would. I didn't want them judging me.

It was still cold outside but the sun had emerged, making it a bright day. Town was busy, like it always was on a weekend. I made my way to Stephen's Green in hopes of finding somewhere secluded. Stephen's Green attracted a lot of tourists and walkers but I was good at making myself unseen. I settled down in the corner of the green, leaning up against an oak tree that hid me from sight. I wasn't really worried about getting caught. How was anyone to know it wasn't a normal cigarette unless they got close enough to smell it? I just wanted the privacy.

Most people in college would normally just buy stuff from the head shops in town. It was legal and therefore much easier to get. I normally avoided them though. Their stuff would have the weirdest effects on me. Sometimes it would be so weak that it was just a complete waste of money, and other times it would be so strong that I would stop after just one puff. I used to buy my stuff from a guy called Matt. He was in my year in college and he grew the stuff in his bedroom. He told me that he was making a nice little profit for himself. I called up two weeks before to buy some more, only to discover that his landlord had found out about his business. He had kicked him out and now he was stuck living with his parents again. Matt told me that he had had to burn everything. He wasn't able to bring it back to his parents' house. His mother was already suspicious of him and she was watching him like a hawk. He said if I really wanted some he knew a guy named Richard who had his own supply. I had taken Richard's number and called him.

'What?' he'd shouted at the top of his voice. He'd sounded a lot older than I had expected and much rougher.

'Hi. My name is Tom. Matt said you might be able to help me get sorted with some weed.'

'Quiet, you fucker! Don't be talking so loudly.'

'Sorry,' I whispered, beginning to get unsettled.

'I can get you the stuff. How much do you want? Two, three kilos?

'Just a half.' This guy seemed odd. I was beginning to wonder if this was a bad idea.

'Only a half? You fucking pansy. Fine, that will be thirty euro.'

'Thirty euro!' I exclaimed. That was nearly double what Matt would have charged me.

'Yes, thirty euro. I need to make some sort of profit here. You can take it or leave it.'

'Fine, fine.' I'd given in grudgingly. 'Where do you want me to meet you?'

'Come to the back of Temple Square tomorrow at nine a.m. There will be a kid named Ronan there. Give him the money, and then wait. Ronan will bring it to me and bring back the weed for you.' It was all getting sketchier by the minute.

'Why can't I just come meet you face to face?'

'Are you kidding? I don't want some spoiled college kid knowing where I do my work. We either do it my way or no way.' I'd had no other option so I'd just agreed.

It had gone exactly how he said it would. The boy who was waiting for me looked no older than twelve and he barely said a word to me. When he returned with the drugs I asked him, 'Where did it come from? Did Richard grow it himself?'

The boy stared at me, confused. 'Who is Richard?'

I rolled the spliff with ease; years of experience meant it was second nature to me. I lit up and inhaled deeply, letting the smoke sink down into my chest. As I exhaled I felt a sense of calm roll over me. The weed was stronger than I was used to. Oh well, I thought to myself. What harm can it do?

I'm not sure how long I sat there, but I could feel the heat of the sun slowly drift away. The weed was strong but effective; I smoked it quickly and then just relaxed. I stopped thinking about my mum. In fact, I stopped thinking completely. I just sat beneath that tree, closed my eyes and listened. I would hear snippets of talk about work, relationships, families, anything and everything. The quiet sounds of distant conversations were calming.

My daze was interrupted by a high-pitched squeal. I opened

my eyes, a little annoyed, to see what the source of the sound was. I saw a small girl with blonde curls being chased by a middle-aged man who was undoubtedly her father. He would nearly catch her and then pretend to miss, as the girl screamed with laughter. A blonde woman with the same curls observed the whole thing, happily smiling. Finally the father caught the child and kissed her on the cheek. The woman came over and kissed her daughter and husband. It really was a picture-perfect family moment.

I turned away, angry. I closed my eyes again and tried to return to the peaceful daze that I had been in before, but I kept hearing the girl's squeal of happiness. I became frustrated and annoyed. Why couldn't they just leave? Surely they must be irritating everyone else in the green? And yet I could still hear them. I put my hands over my ears in hopes it would dull the noise; instead it was now inside my head, getting louder and louder. And then I heard another noise. It was quiet at first but like the squealing it grew louder. It was the sound of someone crying and yelling. I looked around myself frantically. It was almost dark now and people were leaving, I was alone. Then why could I still hear the squealing, and where was this crying and shouting coming from? Suddenly I started to think of my family. I tried to remember when my mum and dad had been together, been in love – before the fighting, before the lawyers, before the divorce – but there was nothing. Not even a hint of a good, happy family memory. There was only crying and shouting. That's all I could hear now – crying and shouting. I put my hands over my ears, yet I felt like it was getting louder and louder. *Stop!* I tried to shout but no sound came out. It was in my head. It was beyond loud now, inside my head. *Stop!* I thought my ears would burst. *Stop!* My head was going to split open with the noise. It was everywhere around me, louder and louder. I can't think. *Stop! Please stop! Just STOP! STOP!*

I think I must have passed out then. I was no longer leaning against the tree but lying face down against the cold earth. I opened my eyes to see darkness. I tried to stand up but I was shaking so much that my legs couldn't take my weight. I sat up and took some deep breaths. I wasn't cold but I couldn't stop shivering. I took my phone out to check the time – 9.30 p.m.; I must have been lying there for hours. There were multiple missed calls from my mum. I should've been home hours ago. I looked to my left to see the stub of the spliff that I had smoked. I picked it up and held it to my face. My hands were shaking as badly as my legs.

'What the fuck was in this?' I asked aloud, throwing the stub into a nearby bush and attempting to stand up again, this time using the tree as support.

I took a couple more deep breaths before I tried to walk, my legs beginning to steady. The street was quiet when I got out of the green. I walked to the nearest bus station, happy to have enough money to take me home – I didn't think my legs could handle much walking at the moment. I opened the door cautiously when I reached my house, unsure of what would greet me on the other side. At first I didn't hear anything and I began to hope that my mum was out. But that hope was quickly destroyed as I heard her running from the kitchen.

'Tom, is that— What on earth happened to you?' she exclaimed when she saw me. Her eyes were red, and I started to feel really guilty.

'Nothing,' I mumbled, hoping that my shakes were not too obvious.

'What do you mean nothing?' she yelled. 'You are ice-white and filthy. It looks like you were rolling in dirt!' She stepped closer to look at me properly. 'There is blood on your face,' she said, sounding more concerned and worried now. I preferred the anger. I put my hand up to my face and felt some small scrapes. I must have had some sort of fit when I passed out.

'I fell. I was walking in Stephen's Green and I tripped,' I explained. I don't know how long she stood there staring at me, scrutinizing me.

'Go take a bath. I think I have some antiseptic for those cuts,' she said finally. She turned away and went back towards the kitchen. She had spoken in a very calm but almost stern voice. I did as she told me. In the bathroom, I turned on the hot water in the bath. As I undressed I was shocked to notice all the small cuts and bruises across my body. *How did I get all these?* My shakes subsided as my body heated up. It was only as my head started to clear that I realized how heavy it had felt.

My mum didn't really speak to me for the rest of the evening. I wished she would say something, but she didn't. She just sat in silence, and as I looked at her I saw for the first time how old and tired she looked. I began to wonder did she believe me. Did she believe that I had fallen? I was sure she didn't. And yet there was no reaction, no anger – just sadness. Did she even care?

'Tom?'

'Yes, Mum.'

'Will you come home more often?'

'OK.' I couldn't help but lie. It was just easier to lie to everyone.

11
Olive

'SO THE CLASSES ARE GETTING EASIER THEN?'

'Yeah, I understand most of what is going on.'

'Well, are you sure that's enough, Olive? I don't want you to be falling behind; maybe coming home every weekend is taking up too much of your study time.'

'No, Mum, it's fine.' It was the same conversation every time she called. Were my classes too hard? Did I need more time to study? Was I keeping up? If only she knew the truth. That as long as we all did the bare minimum to get by, the college was happy.

'Mum, I have to go. I am going to be late.'

'OK. Well, make sure you stay on top of everything and don't feel like you have to come home every weekend.'

'Yeah, whatever, Mum. Bye.'

I clicked the hang-up button on my phone and frantically started searching for my books. The longer I lived away from home, the more disorganized I was becoming. Andy was doing a lot better now. He always replied to my texts and calls, and most of the time he seemed quite positive about everything.

Mum had signed him up for a running club and he now had training twice a week. Mum said he was actually quite good and was really enjoying himself. Hearing this made me feel like I could breathe properly again. I would always feel a knot of worry in my stomach for Andy, but sometimes it wasn't as bad.

I finally managed to gather up all the books I needed for class but I couldn't find my journal which told me the room I needed to go to. I looked at my watch and I was already five minutes late.

'Fuck,' I mumbled under my breath. I saw Beth's laptop sitting open on the kitchen table. I would never normally have used it without asking her, but I was sure she wouldn't mind if I just checked my UCD account. I sat down and pulled the laptop towards me and opened up the internet browser. I always found Beth's laptop difficult to use. She had these notifications that would pop up randomly. It was custom designed for her, which made it difficult for anyone else to use.

As I was about to type UCD into the Google search engine, a small window popped up, saying, *You have received one new email.* I tried to pull it to the side of the screen but instead something clicked and the email opened.

'Shit!' I exclaimed aloud. I tried not to look at the message. I didn't want to intrude on Beth's privacy but the first few words of it were written in capital letters and I couldn't help but look.

The greeting HEY BITCH stared back at me. My curiosity got the better of me and I found myself reading the rest of the short email.

> HEY BITCH. Think you are so fucking great in your posh college with your posh mates. Well I just want to let you know that if you EVER come back to Limerick, me and my mates will kick the SHIT out of you and teach you not to act like such a snotty posh BITCH!!!

The email wasn't signed. I ex'd out of it and had a look at Beth's inbox. She had hundreds of emails from the same anonymous source and they were all titled with things like *Die Bitch* and *I am going to beat you, you posh cow.*

I sat there in shock for a long time. When I finally looked at my watch it was half past. There was no point in trying to make my class now. I didn't know what to think or do. Of course I knew about people being bullied – it had happened in my school, but it had been nowhere near as malicious or violent as these emails were. I began to wonder why Beth didn't just delete them, not look at them, pretend it wasn't happening. But even I couldn't forget the aggression in that email – and it wasn't even directed at me. How could Beth take this without feeling afraid all the time? It suddenly became obvious why she never went home to Limerick on the weekends and why she would often be in a mood where she didn't want to talk to anyone.

I didn't really know what to do next. Do I tell her I know? She might get angry at me for looking at her private emails – but I couldn't pretend not to know. What if nobody else knew? What if she had told no one? If she had, someone would have tried to help, to stop it. I decided that when she got home I would have a serious talk with her. Maybe she would be comforted by the fact that someone else knew. Maybe I could help. Block this email address or encourage her to tell someone. It wasn't fair that she could never go home because of this.

I found it hard to concentrate in the rest of my classes when I finally got to them. I tried to plot out what I was going to say to Beth and imagine how she would react.

It was nearly six o'clock when Beth walked through the door. I was surprised to see her back so early. Normally there would be no sight of her until at least 8 or 9 p.m.

'Ah, it's brilliant, Olive!' she beamed. 'The lecturer was sick, so we have been given an extra week to get our assignments in. I'm thrilled, since there was no way I was going to get it done on time. I am going to have a cup of tea and get started on it now. Do you want one?'

'No, I'm OK, thanks.'

Beth started laughing. 'You don't want a cup of tea? Who are you and what have you done with the real Olive?'

I attempted a smile but there was a sinking feeling in the pit of my stomach. She was in such a good mood and I was going to be the one to ruin it.

She settled herself down at the kitchen table and started sipping her cup of tea.

'How were your classes today?' she asked.

'Fine,' I shrugged, unable to look her in the eye. She was obviously beginning to notice my strange behaviour.

'You OK?' she asked with genuine concern. 'You look a little pale.'

I wasn't surprised at her saying this. The anxiety was making me feel like I was going to be sick.

'Yeah, I'm fine . . . Look, Beth – I need to tell you something.'

'Yes?' she said slowly, looking at me suspiciously.

'I opened up your computer earlier just to check my class timetable. I normally wouldn't do that without asking you first, but it was just literally to check which room I should be in. I lost my journal and I was going to be late. But anyway, some notification popped up and I swear I tried to close it. I didn't want to look through your private stuff but you know how useless I am at using your laptop, and I accidentally opened it. And I know I shouldn't have read it but . . . I did. And it was this really threatening horrible email, and I saw that you had loads of them and . . . I just wanted to see if you're OK because . . . They really are terrible and there must be something we can do to stop them. Do you know who the person is? Maybe we could report them to the Guards or something?'

I said this so quickly that some words practically merged into others. Beth sat there silently, and I was beginning to wonder whether I had made any sense when she finally spoke.

'How *dare* you look at my emails, Olive!' She practically spat the words out.

'I told you – it was a complete accident.' I was surprised to see how angry she was with me.

'Mind your own fucking business, all right?' She stood up and stormed off to her room, slamming the door behind her. I stared in complete shock at the seat where she had been sitting.

The next few days were absolutely awful. Beth wouldn't look me in the face. She pretended that I did not exist. It was even worse in the evenings; Roz was always out so that just left the two of us. She would lock herself in her room as soon as she got home and I would be stuck with a silent dorm for the evening. I tried to talk to her one night. I knocked on her bedroom door but I got no reply. It seemed that she truly hated me and I was only trying to help. Roz, of course, was oblivious to all this. She was only ever there in the afternoons when she would be getting ready for a night out, and she just assumed Beth was studying like she always was. I tried to go out to the student bar some evenings with other people from my class, but I found it hard to enjoy myself. The guilt was eating away at me. I would usually then just make up some excuse and leave early, returning to my silent dorm.

I was actually relieved when Tom arrived on a Thursday evening; it was a nice change from the tension-filled silence. He noticed this as well.

'Is it just me, Olive, or are you actually happy to see me?'

'I wouldn't quite say that now,' I said, smiling at him.

He frowned at me and pouted. 'Uncool, Olive. That hurt.'

I laughed at his pretending-to-be-upset face; he was always so animated when he spoke. I made him a cup of tea. It had become our routine. When I sat down opposite him I noticed a small graze across his right cheek; it was red and looked quite sore.

'You get into a fight or something?' I asked jokingly, gesturing towards his face.

'Oh yeah, with a really vicious tree. If you think this is bad, you should see those branches. Nothing but twigs now.'

We sat on the couch chatting for at least an hour; it was nice that I could finally relax in my own dorm and laugh a little.

'So what was the fight with the branches over?' I enquired.

'Well, now that you ask . . .' He reached into the pocket of his leather jacket and took out one small white flower. He handed it to me and I noticed his face going slightly red.

'Oh wow, thanks!' I exclaimed, genuinely shocked.

'Just remember I had to fight for it.' He was pointing to the scratch on his face.

I smiled back; I was starting to feel a bit giddy.

'On that note, I am afraid I have to go.'

'Oh, OK,' I said, surprised that I felt disappointed.

'Peter, Damien and I are hitting the town.'

'Sounds like fun,' I said, trying not to appear too interested.

'Do you want to come? Don't worry, there will be a bunch of us there so it won't be a date,' he said, winking at me.

I couldn't stop myself from smiling back; however, I heard my voice say, 'No, I think I will stay in.'

He was walking out the door when suddenly he stopped and turned around. The expression on his face showed that he was undecided whether to say something or not.

'Olive. Do you ever just relax and have a bit of fun?'

I was insulted by his question and I went on the defence. 'Of course I have fun. I am just concentrating on college at the moment.' I knew I sounded like an old-biddy.

'OK, well, I am going to tell you a dirty little secret. The lecturers expect you to go out every now and again, and tear it up. I will be in D2 if you change your mind.' I could tell by the look on his face he knew he had overstepped the mark but he left before I could reply.

After he had gone I started making my dinner. I ate it in silence. Beth had locked herself in her room again and Roz wasn't around. I walked into my room and started looking at all my clothes; most of my stuff was completely practical – jeans, jumpers, scarves and runners. I eventually came across a tight black dress that I hadn't worn since I got here. I liked to pretend that I didn't care whether people looked at me or not, but the truth was I loved the attention I would get when I got all dressed up and went out to a club. It felt empowering to sense the stares of lots of guys on you.

Taking out my phone, I texted Roz. *You want to go to D2 tonight?* She texted back nearly instantly. *Hell yeah.*

12

Tom

I KNEW I HAD OVERSTEPPED WITH OLIVE. I HAD SAID WAY TOO much. It was just so hard to hold my tongue with her sometimes. When she acted all responsible and sensible I just wanted to scream at her – urge her to have a little fun, not be so worried about everything. But there was nothing I could do now. I just hoped she wasn't too offended by what I'd said. There was no way she would come out tonight, that was for sure. I was disappointed. Olive was fun and flirty even if she didn't know it. It was hard to keep pretending that her rejection wasn't bothering me. I liked her company, but at this point I was becoming desperate to kiss her, to be with her. It was clear, though, that she didn't feel the same way. I was wondering was it nearly time to give it all up. Maybe it was no harm. I had been feeling a little tense ever since I had smoked that dodgy joint. It would be good to go out with just the lads.

I started making my way to Peter's; we always did our pre-drinking there. I had texted my mum saying I wasn't coming home tonight. She hadn't replied. I guessed she didn't really care. It was 9.30 by the time I was walking out of the UCD main gate. The campus was pretty hectic. Thursday was usually a good night out for students; there would be drink deals everywhere. Girls were wandering around in their short skirts and tight tops, and guys were in their baggy jeans and white T-shirts, usually downing some sort of alcohol.

I could hear voices from the bottom of Peter's stairs. It was obviously more than just Damien and me who had been invited. As I got closer and closer to his door I heard the sound of girls laughing. *Brilliant.* I knocked on the door and was met by an incoherent Damien.

'Tom, you fucking legend!' He was yelling at the top of his voice and leaning up against the doorpost. He put a hand on my shoulder for balance. 'Tom, Peter found these absolute hotties and they are totally DTF. Do you know what DTF means, Tom? It means DOWN TO FUCK.'

I think Damien thought he had been whispering the whole time but he was actually talking very loudly and I decided I had better shut him up before he ruined it for everyone.

'Come, Damien, let's get a drink,' I said, pushing past him and going into Peter's common room. In the room there were four girls, all blonde, all quite attractive, but one was quite plump – which turned me off instantly. I didn't like big girls. Sure, big tits and a large ass were always a bit of fun, but I was a skinny enough guy and I was always worried that they might crush me in the thrusts of passion.

'Tom? Tom, come here.' Peter had just realized that I had arrived. He was also, like Damien, slurring his words but he was managing to stand with a lot more balance. I walked over and he introduced me to the four girls. I instantly forgot three of their names but I remembered the one that I thought was the prettiest.

'So, Danielle, are you in college?' I asked her. She was very tall and slim. In fact, with her heels on, she was a good bit taller than me but I was hoping she wouldn't mind that. With a bit of luck, I would be getting those heels off her later.

'Yeah,' she replied in a strong Dublin accent. 'I am doing a beautician's course in Bray.'

'Oh wow,' I replied, trying my best to sound interested. She was wearing a very low V-neck dress that showed off a lot of cleavage and I was finding it hard to keep looking at her face. Olive might not have fancied me, but it made me feel a lot better to realize that plenty of other girls did.

I got a few drinks into me quickly. I was behind the others and I was doing my best to keep up. I was also careful to make sure that Danielle's glass was never empty; she seemed delighted by my attention.

'Oh, Tom, you're so cute,' she said, patting my shoulder, which then slowly turned into her caressing my arm. She was quite drunk; her eyes were unfocused when she was talking to me. As it got close to eleven o'clock I stopped refilling Danielle's drinks. I didn't want to have to take care of her if she became messy. Everyone seemed to have paired off, leaving the larger girl sitting on her own. We will have to find her someone at the club, I thought to myself, otherwise she is going to be a serious cock block.

'Right, everyone. Time to get the fuck out of my apartment. D2 is waiting.' I was surprised to find that Danielle sat on my lap the whole way into town; she kept on whispering dirty things into my ear and then smiling at me. Damien had been right; these girls were well up for it. There was a huge queue outside D2 when we arrived so we stood in the freezing cold for at least forty minutes. This sobered my girl up quite a bit and she was standing a lot closer to her large friend now than she was to me. Fuck it, I thought. There is plenty more where she came from.

Unsurprisingly, the club was absolutely packed to the brim.

There were girls tottering about the place in skyscraper high-heels and lads looking on lustfully. I was a little surprised that we had managed to get in with no issues. The girls might have sobered up in the cold air but Peter and Damien had gone from bad to worse. Damien actually dropped the full contents of his wallet when asked for ID. This consisted of an age card, a ten-euro note, a couple of coins and a condom. Luckily the bouncers seemed more concerned about reducing the queue than us.

Danielle had run off as soon as she entered the club. She had seen some guy she obviously knew and had lost interest in me. The fat girl and the girl that Damien had been chatting to went off with her. Peter was the only one who had managed to hold on to his girl. He had wrapped his arms around her and rubbed her warm when we had been out in the cold. In hindsight, Damien and I should have probably done the same thing, but it was really fucking cold out there and I didn't want to take my hands out of my pockets. Damien was too plastered to even notice that his girl had run off. He was more concerned about getting to the bar.

'Three Jägerbombs!' he shouted at the barman, waving his ten euro about.

'Damien, you realize that Peter has fucked off and there are only two of us.'

'THREE JÄGERBOMBS!' he shouted even louder, completely ignoring me. When Damien had finally been served, I downed my one quickly, hid the glass and grabbed a second one before Damien had finished with his.

'Where is my other drink?' he asked me, drunk and confused.

'You only ordered two, mate,' I said, trying not to laugh.

'But . . . but I thought I ordered three,' he said to himself. He was like a confused child.

'No, you didn't. Peter isn't here, so you only ordered two, remember?'

'Oh, OK.'

I knew that I should probably feel a bit bad for taking advantage of his drunken state, but it was just too funny. I was actually enjoying my night. I was getting pleasantly drunk and Damien was always endless entertainment when he was in this state.

'OK, OK, Tom. We have to see who can do this the longest!' Damien exclaimed, barely able to keep in his laughter.

'OK,' I said, giggling like a girl myself. We had managed to convince the barman to give us two spoons and we were now seeing who was able to keep it on his nose for the longest. Sober, this would have been easy; drunk, it was near impossible. The barman also seemed to enjoy our competition when he wasn't busy making drinks.

'So this is what you do for fun?' I jumped at the sound of her voice and my spoon dropped onto the floor. Damien screamed with laughter. I turned around to see Olive standing there.

'Hi,' I said, standing up and then sitting back down. Completely unsure why I had done it.

'Hi,' she replied, laughing.

'Have . . . have you been here long?' I asked, stumbling over my words.

'Yeah, Roz and I have been dancing for hours. We just came up here to get a drink.'

I looked around but I could see no sign of Roz.

'Where is she?'

'Well, on the way up here she saw a guy that caught her interest. I thought it best to give her some private time with him. I'll find her again at the end of the night.'

'Oh, cool.' I sat there for a while not quite sure what to say. It was only after the initial shock of seeing her that I realized how great she looked. She was wearing thin black tights with a tight black dress. Her hair looked bigger and curlier than normal and her dark green eyes were striking.

'So you changed your mind then?' I asked with a slight innuendo.

'Roz was coming already,' she shrugged, but she was smiling as she said it.

'Do you want to sit?' I asked, and when she looked as if she was hesitating, I added, 'Just until Roz is done with her guy?'

She nodded at me and took the stool next to me, saying, 'Your friend looks like he has been better.'

I had completely forgotten that Damien had been sitting there the whole time. I turned around and hoped that I would be able to slyly tell him to leave and not reveal our bet, but I then discovered that he had passed out on the bar. I couldn't help but burst out laughing; Olive laughed with me.

I bought Olive one drink. She wouldn't let me buy her any more. She might have come out but she definitely wasn't going to let her guard down with me. Instead I tried to sweet talk her.

'You know, you look absolutely beautiful,' I said, attempting to put my hand on her knee.

'Thanks,' she said, lifting my hand back onto the bar. 'You must be drunk, Tom. You confused my leg for yours,' she said, smiling knowingly at me.

I started rubbing my own leg in hopes to make light of the situation, and thankfully she saw the funny side.

'Do you like this place?' I asked.

'Yeah, it's pretty good. But it's like any other club really, isn't it?'

'What do you mean?'

'Well, you have all the same sort of people you see at every club. For example,' she pointed to a grumpy-looking girl in the corner, 'you have the rich girl who thinks she is above everyone here; then,' she gestured to a lad sitting on the couch with his arms around two girls, 'there is the gay guy seriously over-compensating; also,' she then directed me towards a girl doing some sexy moves with a guy while another guy looked on angrily, 'the girl trying desperately to make her asshole boyfriend jealous – and finally,' she nodded over at a nervous-looking guy awkwardly trying to dance along to the music, 'the virgin who is too terrified to talk to anyone.'

'Is it all that simple?' I asked.

'Yeah,' she replied.

'Then what am I?'

'The gay guy, definitely,' she said, smiling mischievously.

I suddenly felt a sharp tug as someone's arm wrapped around my neck.

'Tom!' Danielle was screaming down my ear and I could smell the Jägermeister on her breath.

'Danielle, you are choking me.' I tried to push her off but she was falling all over me.

'Tom, Tom. You know I think you are *so* cute, right?' She was putting her hands around my waist and trying to pull me out of my seat. I did my very best to stay sitting.

'Tom, do you have anywhere to sleep tonight?'

'Yeah, I do.' Danielle was blocking Olive from my sight.

'Well, if you want, you can stay at mine.' I think she was trying to put on a sexy voice but her words just became more slurred.

'Actually, Danielle, I am talking to my friend at the moment.' I gestured behind her and she swung around to stare at Olive.

'Oh. So who are you?' she asked Olive as if she was a piece of filth.

Olive merely smiled at her. 'Hi, I am Olive,' she said, offering a handshake.

Danielle just stared at Olive's hand and then turned towards me again. 'The club is closing in like ten minutes. Do you want to leave now, babe?' I was about to come up with some excuse when Olive spoke again.

'Ten minutes? Wow, I'd better find Roz. See you, Tom.'

She stood up quickly and started making her way to the dance floor. Danielle looked very happy about her leaving.

'So shall we go?' she asked me again.

'I'm OK, thanks. Why don't you talk to Damien.' I sat Danielle down next to Damien's unconscious figure and went running after Olive. I caught her by her elbow and she spun around to face me.

'Hey, where are you going?' I asked, slightly dizzy from the alcohol.

'I told you, I am looking for Roz. Anyway, I thought you would want to be left alone with that girl.'

'I don't like her.'

'I am not saying you like her, but you *are* attracted to her. Come on, you practically have a boner.' Olive laughed at the fact that I looked down to check.

'But I am *not* attracted to her, I am attracted to you. Jesus Christ, I couldn't want anyone more than I want you right now,' and it was true. I wanted her. I wanted to kiss that smug smile, touch that petite figure.

I started to fear that I had said too much again and that Olive was just going to walk away, embarrassed even to be associated with me. Instead, this odd look of intensity entered her eyes and she walked towards me until her body was leaning against mine and her lips were only an inch away from mine.

'I know there is this raw sexual desire between us, Tom. I have felt it ever since I met you. I tried to fight it, but I can't. I think you should come back to mine tonight and we should go at it like rabbits. You know, just to get it out of our system.'

I could feel the heat of her breath against my face and I couldn't believe my luck.

'Sounds amazing,' I whispered back.

'Tom,' she said, suddenly smiling and the strange intensity

gone from her eyes, 'you are too fucking easy,' and with that she turned around and walked away.

I stood there in complete shock for at least five minutes. Not quite sure what had just happened. Eventually I just mumbled to myself, 'For fuck's sake.'

13

Olive

I HAD NO IDEA HOW ROZ DID IT. I ONLY DRANK HALF AS MUCH as she did and I still felt like my head was going to explode. Even worse than that, I was absolutely starving, but anytime I saw food I thought I was going to be sick. I looked sick also – there were bags under my eyes, my face was white as a sheet and my hair was sticky. Roz, of course, looked as gorgeous as ever. Her make-up was perfectly done before she even left her room in the morning. The thought of putting on make-up made me want to sleep.

'Last night was fun, wasn't it?' Roz was practically dancing around the kitchen.

'Yeah, it was,' I murmured, while resting my head on the kitchen table.

'That guy I met was an absolute babe. He was pretty sound as well. Texted me last night to make sure I got home OK. Like how cute is that?'

'Pretty nice,' I answered queasily.

'So where did you disappear to then? I didn't see you for about half the night.'

'I ran into Tom.'

'Ooh, anything happen there?'

'No, it wasn't like that. We're just friends.'

'I don't think Tom wants to be just your friend.'

I shrugged and didn't bother to answer. I had no clue what Tom wanted with me, but I thought it was better that I keep my distance. At least I knew what game he was playing now, and I could screw with his head just as much as he did with mine.

'I've got to go. I'm meeting Ed for some late breakfast,' Roz said while walking out of the kitchen. No wonder she had made so much of an effort this morning, I thought.

'Roz, can I ask you something. Do you ever go to college?'

She stood there in silence, thinking for a moment before answering.

'I just . . . don't see the point of all of it.' She almost looked a little sad while saying it. It was odd: I had never seen her anything but bubbly and positive.

'Fair enough,' I said, hoping that I had not overstepped. I needed to start watching what I said. She waved goodbye, instantly returning to her bubbly self. It was a talent, Roz's ability to keep everything together and not let life or the people in it affect you. I was jealous of her.

Beth had left at the crack of dawn like she normally did; the tension in the house was honestly becoming unbearable. Last night had been an amazing relief but I knew I still had to fix this. I looked at my watch. It was eleven o'clock and my classes didn't start till twelve today – one of the many joys of being an arts student. I was sick of living in a dorm where I was unable to relax. College was supposed to be my escape, a safe place. It was where I didn't have to worry about other people all of the time. I needed to fix this. I *had* to fix this. Beth hadn't spoken to me for nearly two weeks now. I missed her. I wanted my friend back.

I vaguely remembered Beth saying that she had an hour off at eleven on Fridays. I ran to my room and grabbed whatever clothes I could find. I was going to talk to Beth. I was going to tell her that I was completely in the wrong and that I should never have intruded on her personal business and that I was so sorry. At least outside on campus she wouldn't be able to just block me out like she did when I tried to talk to her at home. She would be forced to listen to me.

Running out of the house I knew I must look awful. I never really bothered with my looks that much for college, but today I had sunk to a new low. I was wearing black tracksuit bottoms and a red hoodie from school. I had not a pick of make-up on and my hair was tied back unattractively. I was getting a horrible stitch from running but I knew I couldn't stop if I wanted to catch Beth. She only had an hour break, and the Medicine building was all the way on the other side of campus. No one looked at me twice. UCD had a habit of attracting students with odd fashion choices and my look was definitely nothing special in comparison with some of the people who went here.

When I finally reached the main entrance to the School of Medicine I was completely puffed out. I bent over and breathed in and out deeply, attempting to get some air. When I felt like I could breathe again I looked up and saw Beth in the distance walking out of a side exit.

'Beth!' I called at the top of my voice but she didn't hear me. I started walking in her direction and I called her name again.

'Beth! Can I talk to you?' Suddenly she broke into a jog, her large bag banging on her hip. I couldn't believe she was actually running away from me. I started to run after her, even though my side was burning with a stitch. I had always been awful at running.

'Beth, come on!' I shouted, as I started to catch up on her.

I came to a sudden halt as I realized that Beth wasn't running away from me. She couldn't even see me. Three very big and rough-looking girls had just caught up with her. One of them grabbed the strap of her bag and pulled it from Beth's shoulder, causing her to come to a stop. The girl then threw the bag as hard as she could against the concrete ground. I started sprinting with urgency in their direction.

'You posh bitch. We will teach you a fucking lesson, think you're so great. Well, look at you now, you fucking coward.' When I reached them the tallest girl, who seemed to be the one in charge, had her hands on Beth's jumper, pulling her up to the same height.

'Hey, what the fuck do you think you are doing?'

The girl instantly dropped Beth and looked in my direction. She smiled when she saw that the voice had come from me.

'Is this one of your posh mates then? Does this bitch need to be taught her place as well?'

'Look, girls, I would just go. None of us wants trouble, OK?' I knew my attempts at a peaceful solution were pointless before I had even opened my mouth; these girls had come for a fight.

'Is this skinny bitch giving me shit?' the girl asked her two friends, both of whom answered with 'teach her a lesson' and 'show her to keep her mouth shut'.

Beth stood in frozen fear. I had a horrible feeling that this wasn't the first time this had happened to her.

'Look, you girls seriously need to fuck off.' I was trying to sound as aggressive as possible but I could feel my knees shaking.

The ringleader walked till she was standing directly in front of me and then she began to eye me up. I did my best not to be intimidated and to stand my ground, but it didn't help. The girl was at least a foot taller than me and probably two stone heavier.

'You are asking for a bollocking. You know that?'

'Go on, hit me. There are people everywhere. The campus police will be here within seconds and you and your friends will get your fat arses arrested.'

The girl stared at me for what felt like hours. I could feel the sweat rolling down my back. The truth was that I had no idea if UCD had campus police and I wouldn't trust any of the few students around to call the Guards if a fight did break out. I have never been punched before, but I knew if this girl hit me, it was going to hurt.

'You better watch yourself,' she said, suddenly turning towards Beth. 'You and your snobby lezzer mate.'

We both stood there completely silent. I prayed that I had some sort of brave face on as the three girls swaggered away. Beth just looked terrified. When the girls were out of earshot I walked over to her and started gently rubbing her arm.

'Are you OK?' I asked.

She looked as if she could faint at any moment. She walked silently over to her bag that had been lying on the ground the whole time, and pulled out her laptop; there was a huge crack across the screen. Suddenly Beth burst into floods of tears.

'Don't cry,' I said, and sat down next to her. 'It's probably just the screen. We can get it fixed, don't worry.'

'It's not that,' she managed to say in between sobs.

'What is it then? Did they hurt you?'

'I have been horrible to you.' She was crying even harder now.

'No, you haven't. I shouldn't have invaded your privacy like that,' but she wouldn't hear any of it.

'I was horrible to you and you were only trying to help. I really am such a bitch.'

I spent the next hour sitting on the ground consoling Beth. We both missed our next class that afternoon but I knew this was more important. Luckily the back area of the Medical

School was quiet, and anyone who did walk by kept to themselves. When Beth had finally calmed down, we made our way back to the dorms. I made Beth a cup of tea and insisted that she eat some biscuits with it. She still looked pale as a ghost.

'You were so brave standing up to those girls back there.' By now, Beth was finally looking more like her old self.

'To be honest, I was completely terrified. I was convinced that girl was going to hit me,' I admitted.

'So was I. Those girls are seriously rough.'

I stirred my tea and thought carefully before I spoke again. 'Beth, who are those girls?'

'They went to school with me in Limerick. They used to . . . beat me up a lot.'

'Why?' The question was out of my mouth before I could stop myself.

'I don't really know. I grew up in a pretty nice area of Limerick and we had nice things and a nice house. But the school I went to – most people didn't even finish, let alone go to college and move out. They just think I reckon I am better than them.'

'Well, you are. They were serious scum.'

Beth started laughing. 'That one with the bad skin actually has a three-year-old kid.'

'Poor kid,' I said with genuine sympathy for the child. Then: 'What were they doing in Dublin?' I asked.

'I have no idea. I nearly died with shock when I saw them. I walked out the back entrance hoping that they wouldn't notice me. That clearly didn't work.'

'Are they the ones sending you the emails, as well?' And when she just nodded: 'Have you told anyone?'

'My boyfriend knows. He wanted me to report it to the Guards.'

'Well, maybe you should,' I said, but she was already shaking her head.

'All they will do is give them a warning, and that will just piss them off even more. Honestly, I just want to pretend it never happened. I am sure they will be gone soon.'

'How long has it been going on for?'

Beth shrugged. 'A bit more than a year, I'm not sure. Since I started school with them.'

'Why didn't you move schools if it was so bad? Did your parents know?'

'No, my parents never found out. There were only two schools in my area, a private one and a public one. I started off in the private school. I loved that school. The teachers were great and everyone was so nice.'

'Why did you move then?' I asked, baffled.

'My parents didn't approve of Michael, my boyfriend. They were horrified that I kept dating him even after they had told me to end things. Michael was not exactly what they wanted as a future son-in-law. They thought he would hold me back. Michael comes from a broken family, you see, with very little money. My parents wanted to send me to boarding school for my final year of school, but I begged them to let me stay in Limerick. They eventually agreed to let me finish in the public school. There was no way they were letting me go back to the same school as Michael.'

'So you went through that hell just to stay close to Michael?'

She nodded. 'He is everything to me. Without him I have nothing.'

After that, Beth changed the subject and I decided it was best not to bring it up again. I know I should have encouraged her more to do something about all of this, but I was so relieved that she was speaking to me again and I didn't want to ruin that. I couldn't sleep properly that night. I didn't realize how shaken

I was from earlier. I had been so scared standing in front of that girl, seeing the pure and utter hate in her eyes. I had never seen someone look so angry and aggressive; I had been truly terrified of what she was going to do to me. I started to wonder how Beth had coped with that for so long. It must have been torture. Always having to worry about getting pushed around, hit, punched, who knows what else. UCD must have been her escape. The drive to be a doctor probably matched the drive to get away from those girls.

It was odd; in a way I felt like I understood her better now. We all have to deal with some sort of darkness in our lives. Beth's had come back to haunt her. I only prayed that mine never would.

14
Tom

IT'S DARK. I CAN'T SEE ANYTHING BUT SHADOWS. SHADOWS THAT rush past so quickly, you're not even sure they were there to begin with. I look around myself frantically. Feel the burning of someone's eyes on me. I can't see anything but someone can see me. I try to speak but nothing comes out, only silence. I cannot be heard.

The shadows fly past again; I try to run after them this time. I run as fast as I can, but I am not going anywhere. I want to get out. What are the shadows? Where are they coming from? Why are they taunting me in this way? I try to scream *stop* but again there is only silence. I put my hands up and try to feel something, anything. I lean down to touch the ground, but it disappears at my touch. And then suddenly out of the darkness comes the noise – the most unbearable noise that I have ever heard. It's in the distance at first but it closes in quickly, cuts through me like a knife. It is attacking me, killing me . . .

I sat bolt upright in my bed. I looked around myself in terror and realized that I was in my room. The back of my neck was covered in sweat and I was completely out of breath. The clock on my bedside table showed that it was 3 a.m. I ran my hands through my hair as I felt my heart-rate slow down, and I whistled quietly. I couldn't help but feel relieved when I heard that whistling sound. My bedsheets were damp with sweat; I threw them off and made my way to the bathroom. I turned on the cold shower and stepped in to try to wash off the remains of the dream. I still had a few cuts and bruises on my body but they were nearly unnoticeable. The cold shower felt good as it slowly dripped down my body and sank through my toes.

When I finally got out, I started to shiver – the shock of going from extreme heat to extreme cold. I wrapped a clean towel around me and tried to warm myself up. As I crawled back into the bed I was thankful that my midnight shower hadn't woken my mum. Trying to explain that I had had a nightmare would be far too embarrassing. As I lay back down in my bed I felt unsettled. I tossed and turned, unable to relax. In the end, I turned my lights back on and started reading a book that was lying on the floor of my room – *A Study in Scarlet*. I felt physically exhausted but my mind was going a million miles an hour. I made an effort to concentrate on the book, but found that my mind could not let go of that disturbing dream.

The next few days were difficult. I was finding it hard to focus and I was constantly nervous. I hadn't slept properly in days; it was making me moody and quick-tempered. Even my friends were noticing. Peter kept asking if anything was wrong. I didn't want to talk about it but I felt like I had to. I couldn't confide in Mum, I would only scare her. Moiraine had plenty of her own problems without my adding to them. Peter and Damien would probably laugh, thinking it was all a joke.

I was left with no other option but to go to my dad's place. It was time to admit that what had happened had really scared me. In that dream I couldn't think, I couldn't breathe. I had never had a panic attack before, but I couldn't think of any other explanation. The only other time I had felt like that was when I was in Stephen's Green. I had blamed the dodgy dope then, but what about in that dream? I had taken nothing; my own mind had created that entire terrifying scene. I couldn't forget the experience – it was haunting me. I had nowhere else to turn but to Paddy. He was my dad, he might know what had happened to me.

I hadn't spoken to my dad in a couple of weeks; we talked less and less as the years went by. It'd been even longer since I had visited him, and even then I would have always rung to say that I was coming. I stood outside his door for about ten minutes, afraid to knock. I knew he wouldn't be working, he mostly did night shifts. But suddenly all I wanted to do was walk away. Only the fear of having to try to figure this thing out on my own made me knock on his door.

Robin answered nearly instantly. On seeing me, she looked flustered. Her blonde hair was sticking out in odd ways and her thin face looked stern as usual.

'Tom.' She plastered a smile on her face, hoping that I wouldn't see the disappointment. 'Paddy didn't tell me you were coming. I have no food ready.' She always made a point of calling my dad by his name when talking about him to me. She never said 'your father'. I knew she didn't want to be connected to me in any way.

'I never called. I was just visiting a friend who lives around here and I thought I'd come and say hi.' Robin's face became even thinner as she pursed her lips at me. She had always made a big show when I was meant to come over – food cooked, house cleaned. She obviously hoped that I would go home and tell my mum what a lovely house she kept. Everything was a competition to her and I knew she felt second to my mum because she had married my dad first.

'Oh well, how nice.' She was always a terrible liar. 'Well, the thing is, Paddy isn't at home at the moment. But you can wait for him inside if you want.'

I could tell she wanted me to say it was fine and that I would go. I was starting to think that might be a good idea when Pamela came running to the door. She was shouting and crying at the same time and I could barely understand what she was saying.

'Mummy, Mummy, you promised we could go to Phoenix Park today. Please, Mummy.' Pamela stopped mid-sentence when she saw me, and a huge smile grew on her face. 'TOM!' She shoved past Robin and hugged me. I never really understood why Pamela liked me so much. I didn't even know if she knew what half-brother meant, but she was always delighted to see me.

'Hi, Pam,' I said, patting her head. She had grown a lot since I had last seen her. I was always so startled to see how much she looked like me and my dad, and nothing like Robin. Her face was round and sweet and her hair was dark brown like mine.

'Mummy, can Tom take me to the Phoenix Park?'

Robin and I stood there silently staring at each other. I had never taken Pamela out on my own before and I knew Robin wouldn't let me.

'Tom doesn't have a car, sweetie, and it's too far to walk.'

Pamela's eyes were filling with tears again and Robin looked like she was struggling for some control.

'I could bring her just for a walk around the area?' I don't really know why I offered. I wanted to go for a walk myself and I guess this gave me a reason to come back and talk to my dad. Robin was chewing her cheek. I could tell she didn't want to leave me alone with Pamela, but then again it would give her some time to herself. Something she always seemed to want.

'There's a Spar down the street. She can get an ice-cream and then come straight back.' Pamela screamed with delight and started pulling my hand down the street. Robin looked torn as we walked away but eventually she turned around and closed the door.

'I can say the alphabet the fastest in my *whole* class, Tom, even faster than Emma and she is supposed to be the smartest girl. But I can also run faster so I don't mind. Did Dad tell you about me winning the story-writing competition? I wrote a story about . . .' I let her just ramble on, commenting every now and again. I started to regret not visiting more often; it felt nice to actually be someone's big brother.

'Tom, Tom – that's my friend Emma.' She was pointing towards a little red-headed girl who was waving enthusiastically at her. Pamela started to pull me over to her friend and I began to wonder how an eight-year-old could be so strong. Emma was standing with an older woman who had dyed brown hair and was undoubtedly her mother.

The two eight-year-olds hugged and Emma's mother said, 'Pamela, how nice to see you.'

My sister pulled at my hand again, saying, 'Emma, this is my big brother Tom.'

At this, Emma's mother's eyes widened. 'I didn't know Pamela had a big brother,' she commented.

I suddenly felt under the spotlight, and hastened to explain, 'Well, actually I'm just her half-brother.'

'Well, well . . . you learn something new every day,' the woman said, an unpleasant smile spreading across her face. 'You two look very alike – you could definitely tell from a distance that you were related.'

'Really?' I said. She spoke in a tone of voice that sounded like she was insulting you, rather than complimenting.

'We better go,' Pamela piped up. 'We're getting ice-cream and then Mummy said we have to come straight home.' Bless Pamela, she wanted to leave as fast as I did.

'Well, it was nice to meet you, Tom.' The woman had her hand out to shake and I suddenly realized that she had never told me her name.

'Um . . . you too,' I mumbled. She walked away with Emma and I suddenly felt like I had said something I shouldn't have.

The walk back was a lot quieter. Pamela was sucking away on her frozen ice-pop shaped like a frog and I was starting to relax in her company.

'Why do I not see you more, Tom? Emma says she sees her big sister every day.' I ran my hand through my hair and pushed it out of my face. It was a nervous habit; I always did it when I didn't know what to say or do.

'Because I'm only your half-brother.'

She looked up at me with those massive brown eyes. 'I don't understand,' she said timidly.

I tried to think of the best way to explain it. I wondered had Dad tried to explain it before, or Robin.

'It means that Robin is not my mum but Paddy *is* my dad.'

She nodded in agreement, but I knew she still didn't understand. When we got back to the house I saw my dad's car outside. Relieved, I went to ring the front doorbell but Pamela started squealing.

'I have a key! I can open it!'

I laughed to myself. She really did get excited about the smallest things. I stood aside and let her open the door herself.

As soon as we walked through the door, I could hear Robin shouting. 'This is humiliating, Paddy. That stupid woman is going to tell everyone.'

I stood frozen. I didn't know whether I should interrupt them or not.

'Robin, calm down. It's not that big a deal.' My dad sounded stressed and tired.

'Everyone is going to know! Everyone! She called me to boast. To tell me that she knew I was your second wife, that you had a family before me. They'll think I'm a home-wrecker.'

I suddenly realized what I had done earlier.

'Robin, you know I was separated when I met you.' Dad was clearly fighting a lost battle.

'She won't see it that way! None of them will! Why is he here anyway – dropping in unannounced like this. He must be in trouble; need money or something. That ex-wife of yours must just let him do what he pleases. He turns up here looking like he has just come from a drinking binge. Think of the example he is setting for Pam!'

I knew I should have just turned around and walked out the door, but a small part of me hoped that my dad would defend me, defend my mum.

'Look, it's hard for her. Tom is difficult. He was such a clever, talented kid but he seems to lack ambition. She was expecting more from him – we both were.' My dad paused, and I heard him sigh. 'When they get back, I will talk to him and tell him to call beforehand, next time.'

I was shaking with rage. I had even forgotten that Pamela had been standing next to me the whole time.

'Tom, what is going on?' she asked, her voice high and scared. I knew Robin and Paddy had heard Pamela.

I told her, 'I have to go,' and started heading out the door. I could hear footsteps coming up behind me and I just started to walk quicker.

'Tom? I didn't know you were here.' My dad could see me now. 'Tom, I—'

I didn't hear anything else because I had started running.

I ran as fast as I could. People stared at me as I raced by. It must have looked odd, a guy in jeans and a T-shirt sprinting through town, but I didn't care. I just kept running. I ran until my sides hurt and I couldn't breathe properly any more. When I stopped, I realized I had run all the way to Grafton Street Luas station. There was a train waiting but I didn't take it. I sat there on the bench and watched as it departed without me. I watched three trains come and go, none of which I even thought about getting on. The rain started and stopped, and still I sat there. My sides didn't hurt any more but for some reason I still found it hard to breathe. At one point I stood up and walked halfway to the nearest bus stop and then I turned around and came back. I must have repeated this half a dozen times. I became paranoid that people were looking at me. I checked my phone – no missed calls, and no voice messages. I was tempted to throw my phone under the tracks, but fear of people watching stopped me. I had nowhere to go, no home, no family, only people who were obliged to take me in. The world started spinning. I put my head in between my knees and took some deep breaths. I thought I was going to be sick. I began to panic that it was going to happen again. *Not now, not for everyone to see.*

But it didn't happen. Slowly, everything stopped spinning. I didn't feel as if I was going to be sick any more. I raised my head and looked at my watch. I had been sitting here for hours; it had felt like nothing. The sun had set and people were starting to head either home or out. I suddenly became angry with myself; I had always known my family was messed up – why did I care? No one else did. I suddenly found that I couldn't stand still; I needed to be going somewhere, to be doing something.

When I knocked on her door, my hands were shaking. I pushed them into my pockets in hopes that she wouldn't notice. I let out a sigh of relief when I saw it was Olive who opened the door.

'Tom, what are you doing here? Are you OK? You look pale.'

She was in fluffy pyjamas, her hair tied back in a loose ponytail. Her face looked clean and fresh. I realized I had never noticed how naturally pretty she was; it made her rather intimidating.

'Um . . . can I stay here tonight?' I was ready for the questions. Why did I need to stay? Why couldn't I stay at home? What was I doing coming here? I stared at my feet, trying to think of suitable responses to these questions and any others that she might ask.

'OK,' she said simply. I must have looked surprised because she smiled warmly as if to comfort me. She gestured me into the sitting room and I sat down on the couch. She sat with me for a while; neither of us spoke. I don't think either of us knew exactly what was going on. Eventually she stood up as if about to leave but then she leaned down and kissed my cheek; her lips felt warm and soft.

She whispered, 'Goodnight,' and walked back to her room.

I woke up before the sun had even risen. At first I panicked, not knowing where I was, and then the memories of the previous day returned. I looked at my phone. Nothing. No one even cared that I was gone. I looked at Olive's bedroom door and wondered should I go in. I doubted that she would ever know how thankful I was for last night. No questions, no judgement, just acceptance. I didn't go in, I just left. It was too humiliating to face her.

15
Olive

IT HAD TAKEN ME A LONG TIME TO GET TO SLEEP. I HAD thought about going back out to him all night. I even got out of bed and walked to my bedroom door a couple of times. But each time I did so, I realized that I didn't know what I wanted to say. I didn't even know what I wanted to do. All I knew was, I wanted to go back out to him. Eventually I settled in my bed and fell asleep. It had been one of those odd sleeps when you feel as if you haven't slept at all. The sun shining in through my bedroom window woke me; my watch showed it was 8.30 a.m. I decided it was too early to go out to him; I didn't want him to think I was interested.

But *was* I interested? The first time I had met him I had been completely repulsed by him. He was messy and unwashed. His attitude was smug, and he clearly thought a lot of himself. And then when he had started turning up here, I was convinced that I had just hurt his ego. He was trying to prove a point to everyone or maybe even just himself. He was a cold person. He might be friendly enough to chat to, but anytime I asked him about his family or his childhood he would just completely close himself off. Make a joke about it and then move on. Why did he do that? Did he not care about anyone, take anything seriously? And then there were those rare moments when I saw something else. Something vulnerable.

I saw it for a brief moment, that night in D2 when he had not expected to see me, and then I saw it again last night. It was as if all his cocky, clever Dick attitude had been stripped away, and all that was left was him. I liked that part of him. Something had clearly upset him last night, and he had felt that he could come to me. Maybe he did have real feelings for me.

I lay there for thirty minutes before anxiety got the better of me and I climbed out of bed. I didn't change out of my pyjamas; he would think it was weird if I did. I did, however, pull my hair out of its ponytail and throw on some make-up, only a little bit though. I didn't want him to think I was getting all dolled up for him. Even though I kind of was.

I strolled out of my room, trying to act relaxed and unbothered, when I noticed that the couch was empty. I had a look in the common room and the kitchen and there was no sign of him. My heart sank as I realized that he was gone. *Why had he bothered coming if he was just going to leave without telling me?* I angrily started to make myself breakfast, slamming the bread into the toaster and shoving the kettle under the tap. S*tupid guy, messing with my head. Who needs him.*

Beth strolled in soon after. 'You're up early,' she yawned, and I just nodded. I was too angry to speak.

I decided to go to the library; my classes didn't start until 1 p.m. and I needed to do something to get Tom out of my mind. I was downstairs in what was considered 'the loud section' of the library – it was here that you found most of the novels and short stories. I had picked up a battered copy of Oscar Wilde's *The Picture of Dorian Gray*.

'That is an absolutely brilliant read, full of sex, drugs and murder. Can't get much better.'

I turned around to see whether that comment was for me or not. In front of me I saw a very tall man, with long blond hair sleeked back; it looked as if it had been perfectly windswept. He was smiling at me, his striking blue eyes alight. The only way to describe him was 'textbook beautiful'.

'Thanks,' I said shyly. 'I have read it before. It is really good – I am just considering whether I will read it again.'

'Well, if that is the kind of stuff you enjoy, I would suggest that you have a look at some of Edgar Allan Poe's stuff. It is a bit more sinister, but incredibly gripping.'

'I have actually read that too.' I was starting to feel a bit more confident. 'I basically love Gothic style, especially during the Victorian era. They just have no fears of crossing boundaries and pushing limits.'

The fair guy smiled down at me. He really was very tall. 'An English student, I am guessing?'

'Yeah, first year – and you?'

'I am in my final year,' he replied.

'My name is Olive,' I said, unable to hold in my giggles for some reason. I hoped that he found me cute, rather than silly.

'I'm Sam,' he said, offering me his hand. 'Well, I'd better be off. Hope to run into you again, Olive.'

I was surprised at his sudden departure. *That is the type of guy I should be with.* Throwing all caution to the wind, I jogged after him.

'Sam!' I said as I reached him. He turned around and looked surprised to see me standing there. A voice in the back of my head told me this was a bad idea, but I decided to ignore it.

'Sam, would you like to get a cup of coffee or something?'

His striking blue eyes started to fill with compassion, which I mistook for eagerness.

Then: 'Oh, Olive, I am really flattered but you are just not my type.' He gave me a pat on the shoulder and began walking off in the direction that he had been heading. I stood there silently, completely stunned. How could I have been so off? How could I have mistaken friendliness for flirting? So I had been rejected twice today. Once by a guy who claimed to fancy me and then again by a complete and utter stranger, who didn't even know a thing about me. Today was not a good day.

UCD campus was absolutely packed. They were having an Open Day for prospective students and there were hundreds of seventeen-year-olds wandering around, clogging up the hallways and lecture halls. Massive queues had built up for the coffee shops and cloakrooms. After standing for twenty minutes outside the ladies toilets I became completely frustrated and decided to go down to the basement and use the toilets there. They were old and filthy – barely anyone ever went down there. I only knew they existed because Roz once showed me; she seemed to know where everything was in UCD. I normally avoided these bathrooms and used the cleaner ones upstairs, but today I was sick of waiting.

I shoved open the heavy door expecting the bathroom to be empty, but I was surprised to see another girl standing by the mirror. The door had made a squeaky noise when I had forced it open, causing the blonde girl to look in my direction. She had a mixture of tears and mascara running down her face, and she was breathing heavily as if she had just been sprinting.

'I'm sorry.' I wasn't really sure why I was apologizing, since this was a public bathroom. It wasn't like I was the one who had made her cry, but it seemed like the only appropriate thing to say in this situation. I walked further into the bathroom. As I got closer, she started to look vaguely familiar to me.

'Alison?' I was standing next to her now. She was just staring at the mirror, make-up smudged all over her face, her hands gripping the sink. 'Are you OK?' She didn't even look at me. I was starting to think that maybe I should leave, when she suddenly spoke.

'An odd thing, isn't it? When we see someone upset, the custom is to ask them are they OK, when it's clear that they're obviously not OK. And the stranger part is that the other person is always obliged to say that they're fine. Well, I don't want to go by that stupid custom. So, no, I am *not* OK. I am far from OK.' She put her head in her hands and I could see the black-soaked tears slip through her fingers.

'Is there anyone I can call for you? I can take you back to your dorm?'

She didn't lift her head from her hands. Her voice was muffled when she spoke.

'No. There is no one – and I can't go back to my dorm, I just can't. No one can see me like this.'

I wanted to comfort her. Say something to get her to stop crying.

'Do you want to talk about it?' She lifted her head out from her hands. She didn't say anything. 'Sometimes things don't seem so bad if you talk about them with someone. It can help.'

Alison started laughing. 'God, you are naive.' She began wiping her face with a tissue. Her lips were quivering. 'My father is having an affair with one of my friends.' She said it with no emotion, as if it was just a fact and nothing else.

'What! Are you sure?'

'Very sure. I went home today to pick up some clothes. I didn't tell my dad I was coming. As it's a Tuesday morning I didn't think he would be at the house. He obviously didn't think I would be there either.'

Alison swallowed. 'I noticed her car at first. Of course I didn't realize straight away that it was *her* car. I just noticed that there was a strange car sitting in our driveway. I didn't think much of it though. People are always popping in to see Katie, my stepmum. I knew something was up though when I walked in the door – I heard shuffling and banging from upstairs. At first I thought it was Katie. I know she gets up to stuff that she shouldn't behind my dad's back, and for once I thought I was finally catching her in the act. I stood at the bottom of the stairs feeling smug. I didn't expect to see the two of them running down together. From the looks on their faces, it was obvious they didn't expect to see me either.'

Alison had stopped crying now. She was still cleaning her face, slowly eliminating the mascara-soaked tears.

'What did you do? What did they say when they saw you standing there?'

Alison started to smile. It was a sad smile.

'He tried to cover it up, of course. He told me some bullshit story about Alex having come to the house looking for me. Alex just stood there like a guilty idiot. She was ice white, her hair and make-up was a mess, she didn't even have her shirt buttoned up properly. My dad got out of there quickly, said he had to go to work or something. Once he left I didn't even have to say anything. Alex just started bawling, confessed completely. I could barely understand her – she was hysterical.'

'Oh my God,' I whispered. 'What did you say to her?'

'I slapped her. Then I told her to leave. I didn't want to hear anything she had to say. That girl is dead to me.' Alison's face was clean now. But her hands still trembled.

'God, my dad is one sick bastard. He used to take Alex and me for ice-cream when we were ten, after our ballet lessons.' She closed her eyes and spoke quietly. I didn't think she was speaking to me any more. I was about to leave when she opened her eyes and turned towards me for the first time.

'You are Rosanna's friend. Your name is Olive, right?' I nodded. Her voice had changed. It was no longer the monotoned tragic voice she had used before. She sounded posh, superior and strong. She sounded the way she had when I had first met her. 'Don't tell a soul what I told you, Olive. Not a single soul.'

'Of course I won't.'

'Then you are a smart girl. Can you leave now?' She turned back to the mirror and started to inspect her face carefully.

'Alison, if you ever need someone to talk to, I am always around.'

She laughed. 'Thanks, Olive. But you and I have nothing to talk about.'

I left the bathroom and returned to the queue that I had been in earlier. I still needed to use the toilet. I couldn't believe the story I had just heard – I didn't know how to process any of it. Alison was so tragic. Her life seemed so perfect on the outside – she was beautiful and she came from a wealthy family. But on the inside it was a disaster. No one cared about her – not her family, not her friends. And yet she seemed desperate to uphold this perfect façade so that no one could see the truth. I didn't want to be like her, I didn't want to let everything fall apart around me.

When I got home that evening I went from furious to utterly depressed. I hated the fact that Tom was able to mess with my head so much when he hadn't actually done anything. That was the point, he had done nothing. He had never said that he was falling for me; he didn't say anything last night. And yet I had convinced myself that he was falling for me, and that he must truly care about me. I felt like such a fool. I knew the type of guy that Tom was from day one – Roz had told me. He was a man-whore who slept with as many girls as he could persuade to do so. Well, I wasn't going to be one of those girls. I was done with him and his stupid games.

Roz could tell I was in a bad mood when I was making dinner. She kept asking what was wrong. Eventually I told her about the guy in the library. I didn't say a word about Alison; I wasn't going to break that promise to her. Tom leaving in the morning without saying goodbye was what was really bothering me, but I was never going to tell her that. She was the one who had warned me about him.

'Gay,' she said simply, when I had finished telling her my story.

'Roz, how can you tell if he is gay? You never met him.'

'Did he reject you?'

'Yes, but—'

'Then he is gay.'

'Maybe I just wasn't his type?'

'Gay.'

'Maybe he is already in a relationship?'

'Gay.'

'Maybe he just didn't think I was good-looking?'

'Gay, gay, gay . . .'

'Roz, seriously, that cannot be the only reason.'

'Describe to me how he looked.'

'He was . . . stunning. His hair was really blond and perfectly done. He had really white teeth and his skin looked really soft and had a nice tan. He was also really well-dressed . . . Oh fuck!'

Roz burst out laughing at my sudden realization.

'Fuck, Roz. I asked a gay guy out on a date. I am an idiot.'

She was actually holding her sides now, she was laughing so hard.

'Olive, you need to seriously update your gaydar because it's not really working.'

I threw one of the small spoons across the kitchen at her. I missed, but I don't think she even saw me doing it; her eyes were welled up with tears because she couldn't stop laughing.

'Don't worry, hun. We have all done it. Sure, I made out with a gay guy once,' she said, trying to comfort me when she had finally stopped laughing.

'Are you kidding?'

'Nope. I even asked him back to my place afterwards. That made for an awkward conversation.'

I smiled at Roz; she really did always make me feel more positive.

'So what is the story with that guy from D2?' I asked. 'You still seeing him?'

'I actually am,' Roz beamed. 'It's weird. The two of us have so much fun just hanging out and talking . . .' She looked genuinely happy with herself.

'That is really great,' I said, truly delighted for her. Roz was the type of girl who made you worry that some guys would take advantage of her.

'It is so weird, a proper relationship. I feel like a grown-up.'

'Yeah,' I sighed. 'I guess we are all growing up now.'

16
Andy

'ANDREW, COME DOWNSTAIRS FOR TEA!' MY MOTHER HAD HER pretend-happy voice on. She always did that when she was worried about me. I didn't want to go downstairs; I didn't want to do anything. I wanted to stay in this room and shut out the rest of the world and everyone in it. But my mother was persistent and she called again. I knew that if I didn't answer this time, she would come up for me.

I sat down at the set table and smelled lasagne, my favourite dish. She was obviously trying to make me happy; it was another attempt at acknowledging my existence. Couldn't she just pretend I wasn't here, that I didn't matter? Why did no one realize that I didn't matter, that nothing mattered?

I heard Dad walk through the front door, and Mum instantly tensed; she tried to cover it up by calling him into the kitchen. It was all just an act, a performance for me.

'Dinner's nearly ready, dear.'

'Dinner?' he asked, walking into the kitchen. 'Surely it is too early.' And then he saw me. 'Andy, why are you not at running training?' He knew full well why I didn't want to go. He talked to me as if I was simple. I am *not* stupid; I hated everyone thinking I was.

'I didn't want to go,' I said under my breath.

'He just wasn't feeling up for it this evening,' my mum said, already looking nervous. Sometimes, I knew she was afraid of me – my own mother feared me!

'Well, that's a pity,' said my dad, pulling up a chair beside me. 'Are you sure? You might feel better once you get there. I could drive you over now if you want?'

'I said I didn't want to go!' I was screaming at the top of my voice. I didn't know why I was doing it but I couldn't stop. 'It is all bullshit, all fucking bullshit.' I was standing now and so was my dad.

'Andrew, do not use that language in this house. Now sit down.' I did want to sit down, I really did. I wanted to say, 'I would love to go to running and thank you, Dad, for driving me' – but I was so angry.

'Fuck you, Dad, fuck you!' I turned the kitchen table over and started throwing anything around me that I could find. I couldn't stop; it was as if there was another, evil, person inside me. Destroying me, destroying everything and everyone around me.

'Fuck you. Fuck you. FUCK YOU.' *Fight, Andy, fight.* My mum was crying now, begging me to calm down. I suddenly felt my dad's arms around my chest. His grip was tight but I did everything I could to get free. *Fight harder, fight harder.*

'Let go of me. Let me fucking go!' My dad's grip became even tighter, and I kicked and screamed against him.

'Calm down, Andy. I will let you go when you calm down,' my dad said, trying to stay calm himself but I could hear the strain in his voice. I elbowed him in the ribs and he yelped in pain, but still his grip stayed like iron.

Eventually the anger slipped away. It is never completely

gone but I was slowly overcome with a feeling of sadness. The voices that had told me to fight now told me that I was worthless. As I eventually became limp, my dad let go of me. I slumped to the ground; I didn't even have the energy to hold myself up. My dad was leaning against the overturned table, one hand against his ribs. He was breathing heavily, as if he had just run a marathon. My mum pulled herself together quickly and began to look over him for injuries. She lifted my dad's shirt to reveal a large bruise on his ribs; he cringed with pain as she touched him.

'Oh dear, I think you have broken a rib.' She didn't blame me; she never does, even though she should. It was my fault, it was always my fault. She started looking over me when she was done with Dad.

'You shouldn't get so upset,' she whispered. I didn't know whether she was talking to me or not. Either way I was too exhausted to reply.

She ran her hands gently down my arms; there were small bruises where Dad had been holding me.

'Andy?' she asked me, but I couldn't even look at her. I just stared at the ground. 'Andy?' she asked again. I tried to lift my head but I couldn't. *What is the point?*

'Are you able to help me lift him? I don't want him sitting on the ground. There is broken glass everywhere,' she said to my dad, who was starting to go very pale. He nodded and knelt down next to me, putting my arm around his shoulder. My mum did the same. My dad groaned loudly as they lifted me, and my mum looked at him, worried.

They carried me to the next room and laid me on the couch. I let my head drop again; I didn't want to look at either of them. My mum knelt in front of me, placing her hands on my knees.

'Andy, can you look at me?' I couldn't move, I didn't move.

'Please, Andy. Just look at me.' She sounded desperate. I continued to stare at the floor. *There is no fucking point.*

'Come on,' my dad said, pulling my mum up from the floor. The two walked into the next room but left the door open. I could not be trusted.

I could hear my mum tending to my dad. She started to rub creams and wrap bandages.

'Oh dear, this looks really sore.' She sounded like she was on the brink of tears again.

'That boy is getting strong.' My dad's voice sounded frail and weak.

'What are we going to do?' Mum asked.

'I don't know. But the two of you can't stay on your own in the house any more. If something like that happens again, and I am not here, he would overpower you and then . . .' He didn't finish his sentence.

'You can't be here all the time. You have work.'

'Maybe we could hire someone, a male nurse or something? We can call up the clinic and ask what they think.'

'I don't think that is a good idea. They will just want us to move him in there and we can't do that to him. We cannot give up on him.'

'We won't, but something has to change. The system we have for him at the moment, it's not going to keep working. He is going to get older and stronger. Even today was close enough.'

'What else can we do? He takes all the medications; we monitor him all the time. We encourage him to do activities, socialize with other people his age and it still happens.'

'I know, but we have to keep trying. We don't have a choice.'

I silently sat there, unable to move even though I wanted to. I wanted to run, run away from them, from everything, from the voices, from life. I wanted to cry and scream. I wanted to go in and apologize. I wanted to be normal. *I want, I want, I want* – but I can't. I can't do anything. I am trapped; I am trapped in my own body, my own mind.

I knew what was wrong with me, I was not stupid. My family didn't talk about my disease in front of me, neither did the doctors. I remembered once looking up schizophrenia on my computer; it was when I was younger, when I didn't fully understand. Before everyone started monitoring everything I did. I knew this was what I had – I heard the doctors talking once when they thought I was asleep. I had all the symptoms, the mild *and* severe ones. All the pills and the medications that the website mentioned – I was on all of them. At the bottom of the page it said that there was no known cure for schizophrenia and that patients might improve with medication. That was when I figured out that everyone was lying to me. My mum promised me that she would help me, that the doctors were going to help and I was going to get better. It was all a lie; I was never going to get better. Everyone lies.

But I wasn't stupid. I was sick and crazy, but I wasn't stupid. I knew more than the website, more than all the doctors who took tests and gave me endless quantities of pills, more than my family. On the website it said: *Schizophrenia is a complex illness. Mental health experts are not sure what causes it.* But I knew, I knew why I was the way I was. I was being punished. The world didn't want me and I was being punished for living, for existing.

Slowly I began to regain control over my body. I was able to lift my head and my arms. I clenched and released my fingers. At first it was hard, it felt like the muscle had become bone, but then gradually it got easier. I shook a little when I stood up first, but my balance caught up with me quickly. I walked into the kitchen. The table was back on its feet, the places had been re-set with new plates and glasses. My mum was standing at the counter, serving the lasagne. She smiled when she saw me. It was a sad smile.

'Are you hungry, Andy?'

I nodded silently; Dad was sitting at the table. He looked very pale, but he managed a smile when I looked at him.

'Feeling better, Andy?'

Again I nodded, trying my best to smile back. I sat at the table and Mum placed my dinner in front of me. If it wasn't for the fact that my dad winced every time he moved, there was no evidence of the incident that had occurred less than an hour ago.

The conversation was forced. My mum tried to talk about everything that was positive in our lives. It was like she worried that if she mentioned anything negative, I would fly off the handle again. Maybe she was right. She talked about the weather, football, friends, family and Olive. I missed Olive so much. We talked every day, and she would always answer when I called, but it wasn't the same. Everything had been easier, calmer, when she had been around. She understood me; no one else seemed to understand me like she did. She treated me like her brother, not a patient, not a nut job. *She left because of me.* Mum said she had to go because of college but I knew it was a lie; she wanted to get away from me. When she came home on the weekends she would spend every minute with me. *But she always leaves again.* She loved me. *She hates you, everyone does.* She had to go. *Because of you.* She would come back, she told me she would come back. *She is lying.*

'Can I go play my X-box?' I asked when I'd finished eating. My plate was basically still full, but I wasn't hungry. My mum looked over to my dad.

'OK,' he said, his voice still sounding strained. 'But leave your door open, OK?'

I got up from the table and started heading towards my room.

The rule in our house was that all doors to every room had to be left open except bathrooms, and there was no lock in any door except for the doors that led outside. Those doors had to be locked at all times and I was not allowed a key.

My X-box was in my room and the majority of the games I owned were football games. I wasn't allowed any games that had any violence in them. John, who had been Olive's friend, had once brought over *Grand Theft Auto* for us to play together. My mum had freaked out when she realized what we were playing and had yelled at John for at least an hour. I never understood why she yelled at everyone else but me. I was the one who was the freak – surely *I* should be yelled at.

She doesn't care enough to yell. My family loved me. *No they don't.* It was too easy to believe that voice. Maybe that voice was the only thing that told the truth. I silently closed the door. I waited in my room, standing perfectly still, listening for footsteps. None came; no one had heard my door close. There was a loose floorboard under my bed that wasn't covered by carpet. I lifted it up without making a sound. I hid things down there that I knew I wasn't supposed to have. There were dirty magazines that I had found in the neighbour's bin, chocolate biscuits – my mum kept me on a very strict diet – and a knife that I had stolen from a restaurant once. Mum counted the knives in the kitchen every day. She would instantly notice if I ever took one of those. I kept the knife because it meant that I could have control over at least one thing in my life.

I took the chocolate biscuits and the knife out and placed them carefully on my bed. I picked up one biscuit and ate it slowly, savouring the taste, the sweet chocolate and addictive sugar. I just stared at the knife, I did not touch it. *What is the point?* I didn't fully understand the question; there were a lot of things that I didn't understand. Why was I different from everyone else? Why was I being punished? Why couldn't I be happy?

Why did no one love me? Why did my mother fear me? Why did Olive leave me? Why couldn't it all just stop? I wanted it all to stop. I wanted it to end.

Was I supposed to do this? This time, the voice had no answers; it stayed silent.

17

Tom

SPENDING THE NIGHT AT OLIVE'S WAS A HUGE MISTAKE. I KNEW that now. What type of pathetic guy does that? A guy who just falls apart in front of a girl he barely knows. I went straight to college after I left Olive's, texting my mum to say I had stayed with a friend. She hated it when I was vague, but I was in no mood to go into details.

Because I had left Olive's so early, Trinity was practically empty when I got there. It was odd walking through empty halls that were usually packed with people. It really made you feel lonely. The strange thing was that I hadn't felt embarrassed at Olive's until I woke up in the morning. The night before, I had been comfortable and calm. It had been like a weird dream. The new day seemed to have shaken me back into reality.

The restaurant on campus made an amazing full Irish breakfast. I hadn't eaten since midday the day before, and as I smelled the rashers and eggs I realized how hungry I was. As I devoured my food I started to feel a little more like myself. The day of classes was long, and I busied myself with excessive note-taking and question-asking. Most of my tutors were shocked. I was normally the guy who sat quietly in the corner, who didn't take notes and didn't have any input. But today I didn't want to be left alone with my thoughts, so I filled my head with facts and information.

As the college day ended I still found myself anxious. I needed to be going somewhere, doing something. I took out my phone and called Peter.

'Hi, Tom, what's up?'

'What are you doing tonight?' I asked, getting straight to the point.

'You sound in the mood to get plastered?'

'That I am, that I am. And I have to admit I am in the mood to get laid. It has been way too fucking long.'

'Thought you were working on that UCD girl. You and Damien have a bet, right?'

I didn't know that Damien had told Peter about our wager; I guessed it didn't really matter, but it annoyed me a little, I don't know why.

'Ah, I am working on it. But it doesn't mean I can't have a little fun on the side.'

'That is the Tom I know and love. Right, we're going out tonight. Bring your alcohol and get your ass over here. I will call Damien.'

'I am on my way,' I said, smiling. This was exactly what I needed.

Needless to say, it took very little to convince Damien to join us. Mention the word 'alcohol' and he was there. Peter had a full bottle of Jägermeister in his apartment that we all happily finished. The only way to describe Jägermeister is that it is like rocket fuel, it gets you drunk like no other drink. Before I knew it, the three of us were in some dodgy Spanish bar in a part of Dublin that I had never been to before.

Even in my drunken haze I could smell the horrible stench of cigarette smoke and tequila. I guess the smoking ban hadn't reached this place yet. The seats were sticky from spilled alcohol and it looked as if we were the only Irish people in the bar. But none of us cared. It was the only place we had tried that hadn't told us we were all too drunk to come in. Peter had managed to create a small fan group for himself; it mostly consisted of large middle-aged Spanish women, but in his current state he didn't seem to mind. In fact, he looked quite chuffed with himself. After a few more tequila shots, a pleasant numbness had washed over me. I was sitting at the bar with Damien, who was worse off than I was, and he was trying to explain to me his brilliant plan to be a millionaire.

'You see, it's just so simple,' he slurred. 'What does every person need?' Damien had been mumbling on for hours and I couldn't care less what his brilliant plan was.

'Dude,' he said, hitting me. 'What does every person need?'

'I don't know,' I mumbled back. I was starting to lose any sense of what was going on. I went to drink my beer, but it was gone.

'So go on, Damien. Tell me what every person needs.' But there was only silence. I turned to him, only to see he was slumped unconscious on the bar. He was starting to make a habit of this. I didn't really mind, he looked comfy enough.

I looked across the bar and saw a small group of Spanish women smiling at me. There was one in the middle who looked slightly younger than the rest. I made my way over, trying my best not to stumble. When I finally reached her, her friends had left and she was standing alone.

'Hi, I am Tom,' I said. She was a very curvy girl. I was finding it very difficult not to stare at her breasts, and she seemed to have a lot of black eye-liner on. Even so, I still found her very attractive. She giggled at me and told me her name was Angelina.

'Angelina, you are the most beautiful girl in this room tonight,' I told her.

She smiled at me and said, 'Do you want to go somewhere a bit more private, to talk?'

'Definitely,' I whispered in her ear. I loved the simplicity of it all. This girl didn't want love, she wanted sex, and I was ready to give it to her.

Angelina pulled me into a small storage room that had a *Staff Only* sign on the door. It stank of stale beer but she didn't seem to mind. As soon as she closed the door she grabbed my face and stuck her tongue in my mouth. It took me by complete surprise. I instinctively kissed her back. I pushed her back up against the wall as my hands explored her body. We continued to kiss roughly, and I wondered if I had a condom in my wallet or not. I was so aroused, there was very little that could stop me. She turned us around so I was now the one up against the wall, and ran her hand down to feel my erection; she then proceeded to kiss my chest while slowly undoing my trouser buttons. At that moment I was so dizzy with arousal and alcohol that I would not have been able to tell someone my own name. When she had pulled down my trousers, she began to kiss my stomach and I knew then what was coming. She took my dick in her mouth, and I was so high, I could feel nothing but pleasure and dizziness. I was no longer angry; I no longer cared about my shit life. All I cared about was how high I was – and I was only getting higher.

Suddenly I heard the door open and a man yelling angrily in Spanish. I pushed Angelina away from me and pulled up my trousers as quickly as possible.

'What is he saying?' I asked in a panic.

'He is telling us to get out. I think we should.' Angelina grabbed my hand and pulled me past the angry Spanish man, through the bar and out the door. All the while I was holding my trousers up because I hadn't managed to do up any of the buttons. I didn't see Peter as I ran by, but I am sure he laughed when he saw me.

We both stood outside in the cold awkwardly. The mood had been broken.

'I don't think he's going to let us back into his bar anytime soon,' I said, trying to see the funny side. I finally managed to get my trousers done up. I still felt very drunk.

'Oh, he will let me back in. He is my uncle.'

'Your uncle?'

'Don't worry, he doesn't mind. He just doesn't want it happening in his bar, you understand?'

'OK,' I said, completely perplexed. Suddenly she walked over to me and pushed her body up against mine.

'Do you want to come to my place and finish what we started?' she asked in a husky voice. I could already feel myself getting turned on again.

It took us the best part of twenty minutes to reach her house. It wasn't far but we constantly stopped to kiss and grope each other. When we had finally got there we both stumbled onto the bed. She had my top and jeans off within seconds, but I was struggling to undo the back of her dress. Frustrated, she eventually took off the dress herself; underneath she was wearing a red lacy bra that barely contained her breasts and a matching thong. It took all my willpower to pull away at this point, but I had been dying to urinate ever since we had left the bar and it was starting to make me feel really sick.

'Back in one second. I just need to go to the bathroom.'

She looked a little annoyed but she replied in a very sexy voice, 'Don't be long. I want you now.'

Her bathroom was tiny; it had a small shower, a toilet and a sink. Her sink was filled with make-up and hair extensions, and the bottom of her shower was stained with fake tan. As I pulled down my boxers I realized that I had a very hard erection and I couldn't work out how I was going to aim at the toilet. I tried to make myself bend right over, but the bathroom was so small that I did not have enough room. Shit, I thought, it will take ages for my erection to go down and she'll wonder why I am in here for so long. I looked around myself in desperation. *Typical – my chance at getting laid and I am going to ruin it.* I suddenly stopped and looked at the shower; I could pee in there and then wash it down. I decided this was the best idea and instantly jumped in. It was such a relief and I began to relax.

I pulled my boxers back up and was about to turn on the shower when I thought that she would probably hear the water running and I had already been in here a while. *Fuck it! The shower is filthy anyway!* I washed my hands and went out to Angelina to find that she was waiting for me completely naked.

'Thought I'd save you the trouble,' she giggled. At that moment I loved her. I jumped onto the bed and within seconds she had my boxers off as well. Afterwards I felt very sober but satisfied. I looked at the clock – it was only 2 a.m. Angelina was lying across my chest and her hand was stroking my limp penis. As I began to wonder if I would be able to go again, she asked, 'You want to get in the shower?'

I quickly came up with an excuse about having to get home and left. She didn't seem too happy with my sudden departure but I decided it was a good idea to get out of there before she went into her bathroom. In my sober state I actually recognized where I was and realized I was within walking distance of home. It was good because I didn't think I would have had enough money for a taxi. This area of town seemed to be very quiet at night, and for the first time all day I allowed myself to think. And there was only one thing on my mind. Actually there was only one person I could think about. Olive's face when she had opened her door last night was etched into my brain. Why couldn't I get her out of my mind? She was a cool girl; I had learned that over the past few weeks. She was really funny when she wanted to be. She was annoyingly tense most of the time but when she did relax she just seemed to brighten up the room. *Oh shit, I actually like her.* It was odd, I had just left a girl I'd had sex with, and yet all I could think about was the girl I had never even kissed. How fucked up was that?

By the time I got home I had it sorted in my head. I was going to try, properly try, with Olive. Not because of the bet, and not to prove anything to anyone – but because I genuinely wanted her. It was going to be hard. She expected a lot more than I had ever given to anyone before, but I had to at least try. If I was honest with myself, I don't think I had ever wanted anything more.

18
Olive

IT FELT STRANGE BEING BACK IN MY OLD ROOM. IT WASN'T THAT long ago since I had left it, but it no longer felt like my room. It looked ransacked, half of my stuff was missing. I had taken everything that I had wanted with me to college and anything that I had left behind I saw as unimportant, irrelevant. I had left Andy behind; I would regret that decision for the rest of my life. *I should have stayed. I should have stayed for him.*

I hated black clothes. Girls wore black because it was supposed to be slimming or something. None of them knew the true reason why people wore black clothes. The true reason was horrible. I made a mental note that after today I was never going to wear black again, and that I would burn the clothes I was wearing now. I wanted no evidence of this day.

There was a picture on my dressing-table. Andy and I were in a cornfield. He was sitting down and I was hugging him from behind. We were both smiling broadly and I laughed as I noticed that Andy was missing his two front teeth. Andy couldn't be any older than ten in that photo. It would have been before any of the doctors or pills, but even then he knew that he was different from any other child. That he would spend his whole life struggling to be normal and to fit in.

My uncle had a farm close by to where we lived. When we were younger, our parents would take us there nearly every day during the summer. We would go horseback riding, help tend to the lambs, and play on the hay-bales in the fields. I had really loved those summers; the farm had been an endless source of entertainment for Andy and me. It was before I had become interested in boys and make-up and started demanding to go to the summer camps that had been set up by the local schools. I remember the days when I would sit around with my friends, all of us trying to figure out what dirty words like 'blowjob' or 'lick-out' meant, or being dared to kiss one of the boys in the camp on the lips. Andy had been, of course, too young to attend those summer camps with me for those first few years, and by the time he was old enough, I was too old. It was the first time that our age difference had come between us.

But this photo was before all that. Before the boy-kissing and the sex talks. Before the make-up and the discos. This photo was when it was just Andy and me, and nothing could have separated us. I don't think I have ever had such good summers as I did on that farm playing in the fields with Andy.

I remember a conversation the two of us had once in those cornfields. It was probably the same year that that photo had been taken. I was young, but I still remember every word that we said to each other. We were both basking in the sun, lying on our backs with our eyes closed. We had been riding my uncle's Shetland earlier. Taking turns to kick as hard as we could, attempting to pick up some sort of speed. My thighs were tingling with tiredness and I was starting to doze off when I heard Andy speak.

'Could you lie down in a cloud? You know, lie down in it like it was a bed?'

'No,' I answered, sure of myself. 'It would fall apart.'

'Why?'

'Because it just would.'

'But why?'

'Nobody knows, but it would. I am sure.' I knew that someone must know, but I didn't, and Andy would always look to me for answers: I liked it when I was able to give them.

A few more moments of silence passed before he spoke again.

'Olive, am I crazy?'

I sat up and looked at him. 'Of course not. Why are you asking me that?'

He was starting to go red with embarrassment. 'One of the boys in school said that I was.'

'Who?'

'Timmy.'

'Timmy? I thought you guys were friends.'

'We were best friends but he won't talk to me now because he said I am crazy.'

'Why? What happened?'

He hesitated before he spoke again. 'I asked him if he ever heard voices in his head. You know, telling him to do things.'

'Why would you ask him that?'

Andy wasn't looking at me any more. 'Because I hear voices,' he said.

I looked at him, unsure how to reply, but Andy couldn't stop talking once he had started.

'They tell me to do things that I don't want to do, and I can't stop them. They make me shout and scream and break things, and I don't want to do any of it. I really don't.' He saw the worried look on my face and started to cry uncontrollably. 'I am crazy, I am. Timmy said men in white coats were going to come and take me away. Please don't let them take me away, Olive. Please. I don't want to go anywhere.'

I rushed over to him and wrapped my arms around him, desperately trying to comfort him. 'Andy, don't cry. Please don't cry,' but his sobs only got harder and harder.

'Andy, can I tell you a secret?' I said, suddenly realizing what I needed to do. He nodded in between whimpers. 'I hear voices too,' I lied.

'You do?' he asked, looking up at me hopefully.

'Yeah, all the time.'

'And do they tell you to do stuff you don't want to do?'

I nodded; he was slowly starting to calm down.

'What do you do?' he asked, sounding desperate.

I thought carefully about what I said before I spoke. 'I tell the voice firmly no, I will *not* do what it wants me to do and then it goes away.'

'And that works?'

'It works, Andy. I swear to you it works. Try it next time for me, OK?'

He nodded and then hugged me. 'Can we not tell anyone about this?' he asked almost in a whisper.

'Of course,' I whispered back into his ear. 'It will be our little secret.'

Staring at that picture, I began to wonder at what age Andy realized I had lied to him. I had created this bond between us, this special link that no one else had, but it hadn't been real. Still, it had made us grow closer. It had been just like the voices in his head – they hadn't been real either, but they had killed him. It was odd that something that didn't even exist could affect a life so drastically. I wondered what would have happened if I had told my parents what Andy had said to me in that cornfield. I had never told them. Even after it was discovered that he was sick, I didn't tell anyone. I had promised him that I never would and maybe it was better that I never did.

Maybe it saved him from even more years of doctors poking and prodding him as if he was an animal. Giving him endless different pills that only seemed to make everything worse. Or maybe I had doomed him; maybe if I had said something then it would have been early enough for them to have fixed him. He could have been happy. I guessed I would never know. It was all over now. But I would keep my promise, no matter what. We had had a bond – maybe it was based on a lie, but it had been real to me and it still mattered. Andy still mattered.

I turned around as I heard my door open. My mum walked into the room. She was wearing a horrible black dress as well. Her eyes were red but her face was dry. She had no tears left to cry.

'The car is waiting,' she said simply. 'Everyone else has gone to the church.' Normally someone who had killed himself wouldn't be allowed to be buried in a church, but because Andy was mentally ill they made an exception. Our local priest knew Andy. He had been kind to him. Andy had never liked him, had always said that he treated him like he was dying. Maybe the priest was right, maybe he was dying this whole time.

I followed my mother downstairs; the house was silent and empty. The past few days had been strange. The house was full of family members and friends, all running about, cooking and organizing and cleaning. My family hadn't had to lift a finger. I knew that they had done this to help, but I honestly think it just made everything harder. My dad had done nothing but stare at the TV, frowning. I think he was only pretending to watch it, wanting to be left alone. My mum ran around the house muttering under her breath, picking up clothes and then putting them back, adjusting pictureframes and then readjusting them. I had done nothing but sit in my room. I hadn't cried, I wished I could. I felt numb all the time; nothing felt real. It was like I had walked into someone else's life and I couldn't get back to my own.

The car journey was silent. My dad sat across from me with that same concentrated frown that he had had all day. My mum sat next to me staring out of the window, holding a handkerchief up to her mouth. I squeezed her other hand, which was on the seat next to me. She didn't look at me but squeezed my hand back. It was a dull day, dry, but the sun was hidden behind clouds. When we arrived at the church the three of us got out of the car and stood together. Three stood where there should have been four.

The next few days passed like some horrible nightmare. Our house was more silent than it had ever been before. Our fridge was full of food that our neighbours had given us but none of us was eating. Nothing made sense any more. I didn't know what I was supposed to be doing. I didn't know how to grieve. I couldn't function without him. I didn't know how to live, how to be me without Andy.

It was the middle of the night. I couldn't sleep. In the past week I had slept less than six hours, and lack of sleep was making me ill. I had constant migraines. I felt dizzy and queasy all the time. I would throw up anything I tried to eat. I felt like my mum was disappearing in front of my eyes, physically and mentally. She had lost so much weight in just a few days and she seemed never to speak any more. It was as if she was in a permanent daze, and she didn't know where she was or who I was.

My migraines had become unbearable. I was looking for Panadol but then I remembered that we didn't keep any sort of painkillers in this house. I lay in my bed, desperately trying to fall asleep, my mind focused on the agonizing pain in my forehead. I tried to think of other things – my friends, college, my family – anything to distract my mind from the pain. I tried to think of Andy. Tried to remember a better time, when we were kids. Before the illness, when everything had been so easy. I thought of the summers that we had spent on my uncle's farm.

The many sunny days that we had passed, just playing with our dog, Mowgli. I recalled one time when we had gone down to the river that was about a mile away from our house. The three of us had gone swimming. That had been a great day: that was the day I wanted to remember.

It was working. The pain in my head was slowly subsiding and I could feel myself drifting off into sleep. I could see Mowgli running at full speed and diving into the water. Andy was quick to follow, pulling off his checkered shirt and jumping into the river. My eyes were heavy now.

Suddenly, the figure that was Andy turned to me and shouted, 'Olive, come in!' but I didn't reply. I just stared in shock. The figure that was supposed to be Andy had no face; it was just a blurred mess. I sat bolt upright in my bed and began to tremble. I closed my eyes and tried to draw a picture of Andy's face in my mind, but I couldn't do it. I couldn't remember.

'No,' I said to myself. 'I can't forget, I can't!' I closed my eyes and tried again. All I could see were distorted features that looked wrong. It wasn't him.

'I can't forget him!' I was shouting at myself in a panic. My head was pounding even worse now. Nothing made sense any more. Why couldn't I remember? I stumbled out of bed and put my hand on the wall for support. The room was spinning and I thought I might be sick.

'I have to remember. I have to remember.' I tried to think, to calm down, but my mind didn't seem to be working any more. I was panicking and I couldn't stop until I remembered his face.

I walked out of my room, still with my hand on the wall for constant support. I don't know what was worse, the stabbing pain in my head or the overwhelming urge to throw up. I opened his door slowly. I didn't want to go in. No one had been in here since that day. But the thought of forgetting him was too scary; my memories were all that I had left – I couldn't lose them. His room was messy; Andy had never been very tidy. Clothes and books were all over the place. His bed was rumpled and some of his football posters were starting to peel off the wall. There had to be something in here to remind me. I didn't want to lose him.

As I walked in further I felt the soft carpet suddenly go hard and crunchy under my bare feet. I looked down to see large dark stains on the ground. It was dim in here; the only light came from the moon outside the window. I assumed at first that they were foodstains. Andy was constantly spilling things. But as I looked closer and saw what was undoubtedly dried blood, I jumped back in fear. My knees crumpled underneath me and I started hyperventilating. I felt like I was drowning, and all I could see was that blood.

I eventually forced myself to stand up. My shakes were even worse now. I no longer cared about the pain in my head and the queasiness in my stomach. I ran to the bathroom and found bleach and a sponge, then returned to Andy's room and started to scrub the carpet furiously. I had only just begun to scrub when I felt a hand on my shoulder; it was my father. The bags under his eyes were emphasized by the moonlight.

'Olive! What are you doing?'

I turned around and continued to scrub the carpet. 'This shouldn't be here,' I muttered. 'I'm getting rid of it.'

'Olive, maybe you should go back to—'

'It can't be here, Dad. It just can't!' I had shouted over him but I didn't stop to see his reaction. I don't think I had ever shouted at my dad before. Eventually I heard him creep out the door but he returned after a few minutes.

He knelt down next to me and I noticed that he also had a bucket of water and a sponge in his hand. Silently he picked up the bottle of bleach, poured a large amount onto his sponge and started to scrub even harder than me. I don't know how long the two of us stayed there, but it was nearly morning before we stopped. The blue carpet had nearly turned white with all the bleach, but there was no longer any evidence of the blood.

Neither of us spoke, but both stared around the room that we had all been terrified to enter. The room where everything had been destroyed. My dad suddenly stood up and walked over to Andy's desk. It was the only thing in the room that was kept neat. DVDs and video games were stacked tidily on top of each other, next to an old computer that he used to play games on. My dad picked up an envelope that had been sitting beside the computer; I hadn't noticed it last night. Written on the front was *To My Family* in what was undoubtedly Andy's messy handwriting. I jumped up from my knees and crossed the room.

'What is that?' I asked. My father was standing silently looking at the envelope. 'What is it?' I was angry but I wasn't really sure why.

'I don't know,' he said. Slowly he pulled out the letter inside. Andy's handwriting was even messier than normal; sentences had been scribbled out and rewritten numerous times. A lump formed in my throat as I began to read and realize what this letter was.

> I am sorry. I am so sorry for so many things. I am sorry for being born and I am sorry for ruining all of your lives. I need you all to know that this is not like the last times. I know I have needed to do this for a long time. I am not doing this because the voices are telling me; I am doing this because I love all of you. I love you and I want all of you to be happy and this is the only way.
>
> I am sorry and I love you. Andy

I thought it would hurt more but it didn't. I think what shocked me most was the fact that it hadn't been a rash decision. He had planned it, thought about it and come to a logical decision. For so long we had all thought he was getting better. All the times that I thought he had been happy, it all felt like a lie now.

My dad stood there staring at the short letter with a frown on his face. I didn't know what to do, how to comfort him. I suddenly felt overwhelmed with tiredness and I just wanted to sleep. I didn't know what to say so I didn't say anything.

I was about to walk away when my dad stopped me.

'Wait,' he said quietly, still gazing at the letter. I wasn't sure if he was talking to me or himself but I stopped anyway.

'Olive. There is something I need you to understand.' He was looking directly at me now. 'You must understand that your brother was a kind and talented boy, but he was ill. Very ill. And the three of us – we did everything we could to help him. To make him happy. To prevent this.' He gestured towards the letter. 'But this world was not meant for him, and I know he is happier now.' My dad sounded like he was trying to convince himself as well as me.

'Do you really believe that?' I asked.

He looked at me with complete certainty in his eyes as he said, 'I have to.'

I never knew if my dad had told my mum about the letter. It was never spoken about, and neither was the stain on Andy's carpet. I still don't have the courage to go back into that room. I sometimes stand at the door, sighing and wondering, wondering what I could have done differently. I hope that one day I will have my father's certainty, his conviction that Andy is happier now. But I still have doubts, and until those doubts are gone, I can't go back into that room. I don't accept what he has done, not yet.

19
Tom

THIS TIME I HAVE GOT IT RIGHT. I HAVE SPENT DAYS PLANNING what I am going to say, what I am going to do. I want it to be right. I am not half-arsing it any more. I am going to get it perfect; I am going to get her. I have the whole scene planned out in my head. I shall walk up to her door with flowers and chocolates – she will look shocked at first, she may even be angry with me, but that's OK. I am ready for it. I will be persistent, stubborn; I won't leave until she hears what I have to say. *Olive, I am falling for you. Give me a chance, no more games, just you and me.* At which point she will see my sincerity and fall into my arms, and admit that she has also felt something these past few weeks.

Sadly, my plan had already gone a little awry. I couldn't afford expensive chocolates and flowers, so I had to settle for Tesco Value chocolates and flowers that I had picked from people's gardens on the walk here. I was sure, however, that she would appreciate the effort.

I was more anxious than nervous; there was no doubt in my mind that Olive felt the same way as I did. I couldn't have created this thing on my own; it must have been coming from her as well. *What if I have created it myself, what if she just stares at me in pity?* I shook the thought away and made myself keep walking. I wasn't going to back out of this now, especially after putting it off all weekend. I had come straight from Trinity and the sun was already starting to set. The winter days were getting shorter and shorter. The UCD campus was still buzzing, people flying by in opposite directions. This place never seemed empty.

Taking a deep breath, I knocked on Olive's door. I tried to shove my hands in my pockets so she wouldn't see them shaking, then realized that I had crushed the flowers while doing this and decided to throw them out the window, hoping that no one was walking by at the time. I hope she likes chocolates, I thought, suddenly panicking. What girl doesn't like chocolates? I was trying to reassure myself. Maybe she is lactose intolerant and she will be offended that you know so little about her. *Shut up, brain, shut up, shut up!*

Beth opened the door – she looked flustered. Her cheeks were red and her hair was in a mess.

'Tom?' She looked surprised to see me.

'Hi, Beth, is Olive here?'

'No, she's at home with her family,' Beth replied quietly. She seemed subdued.

'Oh, OK. Will she be back later then?' I knew that Olive went home most weekends, but I was surprised that she had missed a day of college. She seemed to take her studies very seriously.

'Oh God, Tom. I guess you haven't heard.' Beth looked grim.

'Heard what?' I asked, worried. 'Has something happened to her?'

Beth's eyes looked like they were filling with tears but she didn't let them fall.

'Her brother died a few days ago.'

I stood there silent for a few moments, stunned.

'Was he sick?' I asked finally, more for something to say than anything else.

'No, I don't think so. I am not really sure, to be honest.'

'How did it happen?'

'Olive didn't say, but there was a small bit about him in the *Irish Times* today. They just said he had "died tragically".'

Beth and I stared gravely at each other and I felt a small shiver go up my spine. We both knew what 'died tragically' really meant.

'How is she?'

'I haven't spoken to her since she left last week, but she wasn't good. It was odd when she found out. She was incredibly sad, but . . . it was like she wasn't surprised. As if she had somehow expected it.'

'When is she coming back to Dublin, do you know?'

'She emailed me asking me to tell her tutors that she will be back on Monday.'

'So soon?'

'I know. But that is what she said.'

Beth and I stood in that doorway for a long time. I don't think either of us knew what we were supposed to do. Finally Beth broke the silence.

'Do you want to come in for a cup of tea? I'm not sure if we have milk, though. Olive usually does the shopping.'

'No, no, I am OK.' The whole conversation had felt surreal. Suddenly everything else seemed so unimportant.

I returned on the Monday when Beth had said that Olive would be back. I had skipped my last two lectures and made it to their dorm just after lunchtime. Roz opened the door. It was the first time that I had ever seen her without a smile; she was frowning and looked stressed.

'Tom, what are you doing here?' she asked.

'I came to see Olive.'

'I don't think that is a good idea. She is not handling . . . everything that well.'

'So she *is* here?'

'Yeah, she came home last night.' Roz looked like she wanted to say something more, but she was holding back.

'What's going on?' I asked, a little afraid of the answer.

'Oh, Tom, she really is in a bad way. She hasn't left her room since she got back; she's just laid in her bed all day. She isn't sleeping because I keep checking on her, and she refuses to eat anything. I can't even get her to drink a cup of tea. I thought about calling her parents but I am sure they have plenty on their plate already at the moment. I just have no idea what to do.' She had tears of frustration rolling down her face.

'I just wish she would get out of that bed and eat something,' she sobbed, more to herself than me. I put my hand on her arm; it felt a bit odd but I wanted to do something to comfort her. Suddenly a thought came to me.

'Roz, I have an idea but I need to get some stuff first. Make sure she doesn't leave – OK? I will be back as soon as possible.'

She agreed without any argument. She was obviously desperate.

An hour later I was back and I was knocking on Olive's bedroom door. There was no answer but I had expected that. I slowly opened the door and saw her lying in her bed, eyes wide open gazing at the ceiling. It scared me to see her like this; she looked like an empty shell, her face blank of all emotion, her normally sparkly green eyes dull.

'What are you doing here?' she asked in a frail whisper.

'I brought you a picnic,' I said, sitting on the edge of her bed.

'I'm not hungry.' She wasn't looking at me.

'Well, I know that's a lie. You are always hungry.' She said nothing. 'I brought loads – bread rolls, cheese, ham, butter, Nutella, grapes and even some crisps, and I have set it out all nicely in your common room. You don't even have to get out of your pyjamas.'

'I am not hungry.' She said it slower this time, as if she was talking to someone who was stupid.

'Olive, you can either come out of this room yourself or I will carry you against your will. Either way, it is happening.' I tried to keep my voice sounding as positive as possible, but it was hard when she looked so upset.

She stared at me silently as if to say, *Are you serious?* But I just sat there waiting for her to make up her mind. Eventually she rolled her eyes at me and started to get up. I held back a gasp when I saw her thin frame get out of the bed. She had always been a slim girl, but now she looked like she could snap at any moment. She must not have eaten anything in the past few days. She walked into the common room behind me and sat on the couch, just staring at all the food that I had set up on the floor.

'I am still not hungry.'

'That's OK,' I said, leaning down on the floor to take more things out of the shopping bags.

'I have drinks as well – apple juice, orange juice, Coke and . . . ta da!' I pulled out a small bottle of vodka and some paper cups.

'I will drink that,' she said suddenly, on seeing the vodka.

'Thought you might,' I replied, putting the bottle on my right, placing myself between it and her.

'So here is the deal, Olive. You eat something and I will let you have some vodka.'

'I am not hungry.'

'I don't care. That is my offer – take it or leave it.'

She looked at me so angrily that I thought she might actually hit me. To my surprise though, she picked up one of the bread rolls and started nibbling at the corner.

'Can I have some now?' She practically spat the words at me. I poured less than a shot into a plastic cup and mixed it with some orange juice before handing it to her. I had hoped that it might make her drink it slowly, but I was wrong. She downed it in one and then handed the cup back to me, asking for more.

'No, no, that's not how it works. You have to keep eating if you want to keep drinking.' I think she truly hated me at that moment but I didn't care as long as my plan just kept working. She picked up the piece of bread and bit off another corner.

Even though she was eating, the vodka seemed to hit her like a ton of bricks. Her stomach must have been completely empty. After a while I just started giving her pure orange juice that wasn't mixed with vodka; thankfully she didn't seem to notice this.

'This all tastes the same to me,' she slurred, now eating slices of cheese. 'Cheese, bread, chocolate, all the exact same. Nothing is the way it should be.' I had the feeling she wasn't talking about the food any more; her eyes had begun to well up. 'Everything has gone to shit.' I sat there and let her maunder drunkenly on. I was still shocked how little vodka it had taken, but at least she was eating without complaint now. I just hoped that she wouldn't throw it up later.

'What was his name?' I asked, just to say something; she looked at me in a way that made me think she had forgotten I was there. She wiped the tears away from her face before answering.

'Andy,' she whispered.

'What was he like?'

She thought for a moment before answering. 'He was lovely, really sweet, and he loved sports. When we were younger he always thought of these games that we would play together and they would always involve running or jumping or swimming. He never stopped really.' She sniffed loudly and her eyes looked as if they had stopped watering.

'He loved animals. I think he loved them more than he loved humans. We had this dog once, his name was Mowgli. He was really dark and hairy. Well, when he was a puppy my mum would always make him sleep outside. She said that he had to learn, but Andy used to slip him into the house when everyone was asleep, and when Mum finally caught him and told him the dog couldn't stay inside, he would then sneak out to him at night and sleep outside with him, even if it was raining. My mum would get so mad. Andy constantly had colds and fevers because of it, but he used to tell me that if he ever cried, Mowgli would come and sit with him. So he had to do the same for him. He was closer to that dog than anyone else.'

She had told the whole story as if she was in a trance. I was nearly afraid to breathe in case I broke it.

'Mowgli got hit by a car a few years ago and broke his leg. My parents had to put him down. Andy was devastated. That was when he first tried to . . .' She looked up at me suddenly as if realizing she had been speaking out loud all the time. She looked unnerved.

'I have a little sister,' I said out of the blue, scarcely knowing what I was saying.

'Oh,' she said, looking relieved at my sudden change of subject.

'Well, she is my half-sister actually. She is called Pamela.'

'Do you see her much?' Olive asked, visibly starting to relax.

'No, not much. She lives with my dad and his wife, Robin. Robin doesn't like me that much – I think I ruin her "picture-perfect family" – and Dad just stares at me nervously as if I might lose it any second. But Pam is cool. She looks up at me as if I am the best thing ever. She always has so much to tell me, that little girl could talk for Ireland. I am lucky if I get a word in.'

Olive laughed at my description of Pam.

'I feel guilty that I don't see her more,' I went on, clearing my throat. 'She is starting to get old enough to notice that a big brother should be around a lot more, but it's hard to explain to her. I just don't like going over there. It's . . . uncomfortable.'

Olive nodded with understanding. It wasn't like her to pry, and yet I found that I wanted to tell her everything. I didn't, of course; no one needs to know everything.

We both sat in silence, nibbling at random pieces of food. I smiled to myself as I noticed that Olive had eaten nearly all of it. The food was also starting to have a sobering effect and her eyes began to look a lot more focused. We had been sitting there in silence for so long that I was startled when I heard her speak.

'Thanks,' she said, looking at her feet. 'This was . . . just thanks.'

'No problem,' I replied, also too shy to look her in the face.

'I will pay you back for all the food and stuff.'

'Oh, don't worry about it. Honestly, it's fine.'

'Are you sure? All this food couldn't have been cheap.'

'It wasn't that bad.'

'Tom?' I looked up and suddenly she was staring straight at me. There was an intense look in her eye and she no longer seemed at all shy. She pulled herself closer to me, still gazing at my face. Her lips looked soft and were slightly parted. I moved closer but I was waiting for something, a signal. She suddenly glanced down to my lips, only for a second, but that was enough – that was my signal. I put my hand up to her cheek and brushed her loose hair behind her ear. She closed her eyes and sighed quietly at my touch. I leaned in to kiss her. I was only an inch away from her lips when there was a loud bang and the two of us jerked away from each other in shock.

'Oh my God, oh my God, I fell asleep. I am so sorry.' Roz came racing into the room. Her hair was in a mess and her make-up was completely smudged on one side of her face. Luckily she hadn't seemed to notice anything suspicious about Olive and me.

'It's OK, Roz,' I said, trying to break the tension. 'Unfortunately there is not much food left. Olive and I had a serious feast.'

Only after I had spoken did Roz seem to notice that Olive was also in the room.

'Olive, you are . . . Oh, that is absolutely fantastic,' she said, unable to hide her relief and delight. 'I will make some tea.'

She practically danced around the kitchen, as she boiled the kettle and took out the cups. I smiled at Olive and she smiled back, going slightly red. Roz brought over the tea and settled herself in between the two of us on the floor.

'So, what are you guys talking about?'

'Nothing,' Olive and I replied at the exact same time.

20
Olive

THEY SAY THAT AFTER THE DEATH OF A LOVED ONE, YOU GO through five stages of grief, the first being denial, the second anger, the third bargaining, the fourth depression and the fifth acceptance. I personally think this is all a load of bullshit. Those five stages in no way represent what it is like to lose someone close to you. Grief feels as if someone has cut a huge hole out of your stomach with a blunt knife. The first cut is agonizingly painful but the wound you are left with afterwards is even worse. It's a gaping hole that just feels raw, and you always feel it, no matter where you are, who you are with – it's there.

But as with a wound, distraction is the key. You can never fully forget it, but a good distraction can dull the pain. That was what Tom was; he was the best distraction that God could have put on earth. During the time that we spent together, which was nearly every day now, I began to feel more normal. I didn't think that I would ever feel completely normal again, I doubted that I would ever go back to the person that I was before, but when I was with Tom it was close enough.

It was three weeks since it had happened. I had gone home

every weekend as normal. It was odd. Even though Andy wasn't around any more, I still felt the obligation to go home and I thought I always would. My parents were slowly adjusting; I knew they put on a brave face when I was around. My mum busied herself with needless tasks. She would always have a new project; first it was knitting, then it was puzzles, and now she was repainting every room in the house. Of course, Andy's room was left untouched; I didn't think any of us had been in there in the last few weeks. I knew that I couldn't face it. Sometimes I would catch my mum whispering to herself, usually when she was working on one of her projects.

'Keeping busy, that is the trick, keeping busy.'

Dad seemed to be taking it harder. He had always been such a happy and talkative person but his personality had completely changed; now he was always absent-minded and rarely heard you when you spoke to him.

Going home was hard. When I was at college it felt like I could at least pretend to be someone else, someone who was allowed to be happy some of the time. Tom was over again, sitting on the couch, drinking tea and talking endlessly about some musician I had never even heard of. He got so flamboyant and loud when he was trying to prove a point, it was comical to watch. I couldn't help but laugh out loud at him. The near-kiss hadn't been brought up again, we were both acting like nothing had happened, but I thought about it all the time. When he was on one of his rants like this, I would catch myself staring at his lips, wondering what would happen if I just grabbed him.

'Pete Yorn is possibly one of the best acoustic guitar players in the world.'

'I've never heard of him,' I muttered, my mind in a distant place.

'The music industry is being destroyed by these plastic pop stars . . .' He had grown a little stubble since I had seen him last

– it was very sexy. I wondered what it would feel like against my cheek.

'There is no self-respecting human being with musical taste that would call Avril Lavigne a rock star.' He threw his hands up in an extravagant gesture. I bet he was amazing with his hands. 'And don't even get me fucking started on Justin Bieber.'

Fuck it, I'm going for it. 'Tom, shut up for a second, would you?'

He stopped mid-sentence, looking taken aback.

'OK.' His striking blue eyes blinked at me. How I had never found him attractive before was beyond me.

'Do you want to go out some time? Like on a proper date?' I asked hesitantly. As soon as the words came out of my mouth I regretted being so forward, but luckily Tom answered instantly.

'Yes, definitely. Where do you want to go?'

Trying to decide where I wanted to go was difficult. I didn't trust myself around Tom any more. Every day I found something else that was sexy about him. I was afraid that if I put myself in the wrong situation I might just jump him. It was odd, I had never even kissed him, and yet when I was with him, all I could think about was sex. I needed to be somewhere completely unsexy, somewhere that I could trust we would both keep our hands to ourselves.

'Bowling?' He looked down at me, his eyebrows raised. I hadn't told Tom what we were doing. I had just said to meet me outside the Dart station in Bray. It wasn't until we walked up to the entrance that he knew what was going on.

'Come on,' I pleaded. 'It will be a laugh.' He didn't look convinced but walked in without any further complaint. It was BYOB night – something that had to be illegal, I reasoned. Alcohol and heavy bowling balls? That couldn't be safe. Though the alcohol part did seem to convince Tom that it might actually be fun.

'I'll be right back,' he said, hurrying off in the direction of the nearest off-licence.

The place looked seriously rundown. There were stains on the walls, the carpet looked like it had been pulled up from the ground in certain places, and the only girls' toilet had an *Out of Order* sign on it. I began to think that this had been a very bad idea; Tom was going to think I was so weird. But even with all its faults the place was packed. There were all walks of life, the scumbags in their tracksuits and baseball caps, the slutty girls in their miniskirts and high heels, and the old couples who seemed to have no problem with PDA. I was horrified to realize that everyone seemed to be bowling in their own shoes. I was wearing high heels and I suddenly imagined what I'd look like, falling flat on my face in front of everyone. At least I was wearing jeans, I thought to myself. Some of the girls wearing short dresses gave everyone a peepshow each time they went to bowl. It was like a car crash. You didn't want to see it but it was impossible to look away.

Tom returned with a litre bottle of Tesco Value vodka, looking pleased with himself. I made a gagging noise when I saw the drink.

'That stuff is like paint-stripper,' I complained.

'Well, I couldn't afford anything else, so it will have to do. Anyway, it will make this game a lot more interesting,' he said, winking at me. We were put in the lane next to the girls with the very short skirts. There only seemed to be one empty bottle of West Coast Cooler on their table but they all looked as if they could barely walk.

They were in tight dresses that revealed their amazing figures; Tom had a sly peek when he thought I was looking in the opposite direction. How could you blame him? They were all stunning. I suddenly felt very self-conscious in my dull jeans and long-sleeved top. I had been so happy with my outfit choice when I had left my dorm, but I now felt like I looked really boring.

Tom poured us both a generous helping of vodka and then handed me a bottle of Coke that he had also bought.

'You not using any mixer?' I asked as he started to slug back the pure vodka.

'Nah,' he answered, making a face of disgust at the taste. 'I just want to get it in to me as quick as possible.'

'Alcoholic,' I said, taking a sip of my drink. No mixer on earth could cover up that horrific taste.

'It is better than being boring,' he answered, laughing.

Our bowling skills were definitely not something to be desired. Tom was winning barely, but we both had a gutter nearly every second go.

'I refuse to have bumpers,' declared Tom after his third gutter in a row.

'I just think we both need a bit of motivation,' I said, coming up with a brilliant idea. I was a bit tipsy now, and I was finding it hard even to see straight, let alone throw the ball.

'What were you thinking?' Tom asked, clearly intrigued.

'Every time one of us gutters, we have to take a shot of that foul vodka.'

'Deal,' Tom answered without hesitation. This, of course, led to the complete deterioration of our game. We were now getting gutters nearly every time we bowled, and within an hour I could barely stand.

Unfortunately I started to suffer from word vomit and I began to say things that I knew I would regret in the morning, but still I couldn't stop.

'You think those girls are hot, don't you?' My words were coming out completely slurred and Tom smiled down at me affectionately.

'What girls?' he asked.

I suddenly realized that he wasn't nearly as drunk as I was. I knew I should have stopped talking then but I couldn't.

'Those girls bowling next to us – don't lie, I know you like them. I saw you look at them.'

Tom started laughing. 'Of course I looked at them – everyone is looking at them. Their vaginas pop out every two minutes.' I wished he would take me seriously but he just kept laughing.

'No, no, but seriously,' I tried to argue, 'those girls could have any guy they want.'

Tom suddenly stopped laughing when he saw that I was being serious.

'Those are just ugly girls in slutty dresses with a lot of make-up,' he said.

'No, they're not,' I argued. The alcohol was making me feel emotional.

'Come on, Olive, no one thinks they're good-looking.'

'Then why is everyone gawping at them?' I was being unfair and irrational, but the alcohol had completely taken over.

'Because they're flashing everyone,' Tom practically shouted. 'OK, you obviously can't see how funny this is.' He grabbed my wrist and turned me towards the girls next to us. 'Watch this, please just watch this,' he said as a girl with dyed black hair and a skin-tight white dress picked up a bowling ball. She stumbled a little with the weight of it, then started to giggle – as did all her friends.

'OK,' Tom instructed, 'keep watching.' She stepped forward and threw the ball. As she did so, she bent over, revealing nearly her whole bum and a tiny black thong that left nothing to the imagination.

'And there it is! There is the vagina!' Tom shouted at the top of his voice and the girl, who had clearly heard him, pulled down her skirt looking mortified.

'Tom, shut up, she heard you,' I said, not able to hold in my laughter.

'I am sorry, but if she is going to show it off, I think I am allowed to say it.' Tom was still shouting and the girl in the white dress looked ready to hit him.

'Seriously, shut up,' I begged in between fits of giggles.

'It is indecent exposure, which is against the law. We should call the Guards and tell them that there is a girl here who is exposing herself to us.' The group of girls were whispering to each other now and giving the two of us filthies.

'Tom, be quiet, *please*.'

'Make me,' he said with his typical cheeky grin.

I don't know how it happened, I don't know who started it or even if I had planned it, but suddenly we were kissing. Tom had his hand on the back of my neck and I was gripping his arm. We started off just gently massaging each other's lips, barely opening our mouths, but it soon intensified and I shivered as I felt him nibble my bottom lip. I pulled away first. I was dizzy from the drink and I was afraid that if I didn't stop now I would lose all self-control. He smiled at me when I opened my eyes.

'Well, if you wanted me to shut up that much, you could have just asked.' I hit him as hard as I could, but I don't think he really felt it.

'Ruin the moment, why don't you?' I sulked, but I was secretly thrilled that he had been the first to speak.

At the end of the night we had both decided that bowling was definitely not an undiscovered talent for either of us. We had never finished our game. We had been politely asked to leave after Tom had walked down to the bottom of the lane and kicked all the pins down. It had been after his fifth gutter in a row and he had decided it was the only way he was going to get a strike. Unfortunately this explanation didn't go down too well with the people who worked there.

We stumbled back to the Dart, hoping to get the last one home, and stood there in awkward silence as we waited for it to arrive. I don't think either of us was sure who had initiated the kiss, and I was too afraid to try to kiss him again. But I was dying for him to kiss me.

'I had a really good night,' he told me, staring at his feet.

'Me too.' *Kiss me – kiss me now, you idiot.*

'I have to admit you were right. Bowling was fun.'

'Thanks.' *Come on, kiss me, come on.*

'But next time, I think that I should get to pick the place.'

This caught me by complete surprise. 'OK,' I said, smiling. 'Next time you can pick the place.' As I was talking, Tom stopped looking at his feet and grinned at me.

'Next time then?' He stepped closer to me so that I had to raise my head to look at him.

'Next time,' I echoed, stepping closer so that our bodies were touching. And then he did what I had been dying for him to do. He kissed me.

21
Tom

THE SUN WAS SHINING IN THROUGH MY BEDROOM WINDOW, and the warmth felt nice against my face. I had been lying in bed all day, going from boiling hot to freezing cold. This was the first time all day that my temperature had felt pleasant. I hadn't bothered telling my mum that I wasn't going in to college today. She would have yelled at me and told me that I was being lazy and useless, or she would have panicked over me, worried that I had some fatal disease. There was never any in-between. Anyway, she had a new cleaning job that had her leaving early in the morning and not back till late at night, so she would never know that I hadn't gone in. She was working in the Berkeley Court, a hotel that wasn't too far from our house. This was the first time in years that my mum had managed to get a reliable, regular job. This meant full days of work, but it also meant full days of pay.

I was actually thrilled for my mum, and even though she was working harder than ever, I had never seen her more happy. She seemed more together, and hadn't had a go at me in a whole week. Before, it would have been nearly every day. She told me her good mood was due to the fact that I was around more, which was true. These past few weeks, I had spent nearly all my spare time with Olive, which meant I was nearly always home by ten; Olive didn't like staying out late. She had even come here a couple of times – when my mum was out working, of course. I didn't want the hassle of introducing the two to each other. Sure, my mum had it together now, but I knew it was only temporary. One day she would lose it again. She would start screaming and crying, and Olive didn't need to see that. They were two different parts of my life that I never wanted to cross over. I knew Olive found this weird but she never brought it up. She was good like that – she never asked about my family unless I brought it up first, which I rarely ever did.

My phone buzzed. *I am on my way, will see you soon X.* I had told Olive that I was feeling unwell and she insisted that she would come over and cheer me up. She was cute like that. The truth was, I was thrilled she was coming. After yesterday, I thought I had nearly screwed up everything.

We had been walking around the city centre. The Christmas lights had just been put up in Grafton Street. Everyone was out in their winter clothes and the place was buzzing with Christmas shoppers. The weather was bitterly cold and it felt like it might snow. Olive stayed close to me, claiming that I kept her warm. I knew this was only an excuse for her to keep snuggled up to me. I smiled to myself; I was happier than I had been in a long time. I slipped my hand into hers. For once everything seemed to be working out. I brought her to see all the small, odd and eccentric shops in Dublin that she had never even heard of before. She had looked in awe at all the unusual objects that they sold in George's Street Arcade. I had even brought her to meet Moiraine. Moiraine instantly loved her, I knew she would. It turned out the two had grown up in the same small town in Wexford and Moiraine had known Olive's parents in school. The two talked endlessly without a pause. I didn't even bother to try and join in; it was actually nice and comforting to see the two chat as if they were old friends.

Moiraine had grabbed my arm just as we were about to leave and whispered in my ear, 'She's a good one. Don't mess it up.'

'I know,' I replied, not bothering to whisper. I knew that fact all too well.

We stopped in a coffee shop in Temple Bar to get warm. Olive was looking over all the objects she had bought. This included a pair of knee-high leopard-print socks, very sexy, but definitely not Olive's style.

'I am sure you will find somewhere to wear them,' I said, leaning in to kiss her neck. She was always really tickly there and she squealed with laughter.

'Stop, stop!' she said in between her giggles. She grabbed my face to kiss me and I instantly returned it without hesitation. I loved that I was able to kiss her whenever I wanted. She pulled away first – she always did. I used to think it was because we were in public, but she did it when we were alone as well. I always felt like I wanted her more than she did me, but there was no way I was going to tell her that.

As we released each other, I noticed someone over her shoulder and I felt my body freeze.

'Are you ready to go?' I asked bluntly.

'What?' asked Olive, completely surprised. We had only just got there and neither of us had even started on our coffees.

'I . . . We need to go . . . now.'

Olive stared at me in complete incomprehension. 'Why, what's wrong?' she asked, concerned.

'Nothing,' I said. 'I just need to go now.' Then I made the fatal mistake of looking in their direction and Olive turned around, following my gaze.

Paddy, Robin and Pam were in the line for the café. Paddy

looked tired; he had more frown lines than he'd had the last time I'd seen him. Robin's thin face was set in a scowl and the two were looking off in opposite directions. Pam was gripping onto Robin's hand, looking around the people in front of her. They hadn't spotted me yet and I didn't want them to, especially not when I was with Olive.

'Who are they?' Olive asked, really worried now.

'I'll explain later. Can we just go?' I knew I was overreacting and being rude but I just couldn't handle this.

We quickly gathered up our things and withdrew, leaving our coffees untouched. I walked briskly out of the exit, down the street and around the corner, looking back a couple of times to make sure Olive was following.

'What's going on, Tom?' Olive asked angrily when we were a good fifty yards from the café.

'They were . . . I just . . . I don't really want those people to see me. That's all.' I was hoping she would just drop it there but I could tell by the annoyed look on her face that I wasn't going to get out of this that easily.

'That was your dad, wasn't it?'

I stared at her, completely shocked. 'How did you—'

'You look very alike,' she said, interrupting me.

I felt I had to explain.

'I don't really get on with my dad or his wife Robin, so it is just better to – you know – leave it.'

Olive looked at me sympathetically. I hated it, I felt as if she pitied me.

We didn't talk much after that as we strolled aimlessly around town. Eventually Olive said something about a class presentation due in next week; she gave me a peck on the cheek and started walking off in the direction of the Dart station. She didn't even wait for me to offer to walk with her. I went straight home after that, convinced that I had scared her off. I sat in my room for hours, furious with myself and with Paddy and Robin. Why did they have to turn up at that exact time? If they hadn't been there, none of this would have happened; everything would be fine. I skipped dinner and went to bed early, telling my mum that I wasn't feeling well. Ironically enough, by the time I woke up the next morning, I really felt ill.

The loud knock on my door broke my thoughts. I jumped out of bed, threw on a pair of tracksuit bottoms and made my way to the door. Olive was standing there, her hair looking wild as usual, and she was holding a tub of Ben & Jerry's ice-cream in her right hand.

'Nothing like ice-cream to cure the flu,' she said.

'Brilliant,' I replied, instantly feeling better. I loved ice-cream.

We spent the rest of the day just lying in my bed, talking and eating ice-cream. All the awkwardness and tension from yesterday seemed to have completely disappeared. Olive ate most of the ice-cream herself but I pretended not to notice. I was just thrilled that I hadn't scared her away.

'So, are you feeling better?' she asked, licking the last of the ice-cream from her spoon.

'Much better,' I replied. 'Ben & Jerry's could cure anything.'

She looked at me with a hurt expression on her face and I grabbed her by the waist and pulled her closer to me.

'Of course you are a brilliant nurse too.' She still pretended to be upset, so I began to tickle her waist. She started to squirm and laugh uncontrollably, desperately trying to pull away from me. I pinned her down on my bed and started to tickle behind her knees.

'Stop . . . stop!' she pleaded in between laughter. She tried to push me off the bed, but I was a lot stronger than her. I grabbed her arms so that she wasn't able to move. I was no longer tickling her because my hands were busy keeping her from hitting me. She breathed in and out heavily, completely out of breath. She was no longer laughing but stared at me while biting her lip.

I began kissing her roughly. I released her arms and started exploring her body with my hands. She responded by kissing me back with the same aggression and ran her hands through my hair. I pulled away from her mouth and started kissing her neck; every now and again I would nibble and I could feel her shiver. I made my way down to her chest and then her stomach, constantly kissing every part of her. I was now at her jeans and I started to undo her belt.

'Tom, stop!' Her belt was off and I struggled with the buttons on her jeans, but eventually I had them undone too.

'Stop!' I pulled down her jeans, revealing blue lacy underwear; I was starting to get really excited.

Suddenly I felt her hands against my shoulders, and she pushed me away with such force that I fell off the bed and banged my elbow against the hard wooden floor.

'For God's sake, Olive!' I exclaimed. The blow had really hurt my elbow. 'What on earth was that about?'

She looked at me; her face was in a frown. 'Are you serious?' she said. 'Tom, I asked you to stop twice and you just kept going.'

I looked at her, completely confused. Yes, I had heard her saying *stop* but I had also felt her body shiver when I kissed her. She had wanted to do it just as much as I did.

'It's only sex,' I said, trying to make light of the situation, but she wasn't smiling.

I crawled back onto the bed and made to kiss her, but she just pulled away.

'You don't get it, do you?'

'No, I don't,' I said, failing to hide the annoyance in my voice.

'You will just sleep with anyone, even if you don't like them.'

'That's not true,' I said, desperately trying to defend myself. I didn't know why she was so mad but I decided it was best that I just apologize. 'Look, I'm sorry. I thought you wanted to do it as well. I guess I was wrong.'

'Of course I wanted to do it.'

'Then what is the problem!' I exclaimed in complete frustration.

'I don't just sleep with anyone, Tom.' She spoke as if she was talking to someone who was completely dense. 'Like we're not even committed to each other. Who knows how many other girls you are hooking up with?'

'None,' I said honestly.

'None at the moment, but what if you meet someone tomorrow?'

'Do you want to be committed?' The words were out of my mouth before I realized what I was saying.

'What?' Olive asked quietly.

'Do you want to be committed?' I repeated, knowing there was no going back now.

'Do *you*?' she asked sceptically.

'Yes,' I said, trying not to hesitate, although my stomach was full of knots.

Olive didn't look convinced; she had a judgemental expression on her face.

'You are just saying that so you can get what you want,' she said.

I stood up from the bed and took a deep breath. 'No, I am not. Look, I've done things in the past with girls that I am not exactly proud of,' images of girls like Alison, Angelina and Roz popped into my head, 'but I like you a lot, and I will do anything to keep what we have.' I took her hands in mine and I was thrilled when she didn't pull away.

She started smiling. 'So does that mean you want me to be your girlfriend?'

I couldn't help but smile too. If I was going to do this, then I might as well do it properly.

'Yeah, I do. I like you and I want to keep seeing you. So let's do it.'

'OK.' She pulled me down next to her and kissed me on the cheek. I kissed her back but only briefly. I wasn't going to push my luck again, especially now that she was no longer mad at me.

We spent the next hour talking about college and friends, safe topics. When she left she kissed me for quite a long time, and then whispered in my ear that she was so happy that she had met me. I said I was happy too, but after she left, the knots in my stomach only got worse. *What are you doing? You can't be someone's boyfriend.* I didn't do girlfriends – there were too many expectations and someone would just get hurt. It had been OK before, there had been no commitment, but now there was all this pressure and I was going to make a mistake. I was going to fuck it all up.

22
Olive

'COME *ON*, OLIVE, WE ARE GOING TO BE LATE.'

'I *am* coming,' I said. I could hear Tom pacing about in frustration. He was impatient and I did not normally keep him waiting. We were only going to the local pub for some food and drinks, but I felt like I needed to make a huge effort. The two of us were no longer just *hanging out*, we were a couple, a full-on couple, kissing-in-public, holding-hands and having-sex couple. Well, technically we weren't having sex yet, but after tonight that was all going to change.

It had been a week since the *throwing off the bed* incident. I hadn't brought it up since then and of course he hadn't tried anything either. He had been right when he'd said that I had wanted to too, I was absolutely dying to sleep with him. I shivered with excitement when he would merely brush my hair out of my face.

I dressed up a little tonight. I wore a loose blue dress with thick black tights – too much for a pub, I knew, but tonight was special. It wasn't my first time, I had had sex before. I knew what he would do, what I was supposed to do, what went where. But it was my first time with *him*, so all the scared and nervous feelings were just the same. And I wanted it to be perfect, *I* wanted to be perfect for him.

Underwear had been a tough decision. I didn't actually own sexy corsets or anything like that, and even if I did I don't think I would have had the confidence to wear them. All my plain knickers and bras seemed so dull and boring, I didn't want him to see me that way. Eventually I settled on a black lacy bra and thong to match. It wasn't very comfortable – I didn't normally wear thongs – but it was the sexiest thing I owned, so it would have to do.

Tom was checking his phone when I finally hurried out to meet him; I made a small 'Hmph' sound under my breath so that he would notice I had walked into the room. He looked up and instantly smiled.

'You look really nice.'

'Thanks,' I said, feeling my cheeks heat up. 'Am I a little too dressed up?'

'No, no, you look great. I feel like a bit of a scruff.' He was gazing at me as if he had never seen me properly before.

Suddenly Tom's phone started ringing.

'For God's sake,' he grumbled, the moment completely broken. He answered the phone looking annoyed. 'Damien, I told you I can't tonight – I just can't, that's why. Look, I'll talk to you another time.' I could hear that the person on the other end was mid-sentence when Tom hung up.

'What was that about?' I asked curiously.

'Oh, nothing,' he replied, kissing my forehead.

'It didn't sound like nothing,' I said, getting suspicious now.

'It was just my friend Damien. He wants me to go out tonight to some club called Howl something.'

'Howl at the Moon. Roz said she would be heading there tonight as well. Apparently it's really good.'

'Yeah, well, I would rather be with you.' But his tone sounded forced.

'Why don't we go meet them after dinner?' I asked, watching his reaction very carefully.

'Really?' he said, looking nervous.

'Yeah, I can finally meet your friends.'

Tom looked very uneasy when I said that.

'Wouldn't you rather we just came home and spent time together?' he asked, almost desperately.

'No,' I answered simply, walking out the door. 'I will text Roz and tell her we're coming.'

Tom acted like a nervous child all through dinner; he was very uncommunicative and kept drifting off in the middle of our conversations. I started to feel quite insulted. Was he so ashamed of me that he didn't want his friends to meet me? What was wrong with me? I was smart, pretty and fun. Just because I wasn't like the other slutty girls those boys normally went for didn't mean his friends would be instantly repulsed by me. I wanted to ask him about it, to tell him how I was feeling, but I didn't. Even though I was angry and upset, I still really liked Tom. It was only early days and I didn't want to do anything to ruin what we had just started, so I kept my mouth shut.

The club was packed; apparently Wednesday was their main student night. It was a long time before we could find anyone. After twenty minutes of aimlessly wandering around, I agreed to sit down with Tom at one of the empty tables in the corner. He visibly relaxed as the night went on and we managed to avoid running into anyone we knew. He was even starting to get quite affectionate after a couple of beers. He kept kissing my neck, which made me giggle.

'Let's go home,' he whispered into my ear in between kisses.

'No, we can't,' I said, even though I was now tempted by the idea. 'I told Roz I would meet her here.'

'Come on,' he begged. 'The club is going to close soon. It's bonkers here, you're never going to find her.' I knew that I should have insisted on staying and waiting for Roz, but the thought of going home and being alone with Tom was far too tempting.

'OK,' I murmured, snuggling in closer to him.

Tom grabbed my hand and the two of us started to head towards the exit. Suddenly I heard someone shout, 'Tom!' from the other side of the room.

'Tom, Tom, you fucker. You actually came.' A small red-headed guy who I vaguely recognized was pushing his way through the crowd towards us. Tom looked like he had just seen a ghost.

'Tom, you dry shite. You actually came out for once.' The guy could barely stand straight and had clearly had too much to drink.

'Hey, Damien,' Tom said sternly.

Damien turned towards me. 'Who are you?' he asked rudely.

'I'm Olive,' I said, not really understanding what was going on.

'Olive is my girlfriend,' Tom said, but it sounded forced.

'Girlfriend? *Girlfriend?* Fuck! Never thought I would see you with a girlfriend, Tom. Come on, come on. Peter has to see this, he won't believe me.'

'We are actually leaving . . .' Tom began, but Damien had grabbed the two of us by the wrists and had started to pull us through the club, shouting for Peter at the top of his voice.

Peter was a big guy; he was sitting at a table with a girl on either side of him. Both seemed to be eyeing him up like a piece of meat.

'Peter, this is Tom's "girlfriend".' Damien shoved me to the forefront as if I was a dog on show.

Tom pushed him back aggressively, saying, 'Stop being such a cock, OK?'

Damien looked hurt but recovered quickly. Peter offered me his hand.

'Hi, I'm Peter.'

'I'm Olive,' I said, taking it.

He patted the empty stools beside the girls. 'Sit down, you two. Night's not over yet.'

Tom started to relax once Damien had stopped talking to me; he was now busy trying to chat to one of the girls sitting beside Peter. She didn't even seem to be listening to him; instead she spent her time making eyes at Tom. I wanted to hit her. I kissed Tom obviously on the mouth to make sure she knew to stay away, but she continued to stare. She had some fucking nerve. Tom seemed to cope with the situation by buying endless rounds of drinks. I didn't even attempt to keep up with him. He acted differently around his friends; he was more aggressive and sarcastic when he spoke. I wasn't sure I liked it.

It was about two-thirty when I realized that I really wanted to go. Peter had been OK earlier. He was charming and very funny, but now he was just sucking the face off his girl. The two hadn't come up for air in ages. I had kind of enjoyed Damien's company, too; he was actually quite funny. Unfortunately, he had crossed over from mess to complete and utter disgrace about twenty minutes before, and had now become grumpy because his girl had left. Tom just sat there drinking, saying very little. He had no focus in his eyes.

I cuddled up next to him and whispered in his ear, 'Do you want to leave?'

He just nodded, then stumbled a little when he stood up.

'Jacks,' he explained, before wandering off in the direction of the bathrooms.

'He has so gone to chunder,' Damien said, laughing.

I just looked at him. I was uncomfortable now that Tom wasn't here.

'That guy thinks he could drink anyone under the table, but he is actually the biggest lightweight. I have to say,' Damien went on, 'he really fucking impressed me tonight. I can't believe I am going to have to give him a hundred euro.'

I frowned, confused. 'Why do you have to give him a hundred euro?'

'Because he won the bet.'

'What bet?'

'You know. The bet.'

I just stared, completely baffled.

'Oh my God! The fucker didn't tell you, did he?'

'No . . .' I said slowly, a sinking feeling in my stomach.

'Well, I probably shouldn't say anything then.' But Damien looked very pleased with himself.

'*What bet?*' I repeated angrily.

'Look, this is Tom's thing,' Damien replied, sounding less confident. 'I don't want to get involved.'

'Tell me what the bet is *right now*.' I felt myself shaking.

'We bet a hundred euro that Tom could convince you to sleep with him before the semester was over.' Damien burst out laughing hysterically. 'To be honest, I would have given him another fifty if he had convinced you to film it. Has he?'

I suddenly felt like I was going to be sick. This couldn't be true, it just couldn't. I stood up and rushed away, not really sure where I was going. I met Tom on his way out from the bathroom.

'Hey, babe, you ready? Olive, what's wrong?'

I didn't know what to do. I wanted to run, scream, cry. Before I realized it, I was yelling at him. 'Damien said you guys had a bet about me. Is it true?'

Tom didn't need to speak. The answer was written on his guilty face.

'You disgust me,' I choked. 'You are a pathetic excuse for a human being. Stay away from me.' I pushed past him and started running for the exit. He followed me and grabbed me by the arm.

'Olive, stop—'

'Don't touch me.' I shoved him away and ran out the door as fast as I could. He made no attempt to follow me.

I didn't know where I was running – I just kept going. I could feel the tears starting to sting my eyes and I just ran through them. People stared at me as I ran by. I must have looked very strange but I didn't care. I wanted to get away from them, from everyone, from everything. My sides soon began to hurt but I persevered. I wasn't far enough away, I had to go further. I don't know how long I had been running for when I finally came to a stop. The pain in my sides had become too much for me. I was finding it hard to breathe. I tried to take in air, but it didn't feel like the oxygen was going into my lungs. I sat down, leaning against a wall, and put my head between my knees. This helped.

When I finally started to feel like my heart-rate was slowing down, I lifted my head. It was dark and empty, there was no one around. I stood up and looked about me in a panic: I had no idea where I was. I tried to stay calm, to figure out from what direction I had come, but it was hopeless. I dug into my handbag and pulled out my phone – the battery was dead. I had forgotten to charge it before I had come out. I felt so stupid. The streets all looked the same, dark and abandoned, and in my hysterical state I had been stupid enough to not look where I was going.

Panic set in. I was a young girl on my own in the middle of Dublin. I randomly picked a street and started to walk down it, then as my panic worsened, I broke into a jog. I eventually gave up on the street I had taken, turned a corner and took another one and then another. I must have been walking for hours before I saw a car – it was a taxi. I frantically started waving my hands and it pulled up next to me.

The driver was a large man and he looked at me, concerned. 'Are you OK?' he asked.

I had heard so many horror stories about young girls who took taxis on their own, but I didn't want to be left alone here all night.

'Yeah. I was wondering how I would be able to get back to Leeson Street from here?' That had been where the club was.

'That's a good forty-minute walk from here, and these streets aren't safe for a young girl like you to be wandering around in.' He sounded kind, but I was so afraid. I was afraid to get in but I was also afraid he would leave. 'Look, why don't you hop in and I will bring you home.'

'I don't have any money,' I lied.

'That's OK,' he sighed. 'Look, I wouldn't be able to sleep tonight knowing a young girl like you is alone and lost in this place. Trust me, I have seen some dodgy characters around this area.'

I bit my lip and stood there, completely torn. Eventually I hopped into the car. It had to be the safer option, I reasoned with myself.

'Where can I take you?' he asked after I had closed the door.

'UCD,' I answered, my voice sounding frail and crackly. Most of the journey was spent in silence. I began to relax as I started to see streets that I recognized and realized how lucky I was that this taxi driver had found me before anyone else did. The sun was beginning to come up and when I looked at my watch, I was shocked to discover that it was 5.30 a.m. I had obviously been walking around for hours.

'Have you had a bit of a rough night?' the taxi driver asked as we began to get close to UCD. I could feel tears falling down my face again, but I didn't fight them this time. Instead of replying, I just nodded. I was worried that if I spoke, I would start blubbering.

'Oh, you poor thing. Nobody hurt you, did they?' he frowned.

'No, no,' I said, trying to wipe the tears away. 'I just had a fight with someone and then I got lost and my brother has recently passed away . . .' I couldn't hold it in any more. I began to sob uncontrollably: it was the first time that I had cried since my brother's death. The driver didn't ask any questions or try to comfort me, he just let me cry. I was thankful for that. It was odd, Tom had been the one who had upset me, but now I didn't feel angry at him. I just felt sad and I missed Andy terribly. I don't know whether Tom had triggered my suppressed grief or whether I was always eventually going to explode, but at that moment I cried for Andy and for no one else.

I tried to give the taxi driver money when we reached UCD, admitting that I'd lied earlier, but he refused to take it.

'I have a daughter about your age and I would hate to think that someone wouldn't give her a lift home if she was in trouble.'

'Thanks,' I choked, attempting a smile.

'Now is there someone in there to look after you?' he asked, gesturing towards the dorms. I nodded, flattered by his kindness. 'OK, well, take care of yourself. You seem like a nice girl and there are some nasty people out there.'

'Yeah, there really are,' I replied.

When I finally got to bed, I plugged my phone into its charger and turned it on, to find twelve missed calls, five voicemails and seven texts, all from Tom. I deleted them without even looking and instantly blocked his number. What had happened with Tom had been a nightmare and I was ready to wake up now.

23

Tom

OLIVE, PLEASE CALL ME BACK. IT'S NOT WHAT YOU THINK IT IS. 2.38 a.m.

Olive, please don't be like this. Damien talks shit all the time. 3.02 a.m.

Look, Olive, I am not going to lie. Yeah that bet was how it all started, but I really like you and the bet has nothing to do with anything any more. 3.44 a.m.

Just call me and tell me you are OK. I am really worried now. Just tell me if you're home and safe, please. 4.18 a.m.

Olive, I . . . I think I am falling in love with you. Please, just please call me. 4.50 a.m.

It was 5 a.m. At this point I had given up all hope that she would call me back. It was over, she hated me. She truly hated me. The way she had looked at me when she had found out – I don't think anyone had ever loathed me that much.

I didn't handle it well after Olive left. I stormed back to the table to see Damien looking extremely smug and cocky. He had always been a jealous bastard but I had believed that he would always have my back like I had his. I grabbed him by the shirt and banged him up against the wall before he even saw me coming.

'What the fuck?' I raged. 'Seriously, I know you have no fucking balls, but if you are going to mess with me, you better expect to be beat.'

He stared at me, terrified. 'Tom, I don't know what you are on about . . .'

'You know *exactly* what I am on about, you little piece of shit.' My face was less than an inch from his and I could feel myself quivering with rage.

Peter had his hands on my shoulders, and only then did I realize there was a small crowd of spectators beginning to gather.

'Tom, calm down. You have a few drinks in you and if you start a fight you will get all of us in trouble.' Peter was trying to stay calm but I could sense his agitation. He was afraid. I had never turned on one of them like this before, and I really wanted to hit Damien. I wanted to hit him again and again until he understood what he had done, but I didn't. I don't know whether it was Peter, the crowd of spectators, the fact that the bouncers would kick me out in a second if I did anything, or even the look of pure fear on Damien's face, but I let him go and I walked away.

I walked around for hours looking for Olive, trying to think where she might have gone. I regretted not following her. I sat on the side of the street and phoned her. I phoned and phoned. All the clubs were closed now; there were only a couple of stragglers left stumbling into various taxis. I didn't have enough money for a taxi and even if I did I didn't want to go home but there was nowhere else to go. I couldn't stay sitting here any longer, I had to move. I had to walk somewhere, somewhere that wasn't here.

Just as I began to head in the direction of my house I

discovered an abandoned bottle of vodka that had only been half-drunk, left hidden inside an old doorway. I picked it up and sniffed the top. It smelled like vodka. This isn't a good idea, I thought. An abandoned bottle of vodka at the side of the road? There could be anything in it. But I wasn't willing to listen to the voice of reason. I felt like shit, worthless and unimportant.

Who cared if it was drugged? No one cared about what I did. Olive had cared – at least I thought she had. It didn't matter any more, because I had ruined it, the way I ruined everything. My life was just a series of fuck-ups, so what was the point in being cautious any more? I tried to down the half-bottle in one go but I had to pull it away from my mouth for a moment. It burned my throat raw and I thought I might be sick, but I made myself finish the bottle. It wasn't until I had finished that I realized the taste was off. There was that strong prominent taste of pure vodka, but the after-taste was just . . . not right.

The spirit made me drunk and incoherent. I found it difficult to walk straight and my head felt heavy, but I knew where I was and what I was doing. I began to think perhaps it had only been vodka, but then it hit me. When I am drunk, I sometimes feel like I am having an out-of-body experience. I do and say ridiculous things, but I still know what I am doing. This was nothing like that. Everything became foggy – solid things like buildings and cars suddenly became distorted. I saw shapes and lights fly by me but I couldn't tell what they were or how close they were to me. I became confused and disoriented; I couldn't remember where I was going or even where I was.

After a while I couldn't tell if I was walking any more or even if I was vertical. I was spinning uncontrollably. I wanted to stop, to get sick, but I couldn't. I don't know how long I stayed in this terrifying state, time seeming to no longer exist. There were only lights and moving shapes and then darkness.

When I opened my eyes it was bright. The light burned my

eyes so I instantly closed them again. My head felt like it was going to split open and my heart was beating feverishly. I was strangely out of breath and my chest hurt every time I inhaled. I was lying on a hard and cold surface: concrete – I was lying on concrete. I opened my eyes, this time more slowly. At first all I saw was bright light, but then I started to notice other things. There was a road, and cars. I had fallen asleep in the doorway of an abandoned building. People were walking by – pretending not to see me, of course. I probably looked like a junkie.

I managed to push myself into a sitting position although I was shivering fanatically and found it difficult not to slump over. I sat there for a while before my mind began to work properly and I was able to figure out where I was. I was close to home, very close. I had obviously walked for miles last night. My hands were covered in scabs and dry blood; I must have fallen a lot. I reached for my phone in my pocket, only to discover that there was a huge crack across the front and the battery was missing. The first time I tried to stand up, I instantly fell back down. My chest really hurt and my heart beat even more wildly at the strain of moving. I made an effort to breathe in as deeply as I could before I tried again, this time managing to stand.

I winced with pain when I took that first step. My right leg was in agony and I tried not to put my full weight on it. As I limped home, I walked by a glass window and could see I had a black eye. I was seriously beginning to worry about how I had obtained all these bruises. Had I gotten into a fight? Were my injuries just from falling? It scared me how little I could remember. The walk home would have normally only taken me five minutes or less, but the pain in my leg and chest meant that I had to take breaks every few steps. It was nearly half an hour later before I reached my house.

I stumbled through the door, and found my mum facing me

with swollen red eyes and a phone to her ear. She was about to say something but I didn't hear it. I made it to the bathroom and immediately began to retch. I felt as if I had been throwing up for hours when it finally stopped. My mum was sitting next to me with a glass of water. I took it from her and sipped it cautiously. The cold water stung my raw throat. We sat there in silence for a long while. She looked tired and old, older than I had ever seen her before.

'I'm sorry,' I said hoarsely. 'My phone broke.'

'How?' she demanded. 'And don't you dare lie.' I was a little surprised at her reaction. I expected yelling and crying, but this cold anger was so much worse.

'I don't know,' I said.

She wasn't even looking at me any more.

'Why?' she asked, her voice even chillier, if it was possible. 'Why don't you know?'

'I was drunk . . . and high, I think.'

She barely flinched as if she had expected the answer.

'Do you have any more?' she asked.

I shook my head, but I could tell from the hard stare she gave me that she didn't believe a word I was saying.

'Take a shower, Tom.'

I nodded. I felt like I was going to be sick again.

'You're moving in with your dad today.'

'What?' I practically shouted at her. She jumped at my sudden change of volume. 'I'm not living with *him*. I can't!' The thought of waking up to Robin and Paddy every day, seeing their disappointment, their disgust – there was no way I was going to let it happen.

'It's obvious I can't handle you, Tom. I want you out of this house – you're going today. It is already agreed.'

I looked at her desperately. 'Please . . .' I said, but she was already leaving the room.

I cried quietly for a while – I didn't want her to hear. I forced myself off the bathroom floor and started undressing. I looked at myself in the mirror – I was thin and pale. There were large circles under my eyes, and various cuts and bruises across my body. My hands were still bleeding. I was shaking like a leaf. I ran a cold shower and just let the water soak me; allowed the exposed cuts to feel the sting of the cold water. When I got out of the shower I didn't feel sick any more, just cold and empty.

Going into my room, I noticed that my drawers and shelves had been ransacked and emptied. Sitting on my bed was one set of clothes, and a bag with all my belongings and my guitar. I ran my hands through my hair, as I began to wonder what my mum had found when she had been packing my stuff. There were dirty magazines, condoms, fireworks that I had hidden under my bed, the dodgy weed and a home-made bong that Peter and I had created one night when we were bored. It didn't look good.

I knew I wasn't going to convince her to let me stay, but no way would I move in with Paddy and Robin. I got dressed quickly, and grabbed all my stuff. The pain in my right leg slowed me down and my chest was still sore, but I tried my best to ignore it. I limped down the stairs and went into the kitchen to find my mum sitting at the table with her hands around a large cup of coffee. She opened her mouth to say something but I spoke first.

'I'm going to go to Dad's now, if that's OK?'

Her jaw dropped but she recovered quickly. 'I guess that's OK, but—'

I was out the door before I could hear what she was going to say. I looked in my wallet to see a couple of euro coins.

'Perfect,' I said aloud. I found a payphone and started dialling.

'Hello, Murder's Foulest Things. How can I help you?'

I took a deep breath before speaking. 'Hi, Moiraine. It's Tom.'

'Tom! Hello, darling, how are you? Do you want me to put something aside for you?'

'No, no. I just . . . was wondering if you have a job for me?'

She was silent for a long time before answering. 'Are you in trouble, Tom?'

'No, it's just . . .' There was no point in lying to her. 'My mum has kicked me out and I need some money. But if you don't have a job . . .'

'Of course I do, Tom. Come in tomorrow at nine sharp and I'll start training you in.'

'Thanks,' I mumbled, a little embarrassed at my desperation. I hung up and put more money into the payphone and started dialling again.

'Hello,' Peter said grumpily. Clearly he had been asleep.

'Peter, it's Tom. I need a favour: can I stay with you for a while? I'll pay for my own food and stuff.'

'What the fuck was your deal last night, Tom? I thought you were going to kill Damien.'

'Yeah, I know. I took some dodgy stuff and I don't remember most of what went on last night.' It wasn't really a lie. There had definitely been some sort of drug in that vodka, but Peter didn't need to know that it had been *after* I had attacked Damien.

'Fuck, well, whatever you took, don't take it again. You were fucking nuts.'

'I know, I'm sorry. Look, my mum has just kicked me out and I need somewhere to stay. I'm sure it will only be for a little while.' I didn't truly believe this; my mum had never looked more serious than she had earlier.

'Yeah, no problem, man. Just don't let my dad find out.'

'Thanks, Peter, I'm on my way.' I hung up the phone, relieved. I knew I would eventually have to start paying rent if Peter's dad found out; he was a businessman first and foremost.

Hopefully, by then I would have some money saved up. I tried not to think about my mum and what she would do when she found out I wasn't at Paddy's. I looked into my wallet again – and found another five-euro note. Five euro and fifty cents and nowhere to live.

24
Olive

I SLEPT TWENTY-FOUR HOURS STRAIGHT AFTER THAT NIGHT. IT was a deep and heavy sleep, and when I woke up I felt truly rested. I no longer felt like I was running on adrenaline or fear. I had been taking advantage of Tom – I knew that now. My affection and attraction towards him had suppressed my grief. It had been so easy to be happy when I was with Tom. But lying here now, it was hard to tell if any of it had been real. Did I care for him as much as I thought I did, or had I just created these emotions in my head as a way to cope with the loss of Andy?

The last few weeks seemed like a foggy memory, as if I had been walking around half-asleep. I had felt that if I didn't keep going, keep moving, keep living – that if I stopped for one second and allowed myself to think – I would realize how much I had lost and it would kill me. But it didn't. For the first time in weeks I didn't feel that I had to put on a brave face. I didn't have to keep myself constantly distracted. I just felt like me.

I sat up and rubbed the sleep out of my eyes. Sunlight shone through the window and into my room. Everything seemed so much clearer now, brighter. I walked out into the kitchen to see Roz sitting at the table in her fluffy pink pyjamas.

'Well, hello, sleepyhead. I thought you were never going to rise. Went to wake you yesterday, but you just looked so peaceful, I left you alone.' She was smiling broadly and her voice had a cheerful tone to it. 'How was your dinner with Tom?'

I shrugged my shoulders. 'So-so. The food sucked.' I wasn't lying – it had. 'How about you?' I asked. 'Didn't Ed take you to dinner?'

Roz practically burst with excitement as soon as I asked the question.

'Oh my God, Olive, it was amazing. He is like the sweetest guy in the world. He did the whole romantic flowers and chocolates thing. I was like blown away and then he took me to this really cool jazz bar that I had never even heard of, and we just sat there like listening to music all night.'

'That sounds unreal, Roz. I'm jealous.' I was.

'And then he came in the taxi with me all the way to UCD even though it is like in the complete opposite direction to his house, and he refused to let me pay for anything. He is such a sweetheart and he didn't even try anything at the end of the night. Like we scored, that's it.'

She looked as if she could have gone on and on for hours, but she visibly stopped herself, saying, 'Oh my God, I am just being so rude. Tell me more about your night with Tom?'

I tensed a little at her question; luckily my back was facing her as I was making myself a cup of tea.

'Not much to tell,' I said. 'We went to dinner and then out to meet his friends. So are you seeing Ed this weekend then?'

Suddenly Roz put on a face that made her look like a spoiled child whose doll had just been taken away from her.

'No, he's going off with his family on some camping trip. Apparently they do it like every year so he can't get out of it.'

'Oh, that's a pity,' I said, sitting down at the table next to her, thrilled that I had managed to change the topic without her noticing.

Roz stared at me with a serious look in her eyes – well, as serious a look as a girl like Roz could manage.

'Olive, don't judge me, but I'm really worried about him going away and cheating.'

'But he's going on a family camping trip. Of course he's not going to cheat on you!'

'No, no, I'm not worried about *him* cheating on me. I am worried about *me* cheating on him.'

'What?' I asked, completely mystified. Roz looked embarrassed – it was shocking to see.

'OK, like I say, don't judge me, but I like always cheat on boyfriends. I don't mean to, it's just when I'm out and I have a few vodkas in me, I get really flirty and I am like such a sucker for hot boys. But I really like Ed, and I like don't want to ruin it.'

'OK,' I answered, trying to avoid the whole 'Do you have no willpower?' question. 'If it's only when you drink, then just don't go out this weekend.'

'Oh, I wish I could do that but I know the girls will just annoy me until I come out. I can't be in Dublin this weekend – that's the only solution.' Suddenly her face lit up; you would have sworn a light bulb just went on in her head. 'I know! I will lock myself away in Lahinch for the weekend.'

'Lahinch?' I queried.

'Yeah, it's in County Clare,' answered Roz, starting to sound excited again. 'Oh, it's so lovely there. My parents own a house right on the beach. I spend my days surfing, walking and reading. Oh, and they have like the cutest Irish pub that you can hang out in at night.'

'Sounds amazing,' I said, suddenly getting a brilliant idea of my own. 'Do you want company?'

*

Lahinch was completely different from any other place that I'd been before. I knew it was a cliché, but when you breathed in that sea air, there was just something that made you feel whole again. You felt connected to everything. I had not felt this alive in a very long time.

Lahinch is one of those small coastline towns, famous for its good waves and long empty beaches. Roz had described the place as an escape from reality, and it really was. It was the kind of place where you never saw vandalism or graffiti. No one ever seemed to be in a rush, everyone acted like they were on holidays even if they lived there. You could smell the snow in the country air – it was December now and Christmas was fast approaching. All the small houses had numerous lights and Christmas decorations. Lahinch seemed to possess that small-town charm that instantly made you feel welcome.

Roz drove us; she was a terrifying driver, aggressive and rash, like she was with most things. I tried my best to just enjoy the scenery and ignore the many beeps and flashes from other cars as we drove by.

'For fuck's sake. People seriously need to learn how to drive,' Roz muttered under her breath. I bit my tongue; there was no way I was going to criticize her driving ability. She was letting me stay in her house for the weekend and, to be completely honest, she scared me a little.

I was surprised at how relaxed my parents had been when I told them I wasn't coming home for the weekend. A few months earlier, they would have said that I could go, but come up with multiple reasons as to why I shouldn't. But I suddenly realized that, a few months earlier, I would not have asked. My weekends had been for Andy and nothing could have changed that. My parents were actually going to try and have a romantic few days away together this weekend. Since the day

Andy was born they had never been alone. Andy was so difficult as a baby that my mum didn't want to leave him with sitters, and even as I got older they would never leave the two of us alone for more than a day. I understood it, of course; when Andy had his fits he could be very tricky to calm down. I never told them how relieved I was that they were always around. For nearly my whole life I was terrified that if we were ever left alone, something would go terribly, terribly wrong and it would always be my fault.

When I thought about it properly, it was a true testament to how strong my parents were and how strong their relationship was. I loved my brother, and would have given up anything in the whole world to see him again, but I would be lying if I said I hadn't resented him a little over all these years. At times I had wished I could have had a more normal childhood. As a teenager I wasn't allowed to spend the night at a friend's house or stay out late at parties. Andy liked to know I was home before he fell asleep, and sometimes he would get very upset if I wasn't there. But it was more than that. I resented the fact that none of us could have a normal life, that because of him we would always live in fear. The fear was gone now, but I didn't feel any better.

I had been so angry with myself: I felt like I should have tried harder, done more, but then I realized something. I am human. As human beings, we make mistakes, oh so many mistakes. We are emotional – we do and say things that we do not mean, and sometimes we fall, but the people who love us will always pick us up again. Everyone always assumed that I took care of Andy. That I was the sensible, strong one. They could not have been more wrong. Andy was there for me when I was teased at school, when I had a bad dream or when Mum yelled at me. Andy had loved me and I had loved him – he knew that, that was one thing I was sure of.

*

Roz's parents' house was in the middle of Lahinch; practically on the beach. The town seemed so sweet and wholesome with small cafés and little Irish souvenir shops. The salty air felt amazing and I couldn't wait to walk along that sand. Ed, Roz's love interest, had rung her the minute we had walked through the door; she had practically squealed with excitement when his name had popped up on the screen. I gestured to Roz that I was going out, but she was too distracted to see. I decided to just leave, knowing that she probably wouldn't even notice.

The beach was packed, surprisingly. It was a cold and windy day and the clouds were threatening to pour and yet there were people in the water, surfing and swimming. Kids were running up and down the beach in scarves and hats. The weather didn't discourage anyone from enjoying the day. The rain began as I was halfway down that mile-long beach. I sprinted back to Roz's house but there was very little point in my running as I was soon soaked through. My white hoodie clung to me, weighing me down with rainwater, and my hair was sticking to my face.

'You look like a drowned rat.' Roz was off the phone and getting a pizza out of the freezer for dinner.

'Yeah, it started to lash out there. Everyone's still on the beach though.' I twisted my hair over the sink to stop it from dripping on the floor.

'A bit of rain won't put any of those surfers off, trust me. You'd better get changed – we're going out tonight.'

'We're what? Where?' Lahinch was not the type of place that I thought would have a roaring nightlife. Nor was I in the mood for a night out. I had thought of nothing but Tom on the drive here. I analysed the events of that horrible night again and again. Had I overreacted? Was he sorry? Did he mean anything he said? I missed him – I didn't want to, but I did. But I couldn't face him, I couldn't face any of it. Thinking about what had happened was painful enough; I couldn't go through it all again. Seeing him again would just be too much. I had to move on, I just had to.

Putting a smile on my face, I asked Roz where we were going. She stared at me as if I was stupid.

'The pub, of course.'

Old men, pints of Guinness and blaring Irish music are the perfect ingredients for a night of silliness and fun. Neither of us had bothered dressing up much – we just wore jeans and T-shirts. The pub was small and dingy. It had an odd smell and the people who filled it varied from underage drinkers to men who looked like they were on their second hip replacement.

'I have a son that would be absolutely perfect for one of you young and pretty ladies,' said one old guy.

Roz and I sat with our pints, in absolute hysterics. I was really enjoying all the attention, even if it was from someone old enough to be my grandfather.

'Honestly, girls, he's mad into sports, especially surfing. Studying Medicine – nothing like a young doctor-to-be, eh? He's a little on the short side, I am not going to lie, but a few inches can be forgiven, right?' He was a kind old man. No taller than five foot five, so there was not much hope for the son.

Roz had told me earlier that his name was Pat, short for Patrick. He had lived in Lahinch nearly all his life, and owned two of the most popular surf shops. He even claimed that he still surfed himself, though the image of him in a wetsuit made me think of a shrivelled-up prune.

'I am sorry, Pat, but I must inform you that I am a taken woman,' Roz said, already a bit tipsy, laying her hand on Pat's shoulder.

'Well, I hope that man of yours knows how lucky he is. Well, if I was forty years younger I would be lining up to get a date with you.'

Roz went red with embarrassment and I laughed out loud.

'What about yourself, darling?' Pat said, turning to me.

'What about me?' I asked, still struggling to hold in the giggles.

'Do you have yourself a man?'

'She is dating a musician named Tom,' Roz cut in, before I could reply.

'Musicians are so fickle. A smart and pretty girl like yourself can't be dating one of them,' Pat said jokingly.

'Actually we broke up,' I said, barely above a whisper. I could hear my voice cracking and I started to wish that I wasn't in a pub full of people.

'You what?' Roz asked, completely shocked. I had spoken too quietly for Pat though, and he looked between the two of us with a confused look on his face.

'I am sorry, girls, but have I missed something?'

I took a large gulp of my Guinness and I forced a smile on my face before I turned back to Pat. 'I am actually single,' I said.

'Brilliant!' he shouted, patting me on the back with a bit more force than I would have expected from such a frail-looking man. 'Then you can meet my son. You two would be perfect together – he will be home from college next week.'

'Thanks for the offer, but I'm afraid we're only here for the next few days,' I replied politely.

'Another time then, another time. Come on, girls, it's my turn to buy you a round.'

I found it hard to enjoy the rest of the evening. Roz didn't dare say anything while we were in the pub and surrounded by so many people, but I knew the second we were alone she would want to know everything. *I am over him*, I kept telling myself that, *but I don't want to have to relive it all.*

The moment we left the pub, the questions were practically bursting out of Roz's mouth.

'Olive, oh my God, what happened? Why didn't you tell me earlier? Are you OK? You poor thing, is there anything I can do?'

There was no way around it. I had to tell her everything, about meeting his friends, finding out that it was all a bet, getting lost in town. By the time we had reached her house I could feel the tears rolling down my face.

'What an asshole, like seriously. He is like such a piece of shit. You are like way too good for him.' Roz was doing her best to comfort me, but her constant bashing of Tom didn't help. It just made me feel even more of a fool.

'Thanks,' I told her, angry with myself. Why was I crying over a guy who clearly didn't care about me? It was pathetic. I was so sick of crying, I just wanted to be happy again.

It was odd; a year ago it had all been so simple; now it felt as if happiness was an unachievable goal.

'Do you want me to kill him? Honestly, I would have no problem running him over with my car. He is a skinny guy, he probably wouldn't even like make that big of a dent.'

I couldn't help but laugh at this. It wasn't just what Roz was saying, it was her serious tone of voice, as if she meant what she was saying.

'Thanks, but I wouldn't want you to get a criminal record because of him.' I yawned, starting to feel very tired.

'True.' Roz sighed. 'The turd is not even worth it.' She put her arms around me and started leading me back towards the kitchen. When we got there she placed me in a chair next to the table, saying, 'What you need, Olive, my dear, is a smoke.' She pulled out a packet of cigarettes from her back pocket.

'No, thanks,' I told her, but she was already lighting one up for me. 'Honestly, Roz, I don't smoke.'

'Trust me, at times like this nothing helps more than nicotine.' I stared with hesitation at the lit cigarette in Roz's hand. 'Don't worry – it's nothing dodgy, I promise.'

Grudgingly, I took the cigarette, put it in my mouth and inhaled. I immediately began to cough and splutter. The smoke was caught in my throat and it tasted awful.

'You are doing it wrong,' Roz said, inhaling hers with ease. 'Here, let me show you.' She pushed her chair up next to mine so that the two of us were only a few inches apart. 'Breathe it in slowly and hold it here . . .' she was gesturing towards my chest '. . . hold it for a few seconds, and then exhale it slowly.'

I followed her instructions and tried again. This time I managed not to start coughing. I exhaled it slowly and felt the smoke pass through my lungs. I didn't like it. The sensation was unpleasant and it left a horrible taste in my mouth. But I kept doing it, mostly because I just wanted something to keep my mind busy.

'It helps, doesn't it?' Roz asked.

I nodded. 'Yeah, it does a bit. It's like . . . a distraction. Keeps your hands busy.'

The two of us sat there in silence for a while, lost in thought. When Roz spoke again, her tone was completely different.

'Olive, I have something to tell you. I lied.'

'What? When?' I asked, completely confused.

'When I first met you, I told you that I didn't care what my parents think of me, what anyone thinks of me. Well, I do care, a lot more than I probably should.' The joyfulness was no longer in her voice. She spoke clearly and her voice was serious.

'I am jealous of my brother. My parents are so proud of him. They boast about him to their friends, but they never mention me. Sure, half the people who work with my dad don't even know I exist. I once went into his office to meet him for lunch and his secretary wouldn't let me pass. She didn't believe me when I said I was his daughter. She thought I was some snotty teenager making a practical joke. It wasn't until I found some

ID that she eventually apologized and let me by. I was IDed to see my own father.'

Roz took a large inhale of her cigarette before she continued. I didn't say anything. I thought it was important that I didn't, I just needed to listen.

'My mother is even worse. She is constantly comparing me to her friends' daughters. "Suzie's daughter just got a modelling contract . . . Abigail's daughter is a Med student . . . Joanna's daughter is studying acting in New York". Even when I got into UCD she had something negative to say. "Could you not have gotten into Trinity?"' Roz was no longer looking at me but staring at her feet. I put my hand on her shoulder to comfort her.

'It's not just my parents. I care so much about what everyone thinks – even you, Olive. When I first met you, I wanted you to like me so much. You seemed so genuine and sweet, I was willing to do anything. Some of the people I hang out with, I don't even like. They're full of shit and yet I'm so terrified that if I do one thing wrong they will turn on me and I will have no one.'

I noticed that Roz's hands were shaking; she tried to hide it by taking another puff of her cigarette.

'You know what's funny?' I said. Roz lifted her head and looked directly at me. 'When we first met, I couldn't understand why you were being so nice to me. You seemed so fun and exciting and I felt so dull next to you.'

'You could never be dull, Olive,' Roz said, starting to smile again.

'Neither could you,' I replied. I took a minute and thought carefully before I spoke again. 'You know what I think? Just be yourself, Roz, and if there is anyone who doesn't like it . . . well, fuck 'em.'

Roz started laughing. 'Swearing doesn't suit you,' she said, sounding more like herself again.

'I know,' I said, beginning to chuckle myself. 'But sometimes it's necessary.'

Roz stubbed out her cigarette and I did the same.

'You're right. Fuck my parents!' she shouted.

'Fuck Tom!' I joined in.

'Fuck everyone! At least I am not boring!'

We stayed awake for a few hours, playing card games. Roz was laughing and joking like her normal self. As the night went on, I began to wonder if she really did feel better, or had she just put her guard back up. It was impossible to tell. Eventually my tiredness got the better of me and I was finding it difficult to keep my eyes open.

'I am going to get some sleep,' I said, yawning. I began to walk up the stairs towards the bedrooms when I suddenly heard Roz shout my name.

'Yeah?' I shouted back down the stairs.

'Our DMC tonight – just between you and me?'

'Depends on what a DMC *is*.'

'Deep Meaningful Conversation,' she sniggered.

'Oh, of course. And don't tell anyone about the Tom thing either – not even Beth,' I called down.

'I promise,' she replied simply.

I continued to walk up the stairs and when I reached the bedroom, I pulled off my jeans and got straight in the bed.

I had hoped that telling Roz what had happened would make me feel better, but it didn't; I just felt even more foolish. I wondered did she feel the same. The thing that hurt the most was the fact that I had been so convinced that Tom really cared about me. I had been ready to believe whatever he told me. I didn't want anyone else to know how easily I had fallen for his lies.

25

Beth

THERE IS A FEELING YOU GET WHEN YOU KNOW SOMEONE IS perfect for you. It is a sense of calmness and relaxation. It is a knowing that you have an important role in someone's life and that, no matter what, they will always be there. I am so lucky, since not only have I found the perfect person, but he thinks I am perfect too.

Unfortunately, because Michael goes to college in Limerick and because he works most weekends, I do not get to see him that much. In fact, hardly at all. He is a genius; he got full marks in his Leaving Cert like everyone expected him to. He could have done any course he wanted. To outsiders it looks as if he has all the opportunities in the world, but on the inside his life is a complete mess. His family hold him back; they have very little money and constantly depend on him to save them. He lives with his mum and his grandfather; he has never met his father. His mum said that he ran out once he found out she was pregnant, leaving them both with nothing. Michael has no idea about his father – what he is like, whether they resemble each other. Michael claims that it doesn't bother him. He says his father is a stranger to him, a stranger who abandoned his mother. Even if he had the chance, he says, he wouldn't want to meet him.

He went to Limerick IT because it meant he wouldn't have to pay for somewhere to live. He even had to pay his registration fees himself; working nonstop all summer – and even then he wasn't able to pay the full amount. I lent him 500 euro a month ago, when it looked like the college was going to kick him out. Michael was really humiliated. He hates asking for money, especially from me. I have never had any money issues – my parents pay for everything. I never understood what it was like to have to work so hard for everything in life. Nothing had come easy to Michael, everything was a challenge. But when I heard that he might get kicked out, I had to help. I wasn't going to let him miss out on college.

I didn't tell my parents about the money. They would not have approved, they approve of little when it comes to Michael. We just don't speak about him. They pretend that Michael doesn't exist and I pretend not to care what they think, but I do. They have isolated me; now Michael is all I have. I am their only daughter and they see me as a huge disappointment.

My parents are both doctors and they always wanted me to follow in their footsteps. It was one of the few things that we actually agreed on. I loved medicine; the intricate and complex functions of the human body fascinate me. I read all of my dad's medical journals when I was sixteen, and I got an A1 in Chemistry, Physics and Biology in my Leaving Cert. I felt as if I was born to be a doctor and there was nothing else I could imagine myself doing.

Originally, Michael and I both planned to move up to Dublin together. I wanted to get away from my overbearing parents and he wanted to leave his needy and helpless mother. It was simple for me. My parents would pay for me to go anywhere, as long as I studied Medicine, and I didn't feel the need to tell them who I was going to live with.

It was more difficult for Michael. He had to work in the local Tesco every night after school for four years. By the time we were applying to colleges, he had nearly ten grand saved up in the bank. Suddenly our plan looked like it might actually happen; we might both get to escape. But our dream was quickly crushed. After Michael had finished sitting his exams, his grandfather lost his job. He had slipped on an oil stain while working in the local garage and damaged his back so badly that he found it difficult to walk. Michael's mum had never been able to hold down a job. There were numerous medical bills that had to be paid and without a regular income it looked like the three might lose the small apartment that they all lived in together. Michael was forced to give every penny he had saved for his future in order to rescue his mum and grandad.

I had debated staying in Limerick with Michael, but he wouldn't let me. He knew how desperate I was to get away from my parents and the bullies from my old school. It nearly killed me to leave him, but I knew I had to do it. He was coming up to Dublin tonight and I had not seen him in two months. I was practically dancing about my room with excitement.

Roz and Olive were away for the weekend, which was perfect. Not that I didn't want them to eventually meet him – they would, of course, love him as much as I did – but tonight I just wanted him all to myself. I cleaned the whole dorm and bought lots of food and candles. I was not normally romantic, but tonight I wanted to make the effort. I even tried to put rollers in my hair, so it would go big and curly like Olive's, and I tried to do my make-up like Roz's, brave and bold, but it didn't really work. I ended up tying my hair back and cleaning off my face. I didn't look pretty but I looked like me.

As it got closer and closer to when he was supposed to arrive, my stomach began to do flips. I was so nervous, I couldn't stand it. I busied myself by rearranging all the furniture, only to put it all back where it had been. When the doorbell rang I nearly fell over as I sprinted to answer it.

He was slightly out of breath when I let him in. His thin frame was exaggerated by the fact that he was wearing a black skinny jumper. I loved his short blond hair and blue eyes.

'Hi, Beth, I've missed you,' he said. He spoke with a slight lisp. His Limerick accent sounded stronger than normal – maybe it was because I had been in Dublin for so long. He kissed my forehead and made his way into the common room. I noticed that his hands were shaking – he seemed unsettled and nervous. This made me curious; Michael was not the type of person to get nervous. He was very logical and sensible.

He let out a sigh when he saw the meal I had prepared, and said, 'Oh, Beth, I am seriously impressed.' I smiled, absolutely delighted with myself.

We talked endlessly throughout dinner. Neither of us ate much because we were too busy catching up. He told me about his family, his course – he was an Engineering student, hoping to major in Electrical Engineering. He was fascinated by circuits and the construction of electrical patterns. When he spoke about his course I normally didn't understand half of it. But I loved his passion for it.

I told him all about what I was learning in Medicine and how close I was becoming to Olive and Roz. Michael and I had talked every night on the phone, but it still felt like I had so much to tell him, to share with him. A lifetime didn't seem long enough to say everything I wanted to say. My cooking skills were not something to be desired, but tonight I felt it had all gone successfully. I had bought the Dolmio lasagne set, which in reality is cheating a little bit, and had followed the instructions as carefully as I could. It didn't look as delicious as the picture, but it was edible and even a little tasty once you covered it with salt.

'Did you ever report those girls from your old school to the Guards?' Michael asked suddenly, abruptly changing the subject. Maybe this was what he had been nervous about.

'No, there's no point,' I replied, wishing the topic hadn't been brought up.

'No point? Beth, they broke your laptop and it sounds as if they would have beaten you up if Olive hadn't been there.'

'I doubt they're going to come up to Dublin again. Do you want more food?'

Michael's plate still had plenty of lasagne on it; I just desperately wanted to change the subject. I hated talking about those girls – even thinking about them made me nervous. I'd been sure that I was rid of them when I moved to Dublin, but when I'd seen them that day, I had been terrified. Michael had always wanted me to do something – report them or tell the school, but I never had. I was too afraid that my parents would have moved me to yet another school, so I had forced myself to deal with it. I wasn't sure why I still kept it a secret even after I had left school. I guess I was ashamed, ashamed that I was so afraid and that I was such a coward when it came to those girls. I didn't want anyone to know.

'Well, what if they do, Beth? They could really hurt you. If you tell the Guards, then at least they will go to their houses and give them a good scare.'

'It would only make it worse.' I walked over to the sink and started to pretend to clean my plate. I could feel the tears in my eyes and I didn't want him to see them.

I heard Michael moving his chair out and felt him put his arms around my waist.

'I didn't mean to upset you,' he said, whispering in my

ear. 'I just wish I could take you away from people like that.'

'Me too,' I choked, trying to wipe away the tears.

'I have some news,' he said suddenly.

I turned around to face him with his arms still wrapped around me. 'Oh really?' I asked.

'I got a letter from the University of Melbourne in Australia. They have offered me a full scholarship starting at the end of January.'

I didn't know how to feel. Of course I was thrilled for him. He deserved an opportunity like that more than anyone, but my heart sank when I heard the word 'Australia', and January was so close.

'That's great,' I whispered, but I could feel the tears rolling down my cheeks again.

'Wait, I have more.' His smile broadened and I could feel his whole body start to shake. 'I want you to come with me.'

For a moment I felt the excitement rush through my body. Australia! I could get away from here, from the pressure, the fear. I could apply for colleges when I got there. I had a perfect Leaving Cert, so getting into another Medicine course should be easy. But this feeling only lasted for a moment before reality sank in.

'I am so flattered – but I can't. My parents are generous, but there is no way they will pay for me to live over there, and I have none of my own money saved up.'

'The scholarship pays for everything,' Michael said, still shaking with excitement.

'It won't pay for me to live with you.'

'Actually it will.' I stared at him, completely confused now. 'When I applied for the scholarship, I told them I was married. The apartment they are giving me is for me and my wife.'

I felt like I was a step behind and that I wasn't understanding what was going on.

'But when we get over there they are going to want proof,' I said, bewildered. 'A Marriage Certificate . . . They will take the scholarship away if they find out you were lying.'

He stared at me with a smug look. It was like he was teasing me and wouldn't tell me the answer to a very important question.

'I know,' he said, suddenly serious again. 'That's why I want you to marry me.'

My jaw dropped and I just looked at him in silence.

'Beth, you are amazing. You are smart and so unbelievably kind. The highlight of my day is when I get to talk to you. When something good happens, I feel that I have to tell you first, before I can truly enjoy it. When I think about the future, I think about it with you in it always. Neither of us have had the easiest lives so far and I want to start a new one, together . . . Will you marry me?'

I was crying again, but this time it was with tears of joy.

'I want to spend the rest of my life with you too,' I said in between sobs. 'Yes, of course I will marry you.'

Suddenly Michael also burst into tears; he placed his hands on either side of my face and started to kiss me. When he finally pulled away, he reached into his pocket and pulled out a small blue velvet box.

'My grandad said it belonged to my grandmother. It's not valuable, and as soon as I make some money I will buy you a proper one. But I thought it would be nice to have something to make it . . . seem real.' He opened the box to reveal a ring. It had a gold band with one small and simple diamond. It looked old and a little battered, but it was beautiful. He slipped it onto my finger and I knew instantly that this was perfect. *We* were perfect.

Then a thought struck me. 'My parents! How are we going to tell my parents? They are going to be furious.'

Michael's smile faded for a moment.

'I know. I thought I could come home with you at Christmas and we could tell them then. Whatever they say, we will deal with it together, OK?'

'We will deal with it together,' I repeated, and then he kissed me.

26
Tom

'DO YOU HAVE THE NEW *TWILIGHT* BOOKS?' I HAD BEEN WORKING in Murder's Foulest Things for a few weeks now, and there was one thing that I had learned for certain: I was no good at dealing with people.

'No, we only do murder mysteries,' I said for the third time. This girl looked about fourteen and she had come in nearly every day for the past week, always asking for books that were clearly not murder books.

'But do you have anything like *Twilight*?' she asked again, blinking her big eyes up at me.

'Not really.' I sighed, ready to throw something.

I wanted to walk away but Moiraine had said that we needed more sales if I wanted to get more hours.

'We have murder mysteries about vampires,' I said helpfully, showing her a book with a grotesque picture of some sort of bloody monster on the front.

'Is it romantic?' she asked, clearly repulsed by the picture.

'Yeah, sure, why not?' I lied, my patience running thin with this girl.

'OK, I'll get it.'

'Great.' She was smiling and giggling to herself when I put the book through the cash register and handed it to her; she had a high-pitched laugh that reminded me of hyenas.

As soon as she had left, I rubbed my hands through my hair and kicked the bin on the floor next to me.

'Hey, you break that and you can buy me a new one.' Moiraine was coming out of the back room with two cups of tea.

'Sorry,' I muttered as she handed me a cup. 'It's just that stupid girl has been in here *six times*, and she still hasn't seemed to grasp the fact that we sell murder mystery novels.'

Moiraine raised her eyebrow at me. 'Give the poor girl a break,' she said. 'She has a crush on you.'

'She *what*?' I asked, nearly spilling my tea. 'But she's only a kid!'

Moiraine shook her head and looked at me as if I was the stupid one. Then she said, 'At least you're getting slightly better at dealing with customers. Might be able to give you more hours, after all.'

I smiled at her in thanks. I was going to need all the money I could get.

The day after I had left my mum's house I had used what little money I had to buy a new mobile. It was the cheapest model I could find but it did the job. I rang my mum, explaining to her where I had gone. I knew I had to tell her – she was bound to panic and ring the Guards if I was missing, and I needed to make sure she didn't do that. She had cried nearly the whole time on the phone, begging me to go and live with my dad. She had never once said I could go back and live with her. A small part of me had been hoping that she would, but I guess that was too much to wish for.

I told her I wasn't going to live with Dad and then hung up.

I felt horrible for being so cruel, but it was torture listening to her sobbing. She rang me back on Christmas Day; Peter had gone to stay with his family so I had the apartment to myself. She wasn't crying this time, but I could tell she was on the verge of tears.

'Your college fees need to be paid by the end of the month, don't they?'

'Yes,' I replied. Fees needed to be paid before exams at the end of January, otherwise you were not allowed to sit your exams – and if you didn't sit your exams, you lost your college place.

The truth was, I knew I was bright. I had barely worked for my Leaving Cert and yet I had still done better than most. Even now in college I knew I could do the minimum required and still get away with Cs. I was a coaster, unmotivated to do better than average. But college was important to me: it was one of the only things that I had achieved for myself, and at the moment it was the only thing over which I still had control.

'They will kick me out if it's not paid soon,' I said hesitantly.

'Well, your father . . .' she stumbled at the word, 'and I have agreed that if you don't move in with him by the time the fees are due, we are not paying for you to attend college any more.'

It was a body blow; I felt as if I couldn't breathe. I had never asked for any money off my parents other than to pay for college. Registration fees were only about 1,600 euro but it was still way more money than I had. I wanted to scream at her, cry, beg. I felt cornered, trapped. College was all I had, and she knew that.

'Please.' My throat was swelling up and my eyes were burning. 'Mum, please. I can't . . .' This time it was her turn to hang up on me. I saw one of Peter's pint glasses sitting on his table and threw it across the room. It smashed against the wall and glass went everywhere. I wanted to throw more, break more, but I didn't. This wasn't my home. I had no right to ruin Peter's stuff.

I spent the rest of the day watching whatever DVDs Peter owned, avoiding anything even slightly related to Christmas. I didn't mind being alone and away from my mum for Christmas. In fact, I was quite happy to pretend it wasn't happening. Christmas was probably the hardest time on my mum. She would put so much pressure on herself to get the best tree, decorate our house and cook an elaborate Christmas feast. But something would always go wrong. She would run out of money or perhaps set the oven on fire. Either way it would end the same. She would start crying uncontrollably and I would have to spend the rest of the day comforting her and taking care of her. We would then cancel on any cousins, or aunts and uncles who might have invited us over, thereby ruining all our chances at a happy Christmas. I didn't even know if family members bothered to invite us over any more. I did wonder for a moment what my mother might have been doing this Christmas, but I pushed it to the back of my mind. She had given up on me and I was no longer going to think or worry about her.

I noticed a change in attitude when Peter returned on Boxing Day. He had been relaxed the first few days when I had moved in, but lately I felt that my welcome was wearing thin. He never said anything, but I think that was because he knew that I had no other choice. He only had one bedroom so I slept on his couch with pillows and a duvet that I had bought in Penneys. He said I had to pay for my own food, which I had agreed to. This meant a lot of Tesco Value shopping. I ate food that was cheap and unhealthy. But I knew I was lucky. If Peter's father found out I was living here he would make me pay half the rent, something that I definitely could not afford.

Lately I had begun to feel that my life all seemed to come down to money, and everything depended on how I was going to get more. If I was lucky I made about 80 euro a week with Moiraine. It was very little but I knew she paid me as much as she could. I was aware that she had money struggles as well, and I didn't have the heart to ask for more. My only hope was to try and get another job, but that was difficult in this recessive climate. Even places like McDonald's and Eddie Rockets were not hiring. Also, I was attending college every day up until the Christmas holidays, trying to get as much value out of it as I could before they kicked me out. I suddenly found myself envying the foreigners standing behind the fast-food counters.

'Have you spoken to your mum recently?' Moiraine asked while sipping on her tea. She knew the whole story, about how I had left and was now living on Peter's couch; it had been one of her conditions when hiring me. She said that I had to tell her everything, no secrets. I had worried that she would tell me to leave as soon as she heard about the story with the vodka, but she didn't say anything, she had just looked sad for me.

'She rang last week, asking whether I had changed my mind. I told her no and then she hung up again.'

Moiraine looked at me with those concerned eyes. I wished she wouldn't. I knew she had plenty of her own worries even if she never shared them with me.

'What about your dad?' she persevered.

I just shook my head. My dad hadn't called once since I had left home. I found this a bit ironic, since he was supposed to be the one straightening me out. But it was no surprise; he had never cared before – why would he start now?

Moiraine looked down at her watch. 'It's six. I'll lock up and you can head on home.'

I gave her a smile of gratitude and ran outside the door. It was New Year's Eve tonight so the shop wouldn't be open tomorrow.

I began to undo the padlock around my bike outside the shop. Peter had given it to me; it was old and rusty, but it meant that I didn't have to waste money on bus fares every day. All I ever seemed to think about these days was how I was going to save money. I never went out any more, it was too expensive. I didn't mind, though. I was always afraid that if I did go out with Peter and Damien, I might run into Olive. I would be lying if I didn't admit that I wished I could just blow it all off, get really drunk and pretend that none of these bad things was happening. But they were – and nothing I did seemed to make any of it better.

I had lost Olive's number along with everyone else's when I had broken my phone. It was no excuse, though; I had cycled halfway to UCD and back again six times in the last week alone. It was just less than a month since it had all happened and I relived every moment constantly. I didn't know what to say, what I could do to make it right again. All I knew was that I needed to do something. She had been so angry, so upset. I was desperate to know that she was OK; my biggest regret was letting her run away that night. Where did she go? How did she get home? I wanted to apologize – at least, I think I wanted to apologize. I wasn't sure what I wanted or expected from her. I had thought about that night a lot since it had happened. I knew I had ruined it just like I had ruined everything else. I needed to give up.

I looked from left to right as I was about to cross the road and I suddenly noticed that someone was waving at me. Beth was smiling broadly and she started hurrying in my direction. I had never considered Beth an attractive girl. I always thought of her as the type who blended into the background. But today I took notice. Her face was glowing, her hair was loose, and even as she ran her smile never faltered. I was completely taken aback; she looked very pretty, even beautiful.

'Tom!' she gasped when she finally reached me.

I stepped off my bike and leaned it against a wall. 'Hi, Beth, how are you?'

'I am fantastic,' she said, still puffing a bit after her short run. It was easy to see that she wasn't athletic. 'I am moving to Australia.'

'Oh wow!' I said, shocked. 'When are you going?'

'Next week.' She grinned.

'*Next week?*' I suddenly noticed a small diamond ring on her left hand. 'Are you . . . ? Is that . . . ? Who . . . ?' I stammered, unable to form a coherent sentence.

'I am getting married.' Beth was alight with excitement. 'I know it's crazy, but my boyfriend – I mean fiancé – Michael is just amazing. We have been dating for years and I know he is The One. So we're going to move to Australia together and get married.'

'Congratulations,' I said. The whole situation seemed completely surreal. Beth was younger than me and yet she was making this huge commitment, taking this enormous chance with someone she loved – and she was so sure. She was completely and utterly sure.

'Thanks,' she said. She seemed to be beaming even more now.

We both stood there in awkward silence for a while. I couldn't fight the temptation any more: I had to ask.

'How's Olive?'

Beth gave me a compassionate smile before answering. 'She's good. She and Roz went to Lahinch for a little while. They seemed to have a lot of fun.'

'That's good. Well, I'd better go.' I wished I hadn't said anything. I began to get back on my bike, when Beth spoke again.

'She misses you.'

'What?' I asked, turning to look at her.

'She didn't say that – she actually refuses to talk about you at all – but I know she misses you and I think you miss her too.'

'I . . .' I went quiet; I didn't know what I had been planning to say.

'We are having a going away/New Year's Eve party tonight. It's in our dorm. Olive came back up to Dublin for it. Why don't you come?'

I opened and closed my mouth silently like a goldfish. I was trying to think of an excuse but everything I thought of just sounded so pathetic.

'I don't know why you guys broke up, but – I don't know. Maybe it's because I am so pro-love these days but I think you can fix it. I hope you can come.' She didn't say anything else; she just turned around and walked away before I had a chance to reply.

I was a bit dazed, cycling back to Peter's, and ended up turning the wrong way twice. I couldn't stop thinking about what Beth had said. Over the past few weeks I had convinced myself that Olive was over me, that she didn't care about me. But what if Beth was right? What if she did miss me? What if we were fixable? I was still completely in my own world when I walked into Peter's apartment.

Peter was just getting out of the shower; he gave me a slap on the back when he saw me.

'Hello, Mr Minimum Wage. How was work?'

I leaned the bike up against the wall and went to get myself a glass of water. 'Long,' I sighed, sitting down on the couch.

'To me you look like you need a good night out. Damien and I are heading to McGowan's, it will be hopping tonight.'

I put my hand through my hair in frustration. 'Peter, you know I can't afford to go out. Unless you want me to be sleeping on your couch for ever?'

'Of course I fucking don't, but you have been moping around here for weeks now. You're not still pissed at Damien, are you?'

'No, of course not.' I had apologized to Damien after that night but I still found it difficult to be around him. Every time

I thought about how he had ruined everything I wanted to hit him. But it wasn't his fault, it was all mine; it was my bet. Fortunately he had not been stupid enough to ask for his winnings. I think that would have sent me over the edge.

'Then what is the problem? Is it that girl Olive? It is, isn't it?' I sat there silently; I wasn't in the mood to be slagged. 'If you like the girl so much, then get her to forgive you. You seem to have a way with girls. I'm sure you can pull it off.'

'Doubt it,' I said under my breath, but Peter still heard me.

'Well, do *something* 'cause you're pissing me off.' He threw the towel he had been using in my face and then walked into his bedroom, slamming the door behind him.

'Fuck,' I said, putting my head down in between my legs. I closed my eyes and started to breathe in deeply. *Don't be a fucking coward.* I sprang up and grabbed my bag of clothes that I kept under the couch, pulled out the single shirt that I owned and threw it on. It was a blue and white striped shirt – my mum had bought it for me for my last birthday. I felt strange in it, since I was used to comfy T-shirts, but I wanted to make the effort tonight. I ran to the bathroom and tried to flatten my messy hair with water. It wasn't working and eventually I gave up.

'I am going out,' I shouted to Peter.

'Good,' he replied from inside his room. I was about to leave when I noticed a bottle of whiskey sitting on Peter's counter; it was only just opened and was practically full. I could feel my hand quivering with nerves as I held the door half-open. Just one or two shots to calm my nerves, I thought to myself. Just a couple and then I will go talk to her.

27
Olive

ROZ AND I WERE IN COMPLETE SHOCK WHEN BETH FIRST TOLD us; it was all like a fairytale. The boy gets this amazing opportunity and when it looks like he is leaving for ever, he asks the girl to marry him. They don't care about anyone else, only each other. It was so romantic, and Beth was so happy. But soon reality destroyed the fairytale for me; I couldn't help but think about how crazy it all was.

They were only eighteen. How on earth were they supposed to know if they really loved each other? What were they supposed to do if it didn't work out? Beth said that her parents had disowned her once she had told them. I was stunned when she told me this, but she herself didn't seem the least bit surprised.

'They have always hated Michael. I knew I was going to marry him one day and that when that day came, they wouldn't accept it. It's all just happening a bit quicker than I had expected, but I knew how they would react. I just have to hope they will change their minds one day.'

She hadn't seemed sad or upset when she told me about her

parents' disapproval. I seemed to be more worried about the whole situation than she was. I couldn't imagine being so distant from your family like that, but I guess Michael was going to be her family now. She had told me that she was taking the little money she had left to pay for her flight over and then she hoped to find a job quickly enough.

'How are you going to pay for college?' I asked sceptically.

'I am going to work for a year and then I will apply at the start of the next college year.' Beth was already starting to pack her things.

'Will you make enough money in one year to pay all your fees? Is it not very expensive to attend college over there?'

'I don't know. I am hoping that I will be able to manage it all. I have to stay optimistic.' Her tone was sharp and I knew she wanted me to stop asking questions. I was ruining her fantasy.

I kept all my worries and questions to myself in the days leading up to their departure. In the short time that I had known Beth I had never seen her so happy or content and I wasn't going to be the one to ruin that for her. Roz wasn't as subtle.

'Are you pregnant?'

'No,' Beth replied, laughing.

'Then why on earth are you getting married?'

Beth told us the whole situation about the college scholarship and about how Michael had applied as a married man, meaning that Beth would benefit from the scholarship too.

'But it's also because we love each other and we want to start a new life together.'

'When are you getting married?'

'When we arrive in Australia. A beach wedding, you know? Just the two of us.'

'That does sound amazing,' I said, trying to stay positive.

'I am sad,' Roz said, and Beth and I both stared at her, confused, 'that we won't get to be your bridesmaids.'

Beth smiled. 'I know, I thought of that. But I really don't want to have it here. I would be so afraid that my parents would find out and try to spoil the whole thing. My dad threatened to send me away when we told him at Christmas. I had to remind him that I am eighteen now and he can't legally stop me.' For a moment a look of sadness washed over Beth's face. It disappeared as quickly as it came, but I knew I had seen it. 'I need to get out of this country as soon as possible. I will send you guys loads of photos, I promise.'

Roz was the one to decide that we should throw Beth a going-away party. She had wanted to have a New Year's Eve party anyway, and she saw Beth's departure as a good excuse. She had invited loads of people that Beth and I had never even heard of, but Beth didn't mind. She seemed to be enjoying all of the attention.

It appeared that, like myself, most people had returned to Dublin for New Year's. I had been happy of the excuse to come back. Christmas had been strange this year – not sad, not upsetting – just completely different. We still did the same things that we had done every year, dinner at my uncle's, walking down to the village to watch the carollers. It had even snowed this year, only a light shower on Christmas Eve. By noon the next day it had nearly all melted away. The three of us had done our best to put on a brave face, but there were moments when it was so obvious that someone was missing. Like when my father unpacked our stockings from storage, Andy's name just stared back at him in bright gold stitching. He put it up without hesitation; Andy was still part of our Christmas. Or when my mum cooked too much food for just three people, or when we started to pull crackers. I had always pulled my cracker with Andy and he had always won. Christmas didn't seem real this year. I had expected it to be incredibly sad and at times it was. But there were other times when I had found myself laughing and smiling without it being forced. Times when I had felt warm and safe. A sensation that I came to realize I had missed terribly.

Roz told me she had invited over thirty people to our dorm for the party. I began to panic. Our dorm was small and it could only hold around fifteen people if we were lucky. We moved most of the furniture into our bedrooms so that all that was left was a couch and a few chairs. Roz bought an obscene amount of alcohol – vodka, wine and champagne. She was being incredibly generous to Beth, even offering all her clothes to choose from for the going-away party. Beth took her up on the offer, borrowing a very colourful summer dress. It was completely different to what she would normally wear, but she said she wanted to get in the mood for Australia.

Michael was the first to arrive. He seemed nervous when Roz and I introduced ourselves but he soon relaxed as Beth took his hand. He was quirky and unusual; he talked quickly and seemed to know a lot about everything. It was obvious that he was absolutely smitten with Beth. Every time he glanced at her, he looked as if he couldn't believe his luck. Roz had invited Ed; he was very dark and handsome. But after speaking to him for a while, I realized that he was very eccentric. He talked about myths and stories as if they were facts, and Roz seemed to eat up every word he said. He reminded me of Captain Jack Sparrow, without the beard.

As the night went on, more and more people arrived, none of whom I recognized. Roz and Ed had begun kissing on the couch and they stayed in that position for the rest of the night. Beth and Michael also kept to themselves, staying in the corner, talking animatedly about their plans for Australia. I began to worry that I would be in charge of entertaining these people, but luckily they all seemed to know each other and there was plenty of alcohol to keep them occupied.

'Well, hello there, Olive.' I turned around to see a blonde girl whom I instantly recognized as Alison. I noticed a bulky guy standing behind her looking very moody, and I suddenly felt even more intimidated by her.

'Alison. How are you? It's been a while since I have seen you.' She nodded, giving me her best pout. I didn't want to say too much in front of Cian.

'Fantastic, thanks. Daddy bought me a Range Rover for Christmas. He really is the best.' Alison may have been intimidating but she was a terrible liar. 'I hear you were dating Tom,' she said, suddenly changing the subject.

'Yes, I was. Not any more though,' I said awkwardly, wondering how she knew.

'Good choice, hun. That boy has shagged nearly everything in Dublin. He is such a man-whore. You don't know what disease you would get from him.' I nodded, feeling worse with every word she said. 'And the way girls just fall at his feet is so desperate and sad. Is he coming tonight?' she asked, looking around the room.

'I doubt it,' I said, confused by her odd behaviour.

'Good, good. I personally really dislike that boy,' she said, still looking around the room and sounding a little disappointed.

I muttered some excuse and ran off. I was relieved to get away from Alison but now I had no one to talk to. Roz was still busy kissing Ed and I didn't want to intrude on Beth and Michael. It was their night, after all. For the first time in a long time, I felt really lonely. I didn't have someone like Roz and Beth did; even stupid Alison had a boyfriend who at least cared enough to be with her. And the only guy I wanted, that I truly wanted, had treated me horribly. I was the same as all the girls that Alison was describing: I was pathetic and desperate. It had been weeks since I saw him, and still I felt hurt and betrayed. I could feel the tears beginning to well up in my eyes and I was about to step into my room to take some time to get myself together when I heard the sound of glass smashing. It had come from the other side of the room and I pushed my way through the people to see what had happened.

Tom was picking up shards of broken glass clumsily from the ground. A small crowd had gathered around to watch him. He had knocked over a small table that had a lot of empty glasses and beer bottles on it.

'What are you doing here!' I exclaimed without thinking. He stood up quickly when he saw me, dropping all the glass that he had picked up. I noticed that he had small cuts on his hand from trying to gather the glass.

'Olive! I'm sorry, I didn't mean to . . . I just bumped into the table. Can we talk?'

He was slurring his words and his eyes were unfocused. I grabbed him by the arm and pulled him outside into the corridor. I hated everyone looking. I slammed the door behind us and when I let go of him he stumbled a bit, but recovered quickly.

'What are you doing, Tom?' I hissed. How could he just turn up like this? And he was drunk.

'I need to talk to you.' I could tell he was trying desperately to stand straight and speak coherently.

'You're drunk,' I said with contempt. 'Go home.'

'Well, funny story, Olive, I don't *have* a home. Nobody wants me, nobody cares.'

His voice was starting to crack and I could see tears in his eyes. But I still couldn't help how I felt. I was furious. I tried to walk back inside but he stopped me.

'Please don't be mad at me. I can explain.' He stared at me with those gorgeous eyes that I had fallen for so easily before. I had been like all those other pathetic girls; I was nothing more than a number to him. Suddenly it felt like something inside me just snapped, and before I knew what I was doing, I was screaming at him.

'I have every right to be angry! You are an asshole! You treated me like shit! You made me feel like nothing!' I expected him to look embarrassed. To come out with some pathetic excuse and then leave, but he didn't. He only stared back at me and I couldn't understand the look on his face, what emotion he was portraying.

His eyes became focused. For the first time that night he looked sober. I was shocked to see anger on his face.

'You felt like nothing? You felt like nothing for once in your life? I *am* nothing! I have been nothing every single day of my life. I *have* nothing! My mum has kicked me out, my dad can't even look at me, and my sister barely recognizes me! I have no money, nowhere to live and I won't be able to go back to college – the only thing that I had going for me in my life – and now you stand there wanting me to feel sorry for *you*? When I met you, I thought for once in my crappy life that I could actually be happy, but you can't even look at me now! And as always I fucked everything up. You don't get to be angry any more, Olive, it's my turn. Because once again I have turned everything to shit, and I really tried with you. I am still trying. I want you, and I don't want to give up. I give up on everything, but not this time.' He seemed surprised at how much he had said. He was trembling, and he had gone completely pale.

I stood there stunned, at a loss. I couldn't talk, I couldn't think. I could only stare at him and he stared back. Before I had time to decide anything, Tom moved and within three strides he was standing right in front of me. He put his hand behind my head and kissed me with such intensity that my knees nearly buckled. I wanted to pull away but I could feel my lips moving with his. It felt so good but there was something wrong. I could hear laughter. Damien laughing at me when he told me about the bet, Alison laughing at all the silly girls who fell for Tom, and then I could hear Tom's laughter: he was tricking me again. I pushed him away but he still had my face in his hands.

'I have to go.' I tried to walk away but his grip was firm.

'Please, Olive. Please forgive me.' There were tears running down his face now and I could feel myself starting to cry also.

'I can't,' I said, placing my hands on his. 'I just can't – I can't trust you any more. What you did – it was horrible, and you can't just kiss me and expect it all to go away. I need you to go. Please just go.' I was full-on sobbing now and it was becoming hard for me to speak.

'Olive, I—'

'Go, Tom – please, just leave.' I have no idea what he was going to say and I don't think I will ever find out. He took his hands away from my face and slowly started to walk down the stairs and out of the main door.

I couldn't stop myself from crying. I felt so battered and bruised. I tried to wipe the tears away but it was hard without being able to see myself. I went back inside to the party and made a dash for the bathroom. No one seemed to notice that I had even been gone. There was a queue for our small, dingy bathroom but I just shoved past all of them. One girl started to complain but I just shouted, 'I live here, fuck off!' and slammed the door in her face.

I turned around to look at myself in the mirror. My black eyeliner was completely smudged. My eyes were red and swollen and my bottom lip was quivering. I didn't look like me; I looked like a lost little girl. That wasn't me; I wasn't going to let it be me. I reapplied my make-up, eliminating any traces of redness or tears. By the time I was finished the girl in the queue was practically breaking the door down. I had expected her to shout and swear when I finally opened the door, but instead she just shoved me to the side and ran into the bathroom. She was obviously dying to go.

I walked back out into the party and pretended the last twenty minutes had never happened. When the countdown to midnight started, I disappeared into my room. I wanted to be alone.

28
Tom

MY KNUCKLES WERE BLEEDING AFTER PUNCHING THE concrete wall outside the dorm repeatedly. I didn't even know why I was doing it, or why I'd stopped, I just had. I couldn't stretch my fingers out properly – broken, it made sense. I started to walk away; I couldn't stay here, so close to her, any more. There were people scattered across the campus but I couldn't seem to distinguish anyone's face. There was no point really. I looked at my watch – 11.30 p.m. If I was lucky I could catch the last bus back. I suddenly felt a hand on my shoulder. I turned around to see a large foreign guy wearing a yellow vest with a walkie-talkie in his hand. He was looking down at my hands; there was really a lot of blood.

'What happened to you? Were you fighting on campus?' he asked in a voice that sounded like a bulldog barking. I shook my head but I knew that wouldn't be enough for him.

'Come on, mate, out you go.' I didn't struggle; I wanted – I needed – to leave anyway.

It was strange how calm I had become, no longer angry, no longer sad. I was just numb. As soon as I had stopped punching the wall I knew what I had to do. I had run out of options, there was no other choice left. I managed to catch the very last bus. It was full with people heading out for the night. The driver gave me a funny look when I paid for my ticket but he didn't stop me. I tried to clean off the dried blood with the cuff of my shirt. My right hand was a lot worse; it had swollen to twice its size and I was no longer able to move my fingers at all. It was really starting to hurt.

When I finally reached my stop I knew the bus driver was happy to see me leave. Some state I must have looked. At least I felt sober now. I hesitated before knocking on the door. What was I supposed to say? I looked down at my watch – a quarter past midnight. *Fuck!* I took a deep breath and knocked, using my left hand. I stood there for a while in silence. I was relieved to see that there were lights on downstairs. I had been worried that they might have gone out for New Year's Eve. It was another few minutes before I could hear the keys being scraped in the door.

When Robin finally pulled the door open, she stood there looking at me in complete surprise. She was wearing a light-blue dress and her blonde hair was done up in a chignon. She had a glass of champagne in her right hand.

'Tom! What on earth are you doing? What happened to your hand?' She was staring down at the purple mess that was my hand.

'Is it OK if I move in now?' I sounded pathetic and lost, but still I felt nothing. For the first time ever I saw true concern on Robin's face. True concern for me – it was strange to see.

'Come in.' I noticed that she hadn't actually answered my question, but I was just grateful that she hadn't told me to leave. I had half-expected that. She sat me down in their living room and started to examine my hand. 'That's definitely broken,' she said. 'Let me see the other hand.' I lifted my left hand for her to examine. I wasn't going to argue with her. 'This is not as bad, but there will be some bruising. I have a first-aid kit upstairs.' I looked at her, a little confused. 'I'm a nurse, Tom,' she explained. 'I work in the hospital in town.'

'I knew that,' I mumbled, ashamed and a little sad. I had a vague memory of Paddy telling me what Robin did before. It had been a long time ago, when I had blamed her for my parents' divorce. I had wanted to know nothing about her. I had blamed everything on her, but it wasn't fair, it wasn't her fault. Nothing had been her fault.

I noticed a picture of Robin and Paddy sitting on the table next to me. Robin was in a white dress and Paddy was in a suit. I had been invited to their wedding but Mum had begged me not to go. I hadn't minded at the time. I didn't like Robin and I knew I would have been bored. But looking at that photo made me feel as if I was going to throw up.

Paddy came back in with Robin. He just stood to the side as she started to clean and bandage my hand. I couldn't look at him. I only looked at the floor. It was obvious I had disturbed their celebrations.

'Were you in a fight?' He sounded aggressive – I guess that was to be expected.

'No,' I muttered back. I looked up and I could tell from the expression on his face that I needed to tell him more. 'I punched a wall, I was . . . upset.' He seemed satisfied with that answer for now and didn't ask any more.

'You will need painkillers for that, but I am guessing you have . . . alcohol in your system?' I knew Robin meant drugs but I was not in the mood to defend myself so I just nodded. 'Well then, we'll wait till the morning before I give you anything.' Again I nodded. 'Paddy, go grab him a pillow and a blanket, will you? He can sleep on the couch tonight.'

Paddy was silent in his actions and he practically threw the pillow and duvet at me. His anger would not be so silent in the morning.

It was a long time before I could fall asleep. The pain in my hand had grown really bad. I wished Robin had just given me the painkillers. I could hear the muffled discussion that they were having upstairs. It was mostly Paddy who talked but I couldn't make out what he was saying. It was a good hour before they fell silent.

As the morning came, the realization of what I had done started to sink in. My head was banging and my hand was unbearably sore. I was shocked to look at it and see the amount of damage I had done to myself. Paddy was down to me promptly at 7.30 a.m.; his anger had only grown during the night.

'What the hell do you think you were doing, pulling a stunt like that last night! You scared Robin half to death. She wanted to take you to hospital. Personally, I was ready to call the Guards.'

I stared down at my feet, too ashamed even to look at him.

'Where have you been staying the last few weeks?'

'A friend's house,' I mumbled.

'Stop with your vague shit and look at me.' I slowly lifted my head; the vein in his forehead looked ready to burst. '*Where have you been staying?*'

'Peter Roche's apartment.' I didn't dare look away.

'Does Peter's dad know you have been staying there?' I shook my head. 'Of course he doesn't. The man would rather kick someone out on the street than let them live somewhere for free.' Ironically enough, Paddy used to work for Peter's dad. Peter's family owned a string of bars and restaurants in Dublin, but when the recession hit they had had to close about a third of them. Peter's dad still made plenty of money, but Paddy had worked in one of the bars that had closed. It had left him jobless for months.

'Well, it is Peter's apartment.' I regretted saying it before I had even finished the sentence; Paddy grabbed me by the shoulders and stood me up so that our faces were less than an inch apart.

'Now you listen to me! Snide and sarcastic remarks like that will not get you far with me! Peter's dad pays for the apartment. *He* owns the apartment. Therefore *he* gets to decide who lives there and who doesn't – not Peter!'

He let my shoulders go and started pacing up and down the room. I was unsure of what to do. Did I sit back down? I stayed standing. To be honest he was scaring me and I didn't want to say or do anything that would upset him. He needed to let me stay; I had nowhere else to go, especially now that he knew I had been staying with Peter. He was bound to tell his dad. Peter would be livid with me if I got him in trouble; his dad had an awful temper. He constantly vented his anger on Peter and Peter would just take it; in return, everything he could ever want was given to him.

Paddy was rubbing his chin with his hand, thinking intently.

'You can stay, but there are going to be rules. First of all, no drugs or drink are to be brought into this house. If you ever come home drunk or high there will be serious hell to pay. Secondly, I want to know where you are at all times. You are either at college or here – there is to be no more partying and staying out all night. Thirdly, you are going to come and work with me in the pub after college; you are going to pay rent and earn your keep. Do you understand all that?'

I nodded, starting to wish I had made a runner before everyone had woken up.

'This is Robin and my home. You are a guest in this house.' More like a prisoner, I thought. 'You fuck up and you're gone.' Again I nodded.

Paddy just stared at me silently for the next ten minutes. I could tell that he was already thinking this was a huge mistake.

I stood my ground; I wasn't sure what he wanted me to say. It was true that I had nowhere to go: that fact was far too obvious. But there was no way that I was going to beg to stay. Maybe he wanted me to say thank you. Well, that definitely wasn't going to happen either. I had nothing to be thankful for. He didn't want me here; he was only taking me because he knew he had to. I was his son, no matter how much he wished I wasn't.

Finally the silence was broken by Robin entering the room.

'Are you guys ready?' she asked. She had a red travelling coat on and was wrapping a purple scarf around her neck.

'Ready for what?' I asked. Robin looked at Paddy and he groaned before answering.

'Robin reckons that that hand of yours should be looked at by a doctor. She is afraid you may have done some nerve damage.' I looked down at myself. I only had the clothes that I had been wearing the night before. The shirt that my mum had bought me was covered in blood. My jeans had numerous stains on them – I had fallen a couple of times on my way to UCD. I couldn't go to a doctor's looking like this, they would have me committed. Robin seemed to think the same thing.

'Paddy, will you grab some of your old clothes for Tom. I will wash his stuff when we get back.' She turned towards me. 'You can move in the rest of your stuff during the week.' Paddy turned grudgingly away and did as he was told; his steps were loud as he walked upstairs.

Robin wasn't looking at me; instead she seemed to be trying to fix her jacket, undoing the buttons and then doing them up again. It was odd; her jacket looked perfect to me. The silence was awkward. I had always seen Robin as this cold, self-centred woman, who cared more about her image than the people around her. And yet here she was, vouching for me, getting me clothes and taking me to the doctor's. The more I thought about it, I realized that it was probably she who had convinced Paddy to let me stay.

I started to feel hopeful. Maybe she understood how I felt; maybe she would actually be on my side. I wanted to say something; I wanted to let her know that I appreciated all that she was doing for me.

'Robin, I just wanted to say thanks – you know, for everything.'

At that instant, she stopped fixing her jacket and looked at me with those cold, emotionless eyes that I knew only too well.

'You are my husband's son; I do what I do because I have to – not because I want to.' And just as quickly as it had arrived, the hope disappeared.

29

Olive

THE NIGHT BEFORE HAD LEFT THE DORM IN A SERIOUS STATE. Empty beer cans and bottles of vodka floated about on the floor. Beth and Michael had stayed up nearly all night, just talking about all the things they couldn't wait to do when they got to Australia. Roz and Ed had disappeared to Roz's room fairly early; unfortunately the two were still enjoying their night by the time I went to bed. From my room I could hear a lot that I wished I couldn't.

It was silent and empty as I wandered around, trying to find something suitable to have for breakfast. The cupboards and fridge were completely empty. Obviously any food had been consumed by our many guests the night before. My stomach rumbled. I was starving. After Tom's visit last night I had been too anxious and upset to eat a thing. Only now was my body realizing that I hadn't touched any sort of food since before lunchtime the previous day. I knew that I could just run to the Spar down the road and buy a loaf of bread for everyone else, but the thought of having only toast for breakfast seemed completely insufficient.

I brushed my hair and got dressed in the first things I could find, which was the outfit I had been wearing the night before – a pair of jeans and a loose white string top with a navy cardigan. My belt was on its tightest hole so that my jeans wouldn't fall down. I had regained some of the weight I had lost, but my clothes still didn't fit me properly. I had a habit of not eating when I was upset or nervous, and I seemed to have been upset and nervous a lot these past few months.

The full Irish breakfasts that they made in the restaurants in town were too tempting to pass up. It was greedy, a waste of money and selfish on the others, but I didn't care; there was nothing that I wanted more at this moment. The bus was full of young people clearly on their way home from the night before. Boys with hoodies pulled over their faces to protect their eyes from the daylight, girls still in mini-dresses and make-up smudged all over their faces. Their glamour and beauty didn't look the same in the sober morning light.

With every stop I became more ravenous and I began to fantasize about fried eggs, greasy bacon and buttery toast. The bus was very busy, but I was lucky enough to get a seat. On another day I would have given it up to someone older, someone who looked more in need of it than I did, but not today. I had my earphones on and music was blaring into my head; it was a useless attempt at distracting myself. I didn't want to think about him, about what he had said, about how he had kissed me – but I couldn't help it. I felt as if I was obsessed, and I was almost thankful for my roaring hunger. At least it gave me something else to think about.

It felt like an age before the bus reached town, and I found myself sprinting off it when it finally reached my stop. I saw a blackboard sign at the first restaurant I passed: *Full Irish Breakfast, everything included, ten euro.*

'Perfect,' I sighed to myself.

The restaurant was fairly empty, which meant my breakfast came quickly; I had devoured it in five minutes flat. Eggs, bacon, sausages, black and white pudding, toast and hash browns – it was all delicious and I didn't leave a scrap on my plate. I was impressed and slightly disgusted at my enormous appetite. At least no one was here to witness it, I thought to myself. I paid and left promptly. I was beginning to feel queasy after my feast and I thought a walk might help my digestion.

Town was buzzing; everyone seemed in a hurry, running here and there. Hundreds of faces passed me by, not one even looking twice. My stomach now settled, my mind returned to the one thing that I had been trying to block out for so long. It had been easy to pretend I didn't care when I hadn't been seeing Tom; of course I had thought about him before, but only in weak moments, and I had always reminded myself that he didn't care, he didn't want me.

But now it was all different. He had turned up, I had seen him. And he had told me all those things – he had fought for me. Did he mean everything he had said? Or was it all part of another sick joke? I desperately wanted to believe him, but I was scared. Scared that I would have to go through it all over again. I missed him; I missed his smile, his laugh, his odd sense of humour. I especially missed those rare moments when he let his guard down. When I could see him for what he really was – a sweet, sensitive boy who didn't want to let anyone in. But he *had* let me in, whether by accident or because he wanted to. He had let me see what he hid from everyone else.

A part of me wished that I hadn't sent him away last night. Not because I wanted to forgive him but because last night I didn't see the Tom I knew. I saw a scared and lost boy. A boy on the edge, waiting for someone to push him over. As children we hear stories about the handsome, charming prince who saves the beautiful damsel in distress, since she is unable to save herself. Last night the roles had been reversed. Tom needed to be saved and I had done nothing. I suddenly felt ashamed and scared; the extent of his desperation was only starting to hit me now. I had already lost someone that I cared about; I didn't think I could survive another hit like that. I needed to know where he was, if he was OK.

As if in answer to my thoughts I suddenly saw Peter walking parallel to me on the other side of the street. I paused for a moment, worried that he might think me a fool for asking about a boy who had treated me so awfully, but my worry cancelled out any embarrassment.

'Peter!' I shouted, running across the street. He had been staring at his phone and he looked wildly around himself when he heard my voice. I was nearly next to him before he finally spotted me.

'Olive, thank God. Can you tell me what is going on with Tom?'

My worry turned into panic as I saw true concern in his eyes. 'I was going to ask you the same thing,' I said. 'Do you know where he is?'

Peter gestured to his phone. 'He texted me twenty minutes ago saying that he was at his dad's.' Peter spoke as if Tom had been arrested.

'His *dad's*?' I asked. 'Is that a bad thing?' I knew that the two didn't get along but surely he was safe as long as he was with his family.

Peter was shaking his head at me. 'Tom hates his dad, barely even mentions him. If he's gone to him it must mean he is truly desperate. He has been living with me the past few weeks. I don't know if you know, but his mum kicked him out?'

I nodded silently.

'Olive, what happened last night? Did he go to see you?'

'We were having a party for a friend of mine. He turned up, and he was really drunk so I told him to go home.'

'Drunk? But he has no . . . That's where my fucking whiskey went. I should have known. He must have drunk the whole fucking thing.' Peter ran his hands through his hair in frustration. He was finding it difficult to look me directly in the eye.

'Peter?' I asked, swallowing. 'What is going on? Last night Tom seemed . . . upset. Should we be worried?'

Peter thought for a long time before answering. Was he contemplating whether he should tell me the truth or not? I didn't know whether I wanted to hear it.

'Tom has had it . . . rough. Life hasn't exactly dealt him the best hand. His mum is a psychological mess and his dad has completely rejected his existence – but Tom has always seemed able to deal with all this, you know? Take it in his stride. Fuck's sake, I wouldn't have a clue about any of it if it wasn't for the fact that he has been stranded on numerous occasions and has needed somewhere to stay. Also, I am a nosy fucker.'

I smiled at Peter when he said this, but it was merely to be polite.

'But lately, the guy . . . He's in a bad way, Olive. There is no other way to put it. Yeah, he had been moody and violent at times, but never depressed.'

The back of my throat was burning and my voice croaked as I tried to speak. 'What can I do?'

Peter looked tired. 'I don't know . . .'

The two of us stood there in awkward silence, both a little embarrassed about revealing how much we cared for this one person.

I turned to walk away but Peter stopped me.

'I know it probably won't make a difference, but that boy was on cloud nine when he was with you. True, what he did wasn't cool, but he didn't know you then – and I know that night was horrible but I have never seen Tom so terrified of losing something – and that's from a boy who has lost a lot.'

I didn't speak. I was too afraid that if I opened my mouth I would burst into tears. I just shook my head and walked away; Peter didn't try and stop me this time.

I was in a complete emotional daze on the journey home. Every word that Peter had said just kept replaying in my head, over and over again. I didn't know what I thought, how I felt. Angry, flattered, terrified? All I knew was that my mind couldn't focus on anything else. When I reached my dorm, I was surprised to notice that the lights in the hall had been turned off and the curtains were drawn. Odd, I thought to myself. I was sure that I had opened everything and turned on all the lights before I had left. The door to our common room was also firmly shut, another oddity. We never closed any of the doors, only the bedrooms. I tried to dismiss my paranoia. Then I opened the door to a sight that I was definitely not expecting.

Roz was sitting on our kitchen table with nothing on but a bra and a little mini-skirt that had been pushed up way past her thighs, and Ed, who had his head thrown back in pleasure, was standing in front of her, completely naked, pulling her closer.

'For fuck's sake!' I shouted as I went to turn and run out the door, but in my haste I walked straight into the doorframe. I tried to continue leaving, but I had hit my head hard and before I knew what was happening I saw Roz and Ed looming over me as I lay on the kitchen floor.

'I thought you were out, Olive. I am so sorry. Are you OK?'

My head felt dizzy and heavy and I wasn't able to look directly at Roz.

'For fuck's sake, Roz. You have a bedroom – can the two of you not stay in there?'

Roz's red face made me feel guilty for being so harsh but I

was in no mood to apologize. Ed came towards me with a packet of frozen peas; I didn't even know we had a freezer.

'Hey, Olive, we are awfully sorry. We just got carried away, you know?' *No, I don't know, you sex freak!* I just stared at him. There was no point in making a scene, and I couldn't take back what I had just seen, no matter how desperately I wanted to. Ed's smile quickly faded as he realized that I was not impressed. Roz gazed at him longingly for help. He looked as if he was stuck between a rock and a hard place.

Finally he mumbled, 'Maybe I should go. I'll call you tomorrow, babe.'

As the door closed Roz suddenly burst into frantic apologies that I actually could not understand.

'Olive, oh my God, you have like no idea how embarrassed I am! I am like so, so, so sorry. I swear I didn't think you would be back so soon, and Ed just does this thing with his tongue that makes me go absolutely wild . . .'

'It's OK!' I shouted over her ramblings, hoping that she would stop saying whatever she was about to say. I had managed to make my way to the chair now, the frozen peas still held up against my head; a small bump was beginning to form on my forehead. *Perfect.*

Roz quickly broke the silence. 'So where were you?'

'Nowhere,' I murmured. I had truly believed that nothing could distract me from the conversation I had had with Peter, but once again I was wrong.

Roz didn't stick around for too long after that. She went to go check on Ed. She said that he must feel terribly bad about the whole thing and probably needed to be comforted. I didn't mind. I had a mild headache after hitting my head and even though Roz was only trying to be nice she was making it worse with her constant pampering and concern.

★

It was nearly midday before Beth finally emerged from her room. I was surprised to see she was alone.

'Where's Michael?' I asked curiously.

'He went home early this morning. He still has a ton of things to do in Limerick before we leave.' I nodded. An awkward silence followed. Since Beth had told me her plans, the two of us hadn't been alone together. Roz or Michael had always been around. I realized that now was my only opportunity to make her understand the magnitude of this decision she was making. She was giving up everything she had ever had or known for this one person, so she needed to be sure that this was what she wanted.

'You think I'm crazy, don't you?' She spoke before I had the chance to even think of what I was going to say. I looked up at her; she didn't look angry or sad. She was actually smiling.

'No, it's just . . . Have you thought it through completely?'

'Yes,' she said without hesitation.

'Are you sure?'

'Yes, I am.' She was laughing now. I was beginning to get a little annoyed. 'Tea?' she asked as she walked over to the kettle. I just shook my head as she began to make some for herself.

'How do you know he is The One?' I asked abruptly. There was no point tiptoeing around the subject any more.

'I don't know, I just do. I didn't always know he was The One. I actually didn't think much of him when I first met him. A bit like you and Tom.' I flinched at the sound of his name. Beth noticed as she sat down next to me with her tea. 'I'm sorry, I didn't mean—'

'It's OK,' I said, interrupting her. I didn't want to talk about it any more. Beth didn't know about the bet and I didn't think she had seen what happened last night either. I reckoned she was too preoccupied with Michael. I needed to figure out how I felt on my own.

'Have I ever told you how Michael and I actually met?' Beth said now, and I shook my head, happy that she had changed the subject. 'I was thirteen. Michael was new to our school, no one knew much about him. The town in Limerick that I grew up in was a small place; everyone knew everyone else's business. Michael was this complete mystery and he didn't have many friends, he mostly kept to himself. All the girls made up these scandalous stories about him. It's quite funny to think back on it now. For months we didn't say a word to each other. I mistook his shyness for conceit and I took an instant dislike to him.'

I sat and listened to her, completely sucked in by her story.

'Anyway, nearly a full school year went by and the two of us still hadn't spoken to each other. I didn't think he even knew I existed. You see, we had a big year and I was good at blending into the crowd. As the summer holidays approached I started spending my weekends in the city. My parents worked long hours and I didn't like hanging about in an empty house. My parents didn't know, of course; they would have killed me for wandering around Limerick city on my own. But I loved just sitting in the parks reading all day, watching people come and go. But I was always home before dark; I was rebellious but not stupid.'

Beth and I both laughed. I had never been to Limerick city before but I had heard the stories and it sounded like a scary place.

'But there was one time that I ended up staying out much later than I had planned. It was a complete accident. I had been reading one of the Harry Potter books and got so immersed in the story that I didn't realize the sun had set until it was too dark to look at my page any more. The park I had been sitting in was completely empty – there seemed to be no one around. I ran to the bus stop, only to find out that my bus had gone and there wasn't another for two hours. I was terrified; it was eight o'clock in the evening. I had no phone so I couldn't have called my parents even if I'd wanted to. I made myself stand at that bus stop staring at the empty road in front of me. Every time someone walked by, I closed my eyes and prayed that they wouldn't come near me. At first the people walking by seemed normal, mothers with their children, men on their phones. As the hour slowly slid by I began to feel slightly calmer, convincing myself that I was over-exaggerating. But then it got darker and even quieter, and I started to shiver with the fear and the cold. It had been silent for a long time when I heard another set of footsteps. I did what I had done before. I closed my eyes tight and just waited for the person to pass. But this person didn't go past me; instead the footsteps came closer and closer. I was too afraid to open my eyes, too afraid to see who was standing next to me. I nearly fell over with fright when I heard a male voice whisper my name.'

I was completely lost in Beth's story. I could almost feel myself shivering; I understood the fear she was talking about all too well.

'I don't know whether I was more relieved or confused when I first saw Michael. I was, of course, thrilled to see someone I recognized, but at the same time I couldn't understand what he was doing in Limerick city so late at night.

'"Are you OK?" he asked. I found it hard to get my words out. As the fear began to pass, embarrassment began to set in. I told him I was waiting for the bus and he gave me a funny look.

'"It's pretty late to be waiting for a bus."

'"I missed my first one." He nodded with understanding. "What are you doing here?" I asked, still a little taken aback by his presence. He lifted a plastic bag that he had been holding in his right hand.

'"My mum sent me out for supplies."

'"You live around here?"

'"Just up the road."

'"Must be a long trek up to school?"

'"Forty minutes on the bus. It's not too bad."

'I didn't know what else to say to him but I was desperate for him not to leave. He must have sensed my fear because he didn't go anywhere. The bus was late and we ended up talking about school for a good while.

'"You don't hang out with people from our school much?" Looking back now, I can't believe how blunt I had been with him. I wish I had been a bit nicer. He laughed.

'"No. Everyone at that school is quite intimidating." I asked how we were intimidating. "Different reasons," he replied. "Some of the girls are so smart it's scary, and some of the boys are so good at sports that I feel like they could destroy me if they wanted to." I laughed and asked him if he thought I was intimidating.

'"Oh yes, very." He started to stare at his feet and blushed a little bit.

'"Because I am smart?" I asked.

'"No, no," he said instantly. "Because you are beautiful." We changed the subject quickly after that and he stayed with me until my bus arrived. That was it then. After that I couldn't think about anything or anyone else. He was The One.'

I looked at Beth for a long time before I said anything. Her story was beautiful but it was more the way she had told it that had shocked me. Every word, every detail, was so important to her. There was no fake pride or insincerity, just love.

'You are completely sure, aren't you?' I whispered. And when she smiled at me and nodded, I told her: 'Then I envy you.'

30

Tom

LIVING MEANS YOU BREATHE. YOU MOVE. YOUR HEART PUMPS blood around the rest of your body. If you're lucky, you possess the five senses. You see, smell, touch, taste and hear, but what happens when they no longer work? Your mind and body don't seem to function normally any more, and suddenly everything you felt before is no longer there. Suddenly you just feel numb all the time.

My hand had gone from bad to worse; Robin had to take me to the hospital a couple of times. The doctor said it was severely infected and that I needed a heavy dose of antibiotics. He warned me against taking any drugs or drinking any alcohol. Paddy was not happy, more money being spent on the unwanted child. The antibiotics made me feel sick all the time; I just wished I could do something to make myself stop thinking. It didn't help that Paddy had made all these rules for me living with them – and they needed to know where I was all the time. I felt like a prisoner on probation. One wrong move and I was gone. I wanted to leave so badly except I knew I had nowhere else to go; I had hit rock bottom.

The only thing I liked about this house was Pamela. She was like a small light in what felt like a completely dark situation.

'Do you have a headache, Tom?' Pamela asked, looking up at me with those big brown innocent eyes.

I took my hands away from my face before answering, 'Yeah, a little.'

'Do you want some painkillers?' she asked.

I smiled to myself. It was nice having a little sister around. 'No, Pam, I'm fine,' but I had barely finished my sentence before she started talking again.

'Because I know where Mummy keeps Daddy's special medicine. She doesn't think I do, but I've seen her hide it in a box under her sink.'

'Really?' I asked.

She nodded, bursting with the excitement that she knew something that no one thought she did.

'I can go get them if you want?' she said.

I was about to tell her no, I honestly was. I didn't want trouble with Paddy or Robin. I would also die of guilt if Pam got in trouble for something that she didn't even understand. But she was already gone before I could answer.

She came running back in with a small see-through bottle with the name *Patrick O'Connor* on the side.

'Daddy takes these when he gets a headache.' It was a prescription for migraines; it said to take one daily. I thought for a moment, wondering if what I was about to do could make everything worse. Then I realized there was no possible way that this could be worse.

I popped three into my mouth.

'Thanks, Pam,' I mumbled, putting the bottle in my pocket. I would do anything if it just made me stop thinking for a while. Pam was looking at me with concern. There were moments when it really shocked me how much we looked alike.

'Tom, promise you won't tell Mummy and Daddy. They will be angry at me.'

I chuckled and gave her a pat on the shoulder. 'I promise I won't tell. It will be our little secret.'

She smiled back at me, relieved.

It was a full half-hour before I felt completely numb. My head had become heavy, as if it was filled with stuffing. I spent the rest of the day trying to get myself to Peter's apartment; I was supposed to pick up the remainder of my stuff from him. Everyone was out. Paddy was at work and Robin was at lunch with friends; she had taken Pam with her. They still didn't trust me enough to leave her alone with me. I had been warned severely that I was not to leave the house other than to pick up my stuff from Peter's, and that I had to be back before four.

Soon, walking seemed like a severe challenge, and after that finding the bus stop proved impossible. I couldn't understand it; I walked past this bus stop every day. Eventually I gave up and decided to walk to Peter's house. I took a few more pills along the way, I wasn't sure how many. I didn't want the feeling of numbness to disappear. I didn't want to feel. I don't know how long I was walking or how many wrong turns I took, but it was nearly dark before I reached his apartment. Robin was going to freak, but in my state I couldn't have cared less.

I stumbled up what felt like thousands of stairs and eventually made it to Peter's door. I only knocked once before he answered, half-dressed in a shirt and tie and looking completely out of breath.

'Where the fuck have you been, Tom? You were supposed to be here hours ago. I have called you like thirty times.' It was only then that I started to pat my pockets and realize I had left my mobile back at Paddy's. Luckily the painkillers were still there though.

'Sorry,' I mumbled, leaning up against his doorframe;

standing was too difficult. 'Why are you dressed like that?' I didn't seem to be able to speak properly any more either.

'I'm going to dinner with my dad – some fancy restaurant in town. I told you that, Tom,' he said, looking at me strangely.

I wordlessly pushed past Peter and sat down on his couch. I started to think about what it had been like to live here, working all the time, desperately pining after a girl who despised me. I didn't want to think about her. I didn't want to think about anyone or anything; I wanted it all to stop. I wanted to sleep but my mind would not let me. Olive's face, her laugh, her voice – I couldn't stop thinking about any of it.

I reached into my pocket and took out the small plastic bottle. One more couldn't hurt, and then I could take a nap. It was only when Peter grabbed the painkillers out of my hand that I remembered where I was.

'Are you fucking kidding me, Tom?' He was yelling and staring at the plastic bottle. 'Getting high on painkillers? Seriously, what has happened to you?'

I tried to shout back, to defend myself. To tell him he had no idea about what I was doing or what I had to deal with. I wanted to tell him to fuck off. I wanted to get up and leave, run out the door, but I no longer seemed to be able to control myself. In fact, I could barely keep my eyes open.

'Tom? Tom!' I had never seen Peter look so frightened. I tried to tell him to calm down, that I was fine, but the words just wouldn't come out.

The next thing I knew, Peter had put his arms around me and was lifting me to the bathroom. He shoved me onto my knees, next to the toilet, and sat me upright so I was facing it. I wanted to tell him to stop, that he was hurting me, but only quiet groans came out. Suddenly I felt his two fingers being shoved to the back of my throat. I tried to push him away but he didn't stop until I started to vomit violently.

I'm not sure how many times I was sick, I only remember that the second I stopped, Peter stripped me, dragged me into his shower and turned the water on. The ice-cold water felt like daggers against my skin. I no longer had any problems keeping my eyes open. I started to shiver convulsively. Peter sat next to me, staring at me with pure fear, for what felt like hours. I eventually found that I was able to lift my arms; I reached above my head and turned off the water, using my non-broken hand.

I stayed sitting at the bottom of the shower, aching all over. I couldn't look at Peter. It was only when he started to talk that I was certain he was still there.

'Tom, what the fuck are you doing?'

I don't know why or how, but all of a sudden I found myself telling Peter everything. I wasn't upset or angry; I just needed to get it all out. I told him about my mum, my dad, Robin, Pamela and Olive. Especially Olive – how I loved her and how I had screwed everything up because I didn't deserve her, and how I felt that I was never going to achieve any sort of happiness. I knew I was being irrational and pathetic, but at that moment I hated myself and I couldn't stop. It all kept rushing out until I no longer had anything else to say.

I looked up at Peter to see him staring down at his feet; he was completely silent. I tried to stand up, but found I wasn't able to support my own weight and I slipped back down. Peter looked at me then.

'Do you need a hand?' I just nodded. He passed me a towel before helping me stand up. He put another towel on the floor in the corner and placed me sitting on top of it. I wrapped the other towel around me and tried to stop shivering. At least I had stopped talking. My head didn't feel heavy any more but I ached all over. I began to wonder would Peter ever talk to me again after this.

'Tom, you have got to man up.'

I was shocked by this. Of all the things I expected to hear out of Peter's mouth at that moment, this was not one of them.

'Your family is shit. Well, we all have that. For fuck's sake, every time I go home I have to pretend that I don't know my dad is screwing some twenty-five-year-old waitress.'

I had never known that about Peter, and I started to feel guilty. He went slightly red; I don't think he had meant to reveal such a personal detail.

'You have screwed everything up? Fine, then fix it. You want to not have such a shitty relationship with your parents, then go back to your dad's, cop on to yourself and show him you're not a screw-up.' Peter took a deep breath before he continued.

'And if you're in love with Olive, then tell her that. At least you'll know you gave it an honest shot.' He said the last bit slower than the rest as if to make sure I understood it.

The realization of what was happening seemed to hit both of us at the same time and self-consciousness set in. I thought about saying that I hadn't meant anything I had said. That it had been the drugs talking – but that would be the cowardly thing to do and I didn't want to be a coward any more.

After a while Peter got up and offered his hand to help me. I looked out the bathroom window to see it was pitch black outside. I knew all hell must be awaiting me back at Paddy's.

'I'm late to meet my dad. Are you OK to get home on your own?' Peter asked.

'Yeah,' I mumbled, but he didn't look convinced. 'I'm sure, Peter. I'll just get cleaned up and then I'll go straight back to my dad's.' I was still aching all over, especially my hand, but at least I was able to support myself.

'Peter, I am really sorry. I—' I didn't know what I wanted to say, but it didn't matter because Peter cut me off anyway.

'Don't get all heart-to-heart with me. It's kind of gay.' He gave me a cheeky smile which I could not help but laugh at.

*

I was barely in Paddy's door before the roaring began. Paddy grabbed me by my T-shirt and threw me into the kitchen.

'Where the fuck have you been?'

'Paddy, calm down. I don't want Pamela to hear you shouting like this.' Robin had her hands on his shoulders and she looked genuinely scared of her husband. I tried to keep my voice calm as I spoke.

'Paddy, I am sorry. I left my phone here. I know I should have called.'

'You didn't answer my question!' He was no longer shouting but there was still the same amount of menace in his voice.

'I was at Peter's.'

'For six hours? Where is your fucking stuff anyway?'

I suddenly realized that after all that had happened, I had forgotten to pick up my things. Paddy's hands were grasping my shirt again.

'Tell me the truth, Tom. I am serious.'

I didn't say anything. I just handed him the painkillers that I had stolen earlier. At first he looked confused and then his eyes widened in complete shock when he saw what they were.

'How did you get these?'

'I found them,' I lied. I wasn't going to let Pam become involved. He quickly realized that the bottle was practically empty.

'How many of these did you take?'

'I'm not sure.' But I knew this was not a sufficient answer. 'Five or six, maybe.'

Paddy let go of my shirt, while Robin let out a small whimper. He looked at me, no longer angry. He pitied me.

'You are on antibiotics, Tom.'

'I know.'

'And you overdosed on prescription painkillers.'

I just nodded this time.

Paddy hesitated before he spoke again, clearing his throat. 'Were you trying to kill yourself?'

'No,' I said firmly. I had expected the question. I hoped that he believed me.

'How are you? Sober now?'

'I . . . Peter got me to throw up – a lot. The pills are out of my system now.'

Paddy sat down and buried his face in his hands. When he rose again he looked old, older than I had ever seen him before.

'Do you not realize you could be dead right now? All that shit you put in your body, it will eventually kill you. Do you understand that? Do you?'

'Of course I know.' I was finding it hard to stand there and be spoken to like an idiot. Robin could sense my agitation and I knew her body had just tensed; she was ready for war to break out.

'Are you actually being cheeky with me?' Paddy roared. 'After all I have done for you? After everything you have put this family through?'

He nearly fell over with shock when I started laughing at him.

'After all you have done for me? Please, Paddy, name what you have done for me. You conceived me, and then left. Leaving my mother to be looked after by a child, a child who was bullied and forced into a decision about who he should live with – a decision that I should never have been allowed to make. Then you decided to cut me out of your life completely. You have had *twenty years* in which to have a relationship with me, to do something for me – and you have done nothing. Even now, you only have me here because you have to. You wished I had died tonight, don't you? Then your estranged son that you have secretly always hated can just be a tale of warning for the child that you really love.'

Robin had her hands to her mouth and there were tears running down her face. I don't know what emotion was on Paddy's face; he just looked at me in silence.

I was thankful for that silence: I had more to say.

'I am sick of blaming you, Mum and everyone else for the way I am. I have been obsessing about the past my whole life. I don't want to do that any more. I no longer want to be the worthless child. I want to be . . . I *can* be worth something. I know I have messed up again and again, but I just want one more chance. Please. I swear I can be something, someone. Please.' There were tears in my eyes now, but I wiped them away quickly. I wasn't going to break down; I wasn't going to let them see me be weak.

Paddy looked as if someone had hit him. His mouth hung slightly open, and his eyes were in an unbroken stare but not really looking at me or anything. I waited, terrified, truly terrified because I now had something to lose. When Paddy finally spoke, his expression didn't change.

'Fine, Tom. Fine. Prove me wrong.'

31

Olive

I KEPT THINKING THIS WAS A MISTAKE, THIS WAS A BIG MISTAKE. What was I doing? What was I thinking? This wouldn't work; I was going to look like a fool. I wasn't even sure what I wanted to say or what I wanted to happen. All I knew was that I had this urgent need to *do* something. Oscar Wilde once said that the only way to rid oneself of temptation is to yield to it. So that was what I was going to do. I would yield to temptation, whatever that might be. I tried to ignore the fact that Wilde was arrested and exiled for yielding to his temptations.

It was three weeks since my conversation with Peter. The Christmas holidays had ended and everyone was beginning back in college. I had tried so hard to distract myself by getting a head start on college reading, and any free time I had, I spent with Roz. But it wasn't working. I couldn't stop thinking about him. I had heard nothing more of Tom, and this had been slowly killing me. For the past three weeks I had thought of nothing but how he was, where he was. Did he think about me? Did he miss me? Hate me? I had become completely obsessed. I felt as if I couldn't move forward until I knew he was OK. I was stuck, stagnant. I needed something to jerk me out of this state of anxiety. I needed *him*.

Of course I had considered doing this more than once. But not until today had I acted upon it. He no longer lived with his mum and I had no idea where his dad was or even if he was still there. My only hope was that he might be at college today. I knew that the Trinity exams were on at the moment, and I reasoned that he must be in college taking his exams or at least studying for them. I had already sat mine; one of the advantages of studying in UCD was that exams took place before Christmas. They had been extremely intimidating – thousands of students sitting in one hall at old and creaky desks. I wouldn't get my results for another while but I had felt that everything had gone OK. At least I didn't have to face the cruel task of sitting exams after the Christmas holidays, like Trinity students had to. Trinity was huge, not as big as UCD but older, historical, more daunting. It had snowed during the last few days and the place looked almost magical in the snow.

Sitting there alone, I began to think back on all that had happened, about all the people who had come into my life and those who had left it. I was shocked at how everything had changed. How I had changed. The boy I had thought I was in love with a few months ago had now become a complete stranger to me. New friends now knew more about me than anyone else in my life ever had. And my brother, I missed him so much; nothing could fill the gaping hole that his absence had caused. His death had taken me to dark places inside myself that I never knew existed. I still had Andy's phone number. It had been disconnected long ago, but I didn't feel right deleting it. Before, I would have gotten about six or seven texts and calls from him a day. Now I found myself checking my phone constantly. I still felt a sting of sadness every time I saw that blank screen.

There was a time, a short time, when I was sitting in my bedroom, staring at the ceiling, that I thought life had become pointless. I no longer knew how to keep going, how to be me. Tom had been there for me when I had felt so desperately alone. I don't think I had fully understood until now the huge impact that he had had on my life.

I told myself that I was leaving it all up to fate. Trinity is a big college; thousands of students walk in and out of the door every day. I would wait at the main gate for one hour, and if he walked by, then it was fate. I had butterflies in my stomach. This was impossible, I told myself. There were so many reasons why he might not walk through those gates during that hour. Perhaps he had no college today? Perhaps he would leave through another entrance? It wasn't time for him to leave; it wasn't time for him to come in. The hour dragged on slowly. Every minute felt like a lifetime. I wanted to give up and leave, but I made myself stay. I had made a promise to myself, and if he didn't turn up, then I could walk away safely, knowing that it wasn't meant to be.

There were only two minutes left in the hour that I had allowed myself, when I finally saw him. At first I wasn't even completely sure it was him. He had his head lowered with a beanie on, reading a book as he walked outside, surrounded by a crowd of students. I edged closer to make sure it was definitely him. His floppy hair, hidden under the hat, looked like it had been cut shorter, and he had a large bandage wrapped around the hand that was not holding the book, but it was undoubtedly him.

I didn't have time to hesitate. He was already heading in the direction of the bus stop and he was within a shell of people. I didn't want to shout out his name, although I felt desperate enough. This meant I had to rudely shove past half a dozen students before I was able to tap him on the shoulder. He looked up from his reading. I was close enough now to see the title of his book. *Irish Genetics* – it looked like a heavy text.

'Olive?' he said, shocked.

'Hi,' I mumbled, the butterflies at full force. People were bumping into us as they tried to squeeze past. 'Do you want to go somewhere less busy?' I asked.

'Um, yeah, of course,' Tom said, looking flustered and shoving his book into his bag.

I followed him through the Trinity campus towards the Buttery Café. Even in my state of complete anxiety I couldn't help but notice the beauty of the old buildings and cobble-stoned pathways, made only more beautiful by the light dusting of snow. It was easy to imagine a Victorian horse and carriage trotting by, carrying young scholars and idealists. The Buttery Café brought us straight back into the twenty-first century; it was painted white and green, and was more like a canteen than a coffee shop.

Tom offered to buy me a coffee but I just shook my head. I had tried to rehearse what I was going to say when I was waiting at that gate – composing amazing speeches in my head: declarations of love or scornful, hateful words – but none of them had seemed right. I couldn't express what I was feeling in words. There was too much, too much emotion, to be expressed that way. Maybe I could slap him, or cry, or kiss him. I wanted to do all of those things. And yet none of them seemed like enough.

Suddenly, words starting pouring out of Tom's mouth and I found it hard to keep up.

'Olive, I am so, so, so sorry for what I did. It was a really stupid, selfish, horrible thing. I didn't know you then – which is not an excuse, I know – but once I started to get to know you, I really liked you and had so much fun with you and sex was the last thing on my mind . . . well, not the last thing, obviously. You're really hot and I obviously did think about it, but the point is, Olive, the bet doesn't mean anything. It was stupid. I do stupid things sometimes and I am trying to stop and – and I am sorry.' He was out of breath when he finally stopped talking. He looked as if he wanted to say more, but decided it was better not to.

'I think I love you.' It was out of my mouth before I could stop it. I hadn't thought about saying it, I hadn't planned it. It just happened.

Tom no longer looked as if he had words bubbling up inside him; instead he looked as if someone had just hit him. His eyes had widened and it took him a while to make sounds.

'Olive, I . . .' There it was – the hesitation. The dreaded pause that every girl fears after she has told someone she loves him. I couldn't sit there and listen to the excuses and apologies that I knew would come. Not from someone I had been so sure loved me back.

I stood up and ran for the exit. I knew it was a bit dramatic but I didn't care. I could feel the tears beginning to burn my eyes and I didn't want him to see me cry. Tom didn't hesitate in following me. He called my name and raced after me. I was outside the main gate by the time he caught me.

'Olive, what are you doing?'

'It's fine, Tom. I get it.'

'Get what? Why do you always have to run away from me?'

'I get that you don't feel the same way. It's fine, just let me go home.'

Tom grabbed me by the arm and made me look him in the eye before he spoke again.

'Olive, I love you too.' And then he kissed me, and it was with such passion that I couldn't help but let myself melt into him.

I don't know how long we stood there kissing, but it felt too short. I would have happily stayed there all day, but passers-by were laughing and wolf-whistling. I eventually pulled away and looked at Tom properly for the first time that day. He had never looked so good. His eyes were bright and alert, his face seemed fuller, not so thin, and his smile seemed genuine, honest.

'I am done with fucking this up, Olive.'

I smiled back at him and replied, 'I am done with running away.'

He brushed my hair out of my face. 'So, we are going to give this a real shot? You and I? No more bullshit?'

'Yes,' I said with complete certainty. 'You and I. No more bullshit. Let's do it.'

32

Everyone

Olive

IT'S AMAZING TO THINK THAT SO MUCH CAN CHANGE IN SO little time, and then months and months can go by when you remain in the same pleasant state of joy. I turn around as I hear the clatter of books behind me. A small blonde girl with a red face is down on her knees trying to gather everything she has just dropped. Her hands are shaking and she keeps her head low as she turns towards me.

'Excuse me. Do you know where the programmes office is?' I smile compassionately, and point her in the right direction. She mumbles her thanks and stumbles off.

It's the first day back after summer and UCD is swarming with new, vulnerable and terrified first years. As I watch the blonde girl move away, I wonder had I looked so scared on my first day? In reality I had probably looked even worse.

The summer had been unusually wet, but now that September has started the sun has finally arrived. I feel my phone buzz in my back pocket; it is a message from Tom.

Meet you after college today? X. I stand there smiling to myself as I write my reply.

Tom and I had been practically inseparable this summer. We had spent most of it in my house in Wexford. My parents had decided to do a tour of Europe and had been gone for several weeks. I was shocked when they first told me their plans. I had never even known that my parents liked travelling! It turned out there were so many places they had wanted to see, so many things they had wanted to do – and now they were finally doing it all.

Before they left, my mum took me aside one night. 'Olive, is what we are doing wrong?'

Her eyes were full of doubt and tears. At this stage they had already told me their plans and I was thrilled for them. This sudden sadness and doubt from my mother surprised me.

'What are you talking about, Mum?' I placed my hands on hers; she looked as if she might cry.

'I loved my son – I still do.'

'I know you do, Mum. Why are you upset?'

She took a deep breath before she spoke again. 'When you and Andy were kids and before we knew about Andy's . . . problems, your dad and I always spoke about all these things we wanted to do when you guys got older and were able to take care of yourselves. And then, when we found out about Andy, I just accepted that all our plans . . . that they just couldn't happen. I wasn't angry. I wasn't sad. I loved my son and I would always put him first. I knew that when I became a mother, even if I didn't know to what extreme. I had accepted that my life would be completely devoted to keeping him well and happy, and now – and now he's gone. And suddenly we can do everything we ever wanted and I feel guilty. Please, Olive – you have to tell me if you think that what we are doing is wrong.'

I caressed my mum's hands and chose my words carefully before I spoke. There were silent tears running down her face.

'Andy would not have wanted you to feel guilty for anything. He knew how much we loved him. How much we still do, and he would want us to enjoy life.' My mum nodded and then hugged me. I understood, since I had the same guilt. I felt guilty that I was able to enjoy things that I wasn't able to when he was alive.

My parents emailed me weekly, telling me about all the adventures they were having and everything they were getting to see. They sent me pictures of them standing on top of the Eiffel Tower, sunbathing in Greece and shopping in London. They had returned to Ireland, though, for a couple of days in the middle of the summer to celebrate Andy's birthday. We had decided a long time ago that we would celebrate the day Andy was born and not the day he died. We wanted to celebrate his life, not his death.

We had spent the day looking over old photos from when we were young. There were pictures of Andy and me playing with Mowgli and sitting in the grass with ice-creams in the summer. We even had a couple from the hospital on the day he was born. My dad told the story proudly.

'When I came home, Olive, and told you that you had a little brother, you were so angry. You had wanted a little sister so much.' Mum and I were laughing as he told the story. 'And then the day came when your mum and Andy returned home from the hospital and you saw your little brother for the first time. Well, it was love at first sight, I can tell you that. You just stared at him for hours, and I never heard you say you wanted a little sister instead ever again.'

I smiled, comforted. I had adored my brother and was glad that it had been easy for everyone to see.

Andy's room remains untouched. My mum keeps it clean, so that it doesn't look abandoned. But nothing is ever moved, nothing is ever taken away. His football clothes are still bundled up in the corner covered in grass stains, his socks are overflowing on the bottom shelf. His posters still hang on every wall of the room. If you were a stranger looking in, there would be no evidence to say that this wasn't the current room of an average teenage boy. But Andy had never been average, he had been so much better.

Guilt is something that I have learned to live with. Sometimes I feel that I don't deserve to be happy, but I *am* happy. Tom makes me happy. My parents' many travels mean that my home in Wexford is nearly always empty. Tom and I have great fun playing house there, but only at the weekends. He still lives with his father, and Paddy has many rules. I think he is slowly beginning to trust Tom, but I doubt he will ever let his guard down fully. Roz often comes to stay as well, bringing Ed with her. The two seem to have the most melodramatic relationship, breaking up and getting back together nearly every week, but I think they truly care for each other, and I am convinced that Roz secretly loves all the drama. Even though she would never admit to it.

Beth writes to us constantly. She has sent us pictures of her and Michael getting married on the beach. She looked beautiful and the two were smiling broadly, but it makes me sad, thinking that no one was with them. No family, no friends. In her letters she is positive. She tells me how well Michael is doing, and says that she has already been accepted to numerous medical schools over there, although her semester won't start for another few months. I can't help but notice in her descriptions of her life that she seems to be alone a lot; I worry that in a big country like Australia she will become lost.

I love the weekends when it is just Tom and me alone in my house. When we are alone and we block out the rest of the world, it feels like nothing else matters, only the two of us. But unfortunately this feeling never seems to last. When we are out in the world I get scared again. I am scared of being so vulnerable. Tom has the power to really hurt me and I pray that he never does. He has told me everything – about his life, his family. It was only then I realized how strong a person he really is. I feel safe with him and it makes me love him even more. I don't know what the future holds, but I have learned for certain that it is impossible to predict. As I look up from my phone and see the blonde, nervous-looking fresher go round the corner, I can't help but wonder what this year has in store for her.

Alison

I got stabs of pain in my stomach as I threw up convulsively. When I had finally finished, I washed my face and reapplied my make-up. No one had noticed my absence, and even if they had, they wouldn't bother coming to look for me. My friends were probably busy bitching about me, saying that I was a mess who couldn't handle her drink. I saw my boyfriend flirting with some girl earlier; he had more than likely used my absence to make his move. He would convince the girl to leave with him, telling me some pathetic excuse. I didn't know why he even bothered lying any more. He would then turn up at my house the next day with flowers and chocolates; he might even buy jewellery if he was really worried about getting caught. My friends, if you could even call them that, never tell me what they see or hear. Usually because it is one of them that he has taken home. I have no one to blame but myself; this was a life that I chose a long time ago, one full of money, excess, lying and cheating.

Cian and I had been together for two years now; my dad would constantly drop unsubtle hints about marriage whenever he was over. It was undeniable that this was the track we were both heading on, but I wasn't the least bit happy or excited about it; nothing about our relationship would change if we got married except that I might get a bit of money one day when all our bullshit went public.

Of course, Cian hated the idea of marriage and would just grunt if it was ever brought up. All he cared about was rugby and how much bigger and stronger he could get, and what supplements he needed to take. But I knew his family was putting pressure on him to propose too. I was good-looking, rich and came from a well-recognized family. I was the perfect trophy wife.

Katie had her baby – a boy, to my dad's delight. He resembled my dad, very much to my disappointment. Dad had always wanted a son and now that he had one, he suddenly no longer cared about where I was or what I was doing. He didn't even comment when I told him that I had failed my first year of college and that he would have to pay 2,000 euro extra for me to re-sit the year. At first I was thrilled about the lack of attention. I no longer had to pretend to like Katie or tell him why I was spending so much money and where it was going. But the fact that he truly didn't care about me began to sink in slowly, and then the realization that *no one cared* hit me. People either hate me or are jealous of me. That's it.

Katie named the baby Connor. I have only visited him twice since he was born. Katie tried to make conversation by saying that she could see similarities between Connor and me, but I ignored her stupid remark. Connor is blond and fair-skinned like Katie. I am also blonde, but my hair is bleached, and I have very dark skin like my mother. The baby and I look nothing alike. Katie no longer tries to be my friend. Mostly because she now has her own child to 'bond' with, but also because she knows she no longer has to.

I didn't normally get as drunk as this but tonight I had just wanted to try and forget everything. I had seen Tom earlier today. He was in a café in town with Olive. I was still humiliated and ashamed that I had broken down in front of her, that time in the basement toilets. I had told her so much; I told her things that I have told no one else. I guess it doesn't matter – *she* doesn't matter.

I had completely isolated Alex from our group after what she had done. If I had no other power, at least I had the power to do that. My dad still denied everything. Even after I told him that Alex had confessed he continued to laugh it off, saying that the girl had a silly crush. I knew Katie wouldn't believe me if I told her. I had wanted to tell her originally – not to help her or protect her, but because I wanted to punish my dad. I wanted to hurt him as much as he had hurt me, but I knew I couldn't do it. I was powerless when it came to him.

I was thrilled to see Tom; the boy had never said no to me and I knew that what I needed more than anything was a confidence boost. The two were being disgustingly romantic, kissing, holding hands, laughing and smiling. But I knew Tom and he was a master at telling girls what they wanted to hear. I waited until Olive had gone to the toilets before I went over to say hello. Tom looked surprised to see me and not that happy.

'Alison, hi. How are you?'

I sat down where Olive had been sitting and flicked my hair. 'I am good. So who is the girl?' I said, gesturing towards the bathroom.

'Oh, that's Olive. She's my girlfriend.'

I laughed but Tom didn't look like he was joking. 'Are you serious?' I asked, when I noticed that he wasn't laughing with me.

As he nodded, I saw Olive come out of the bathroom and decided to leave before she realized what I was trying to do. I smiled at Tom and walked out of the café. As I was walking down the street I took out my phone and starting texting. *When you are done with your 'girlfriend' you should come over to mine. We need to catch up!* ☺ X. I was nearly at the bus stop before I got a reply. *Sorry Alison, can't.* It was blunt and brutal and it felt like a slap in the face.

When I had finally finished reapplying my make-up, I stared at myself in the mirror. I wasn't that pretty, not really. I bleached my hair because it was a disgusting mousy brown. I put on loads of eyeliner and mascara because my eyes were dull and lifeless, and I wore fake tan because my skin was lifeless too. I pretended to be pretty just like I pretended to be happy.

I didn't want to be this way any more. I didn't want to become my parents. I didn't want to marry Cian. I wanted to be different. I wanted to be happy. I left the club without saying a word to anyone. I didn't look back as I walked away. I never wanted to look back.

Beth

My skin is tender as I lather on the sun cream; I am still not used to the Australian sun. My Irish skin burned the day we arrived and I have been paranoid ever since. I just pray that no serious damage has been done. As a medical student I know all the dangers that the sun can bring to you. Michael is not much better; he hides under long-sleeved shirts and big sun hats. We couldn't look more like tourists if we tried, and yet we have been living here for months now.

The apartment that we live in is small, but everything in it is new and modern. It's a five-minute walk from Michael's college and a ten-minute walk from the local town. We are usually woken in the night by screaming babies. We live in the dorm for married couples and we are one of the very few who don't have children.

Our first few weeks here were madness. When we arrived we had only a short time to get married before Michael's term began. This meant finding a location, a dress, witnesses, a priest and a marriage licence. I never imagined myself as a beach wedding type of person, but the long white strands of beautiful paradise in Australia were impossible to resist. We kept the whole thing very casual. Michael wore a white shirt and cream trousers and I wore a white sundress. Finding witnesses was the hard part. Eventually we had to ask two passers-by if they would mind stepping in. They were an older couple, late sixties possibly. They were shocked when they found out we were being serious, but agreed immediately. They were very kind and even insisted that we join them for drinks afterwards to celebrate.

The day had been wonderful, simple and beautiful. But it wasn't long before reality broke our small fantasy. The older couple were named Orla and Joshua as they told us over drinks; they had lived in Australia all their lives and had been married for thirty-five years. Orla gushed over how young and attractive I was. I felt my cheeks go red with embarrassment; I wasn't used to so much attention.

The two guys were talking about some football championship that I had never heard of when I felt Orla place her hand on mine. Her face seemed to be full of concern.

'I don't want to be rude, darling, but what age are you two?'

'Eighteen,' I said, barely above a whisper.

She began to frown. 'You are only children. Why are you getting married? And without your family? Where is your mother?'

I cleared my throat before I tried to speak again. I didn't want to act like a silly child but secretly I was a little ashamed of myself.

'My mother does not approve. I love Michael, he is The One.'

Orla said nothing more on the topic, but I could see her eyes fill with sadness.

When the day had ended and we went to say goodbye to the

older couple, Orla took Michael's hand and mine in hers and said, 'I wish the two of you the best of luck.'

We both said our thanks and goodbyes, Michael naive to Orla's double meaning. I could see in her face that she thought we were making a huge mistake.

I knew that Orla's reaction was to be expected, and that I would have to get used to other people's disapproval, but I found it extremely difficult to shake off the doubt and worry that she had sown in me. It made me think back to the morning of our wedding. I had been so happy and so hopeful; everything was working out. Michael was beaming, and our new life seemed to have so many possibilities.

Michael was in the shower as I was trying to pin my hair back in order to look bride-like. Other than the sound of the running water the room was completely silent. I knew I would have to start to get used to that now – the silence. It really was going to be just the two of us. For a moment the thought seemed more daunting than exciting, but I shook the feeling away and continued to get ready.

I jumped as I heard my phone ring. I assumed it was Roz or Olive. The two had said they would ring later on today to see how everything had gone. I began to wonder had they gotten the time difference wrong. I picked up the phone without even looking at the screen.

'Hello,' I said, looking for a shade of eye-shadow that didn't completely offend me.

'Hi.' I recognized my mother's voice immediately. She sounded tired. I dropped the make-up that had been in my hand.

'Mum . . . how are you?'

A moment of silence followed before she spoke again.

'I am scared, Beth. I am really scared that you are going to do something that will ruin your life.' My mother hadn't contacted me since I had told her my plans. There was no possible way she could have known that today was my wedding day unless she had spoken to Michael's family – and I doubted that in the extreme.

'I am not ruining my life. I am just choosing a new one.' I wanted to sound brave and confident but there was fear in my voice.

'You have no idea about what you are doing, Beth. You are a child.'

'I am eighteen,' I said angrily.

'Marrying someone is a huge thing and you are not ready. You are running away from everyone and everything you know. You are going to be completely alone.'

'I have Michael.'

'You are going to be alone, Beth. Trust me.'

Tears were starting to well up in my eyes. I was glad that she couldn't see them: her words felt like daggers.

'I can't stop you, Beth. I can't force you to do as I say. I can only give you the option to stop and realize that what you are doing is wrong. You can come home and we will work everything out from there, but if you . . . if you do this, if you marry him . . . well then, I am sorry, Beth – but you will not be welcome home. I will not help you any more. You will be alone.'

I wanted to shout, scream, cry, tell her she was wrong. Tell her I hated her – but I didn't get the chance. She just hung up on me.

Michael didn't know about the call, about the things my mother had said. I knew if I told him he would just feel guilty and it would make him think that what we were doing wasn't right. Michael is aware that he comes between my family and me. It makes him unhappy. Michael is logical; he believes that every problem should have a solution. Unfortunately, life is not an equation; not everything does have an answer. Some things are unknown.

*

Our first few months were harder than I had anticipated; my fantasy of married life was quickly destroyed as soon as Michael started college. His workload was heavy and his hours long. He left at 7 a.m. and didn't return until 9 p.m. He came home exhausted and worn out. Sometimes he said less than two words to me before falling asleep. I didn't complain – I couldn't, he was under too much pressure. Michael had to keep a perfect GPA if he wanted his full scholarship to continue. I knew he worked so hard so the two of us could stay here, but it didn't stop me from being incredibly lonely.

I eventually got a job in a nursing home. I work mostly with people a lot older than me, but it helps that I now have something that gets me out of the house. The other nurses are constantly whispering behind my back. It is to be expected, a young girl with a wedding ring on her finger, desperate for a job. I have been accepted into med school but I am still unsure whether I will have enough money saved to pay the tuition when it starts. It looks like my dream might have to be delayed once again. I guess it is OK to give up one dream to achieve another. I just hope I have made the right choice.

As I think these thoughts, Michael is lying in bed breathing heavily. It is a Bank Holiday over here and we took the opportunity to have a romantic night together, knowing that Michael could sleep in this morning for the first time in a long while. It is only as I sit here, applying the sun cream over my whole body, that I realize that last night was the first time we have slept together in three months. This shocks me, and it is soon clear that last night was also the most time the two of us have spent together in a very long while. I turn to look at Michael. He is lying on his side, fast asleep with large bags under his eyes. He is always so tired these days. I gently brush his hair out of his face, but he doesn't stir.

I lean in and gently whisper in his ear, 'I have fought to be with you. I will always fight to be with you. Please always fight for me.'

Tom

'Why are you awake so early?' Olive groaned while trying to pull me back into bed.

'I have to be back in Dublin by one p.m. to meet my mum. The bus will take at least an hour,' I said, pretending to push her away but actually enjoying the attention. It was only 9 a.m. but Olive was definitely not a morning person. A bomb could go off in the house and she would still stay sound asleep. We were in her family home in Wexford. Her parents had been away most of the summer and the two of us had essentially moved in on the weekends. Unfortunately I still had to go back to Dublin a lot. My dad and I were getting along much better now, but he still didn't completely trust me. I often think that he is just waiting for me to fly off the handle again. That he doesn't believe I have really changed; well, I guess that is to be expected.

When Olive first told me about her parents' travelling plans I was worried. She wouldn't want to admit it to herself, but Olive depends on the support of her family a lot, and it made me fear what might happen if all that was taken away. She doesn't like to speak about it but I know her brother's death still haunts her. I often catch her looking at old photos when she thinks I am not around. Sometimes she even comes out of the bathroom with red eyes as if she has been crying. I asked her once before if she was OK. She snapped at me, telling me to mind my own business, but she apologized nearly instantly. Even so, I decided it was best not to ask again. If there is something I do understand it is someone not wanting to talk about their problems.

'Are you nervous?' Olive asked, her voice still sounding a bit sleepy.

'No, I am actually OK,' but she couldn't hear me. She had already fallen back asleep. She was lying on her stomach and her hair was covering most of her face. I laughed at her, she looked very funny. She was wearing my T-shirt from the night before. As I saw my boxers and her silk slip wrapped together on the floor, I smiled to myself. The two of us certainly knew how to enjoy ourselves.

Olive's back rose and fell as she took deep breaths. It seemed so long ago when we had spent our first real night together. Summer had just begun. The stress-release of exams ending meant that the two of us were in high spirits. I avoided most after-exam parties. It's not that I have given up alcohol; I know – well, at least I think – I am not an alcoholic, but I don't trust myself under its influence, and for the first time ever I have something that I don't want to lose. Olive doesn't drink any more either. She claims that it has nothing to do with me and that she just wants to save money. I know she is lying but I don't argue. Secretly I am thrilled. The temptation is a lot easier to avoid when she is sober with me. Even though neither of us wanted to go out clubbing we still wanted to do something to celebrate the end of the college year.

When Olive invited me down to her family home I was extremely nervous. I never pictured myself as the boy you bring home to the family. If my own family thought I was a mess, there was no doubt in my mind that Olive's family would hate me, and I knew how important her family was to her. My nerves disappeared, though, when she told me that they were actually away, but then I was left with new concerns. Since Damien had revealed the bet to Olive, the topic of sex was completely avoided. Even after months of being together and really getting to know each other, I didn't dare speak about it. I respected her but I was also extremely attracted to her and I didn't know how to show her this without ruining everything.

I kept my fears to myself and the two of us headed to Wexford. Her house was beautiful, bigger than I had expected. It was red-bricked with two storeys and a large garden. I was a little stunned when I saw it. I had always known Olive was wealthier than I was, but I had not quite expected this. It was another thing that made me think, Why is this girl with me? We spent the rest of the day lying in the hot sun, talking about music, friends, life, anything and everything. She made me dinner. Cooking was not one of Olive's talents but I enjoyed watching her pretend to know what she was doing.

It had been relaxing and fun until the night had set in and the awkward question of who was going to sleep where hung in the air. In a way I kind of wished that Olive's parents had been there and then we would have had to follow their rules. It would have been out of our hands. But they weren't there. It was just the two of us and neither of us seemed completely sure of what to do or say.

Eventually Olive was the one to break the silence.

'I am getting pretty tired. I think I am going to go to bed,' she said, not really looking me in the eye.

'Yeah, me too,' I mumbled. 'So I will just grab the couch then?' I wanted to ask her did she want me to come with her, but I chickened out. What if she got offended, upset. I wouldn't know how to deal with any of that.

'Oh . . . OK. I will grab some pillows for you.' She ran upstairs before I could say anything. I had no idea how to judge her reaction. Was she surprised? Insulted? Relieved? It was impossible to tell. She came back downstairs with white pillows and blankets; she placed them neatly on the couch in the room that we had just been talking in. She wished me good night and gave me a quick kiss before running back upstairs. It was the type of kiss that you did out of politeness; it wasn't because you really wanted to do it.

I tossed and turned for hours, unable to sleep and debating whether or not I should go to her room. I knew where it was. I had seen it earlier when she had given me a tour of the house. But what would I say? What would *she* say? I tried reading a book for a while to distract my mind but it was hopeless. Eventually I gave up and shoved my face in my pillow, determined to get even a little bit of sleep before the morning. It was close to 3 a.m. when I heard someone creaking down the stairs. I had dozed off and at first I thought I was dreaming it, but then it got louder.

'Olive?' I asked, turning over and staring into the darkness. It took my eyes a few seconds to adjust but I was soon able to see her in front of me clearly, standing in a blue string top with matching checked shorts.

'Are you OK?' I asked, trying to rub the sleep out of my eyes. She didn't say anything but sat down on the couch next to me. She closed her eyes and leaned in and kissed me. When we stopped, I could see she had a fiery look in her eyes. Nothing more needed to be said.

Afterwards I had watched her, listened to her light breathing, her chest rising and falling slowly in time with her breath. Her mouth lay slightly open, her eyes were tightly shut. As her warm body came into contact with mine, I closed my eyes and tried to enter that perfect state of bliss that can only be achieved in dreams.

Sitting here months later, it seems crazy, how nervous I had been. Now being together feels like second nature to me. I kissed Olive on the forehead, careful not to wake her, and then headed out the door, hoping that I wouldn't miss the bus. I managed to catch it barely. I found that these countryside drivers liked to work by their own time, whether it was five minutes early or thirty minutes late. It was impossible to guess when a bus would arrive.

I went back to my dad's first to shower and change. Everyone was out, as usual. I didn't mind though. I still found it difficult to get along with Paddy and Robin, but luckily there had been no major arguments since the incident with Peter. I had to be grateful; they were paying for college and my doctor bills. My hand still had small white marks where the wounds had healed. The doctor told me I was very lucky that there had been no permanent nerve damage, but that I would probably be left with scars. Every time I look down at my hand, it is a constant reminder of what happens when I lose it. I have never told anyone, but on that night I had seriously scared myself.

I still work in Murder's Foulest Things with Moiraine but only on weekday evenings. Olive makes fun of me and says that Moiraine is more like my therapist than my boss, and in a way she is kind of right. This also keeps Paddy happy. Originally he wanted me to work in the pub with him, but he agreed that as long as I had a job I could work where I wanted.

I have talked to my mum a lot since I moved out, but I haven't actually met up with her until today. I had been avoiding her till now, making up excuses every time she tried to organize something. A part of me was still angry with her. I know in her own way she was trying to help me, but I still can't shake off the feeling of abandonment. She gave up on me, and I wasn't sure if I could forgive her for that, or whether she would forgive me for forcing her to give up on me. I flattened my hair with water and wore one of the shirts that Robin had bought for me; I wanted to look nice for her. We had planned to meet in a café on Dawson Street at 1 p.m. but I was early. I sat down, wishing I had brought something to keep myself occupied. Normally I would carry a book with me but today I had nothing.

I saw her before she saw me; she looked thin and frail, even worse than I remembered. Her hair was greying and she wore a blue dress that looked too big for her. She was slightly hunched over and looking around herself frantically. I suddenly felt enormous guilt. The stress that I had caused was what had made her look like this. I was the one who had aged her so much, made her so emotional and unstable.

She scrambled over quickly to my table when she finally saw me. To my great surprise she hugged me before sitting down.

'You look really great,' my mum said, pulling her chair out. 'Robin has you looking like a young gentleman.'

I didn't really know what to say to this so I just told her that she looked great too.

'Oh, don't be silly. I am just out from work and I found this,' she pulled at the sleeve of her blue dress, 'in a second-hand shop in Temple Bar. It is very ugly but it does the job.'

The two of us sat there silently for a long time. All the months and everything that had happened – it had created this great distance between us. I felt like she didn't know me any more.

'You seem to be doing better?' she said, trying to break the silence.

'Yeah,' I mumbled. 'It has been going better.'

'Good,' she replied, her voice getting quieter.

'I miss you, Mum,' I blurted out.

She looked at me, surprise on her face.

'You do?' she asked hopefully. 'But you seem to be doing so much better, living with your dad.'

'I am doing better but . . . I am still scared. Scared that something will happen. That I will ruin everything that I have worked so hard for. Everyone expects me to. I finally have things going right. I feel that for once I have control over my life. But I'm afraid. I always ruin it. I always ruin everything.'

I needed comfort and reassurance. I wanted her to believe in me. I needed someone to believe I could do this.

My mum looked at me silently for a long time before placing her hands on either side of my face. She forced me to look at her. 'You won't ruin it,' she said gently. 'I believe you won't.'

'But what if I do?'

'Then I will be there for you. You are not alone.'

And in that moment, I knew I wasn't.

Acknowledgements

I would like to thank my literary agent, Marianne Gunn O'Connor. Without her this story would never have been told. I am for ever grateful for her suppport and the faith that she has in me.

I would also like to thank Catherine Cobain and everyone else at Transworld Publishers. They have been endlessly helpful and encouraging.

Finally I would like to thank all the Irish college students who I have met over the years: you have all been a greater influence than you will ever know.

About the author

Emily Gillmor Murphy was born in 1990 in County Dublin, Ireland. She is currently in her final year studying Arts at University College Dublin, majoring in English and History.

Emily lives in Enniskerry, County Wicklow, with her two older sisters and her parents. She is also a competitive show jumper, travelling across the country to events with her sister Lucy.